The Man
From
Buzzard Roost
Priceless Dirt

David Powers

THE MAN FROM BUZZARD ROOST: PRICELESS DIRT

First Edition - July 2015

This book is a work of fiction. Names, characters, places, and incidents either are a product of the author's imagination, or are used fictitiously, and any resemblance to actual persons, living or dead, business establishments, events, or locales is entirely coincidental.

Library of Congress Cataloging-in-Publication Data
Powers, David.
The man from buzzard roost: Priceless dirt/David Powers.
256 p. 22 cm.

ISBN 978-0-9914248-6-3 (hardcover)
ISBN 978-0-9914248-7-0 (paperback)
ISBN 978-0-9914248-8-7 (ebook)

1. Murder--Investigation--Fiction. 2. Mystery--Fiction. 3. Seances--Fiction. 4. California--Fiction. 5. San Diego (Calif.). I. Title.

Library of Congress Control Number: 2015910069
Printed in the United States of America

Eerie Forest
www.eerieforest.com

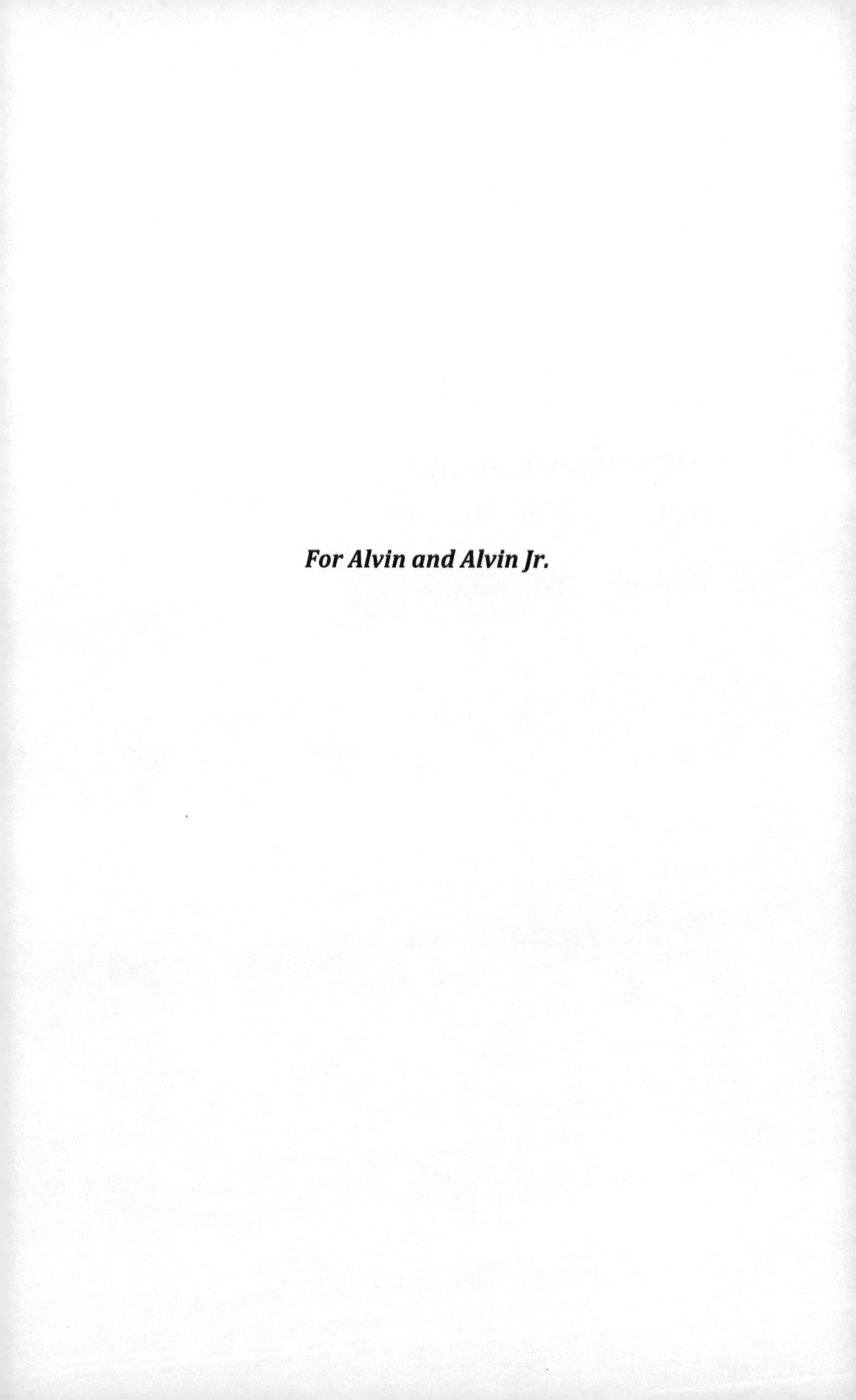

For Alvin and Alvin Jr.

ALSO BY DAVID POWERS

UNBURIED MEMORIES
TIDINGS FROM THE ABYSS

Preface

FOURTEEN THOUSAND YEARS AGO, the San Dieguito people crossed what is now the Bering Strait to populate Southern California. San Diego has always been a beautiful place to live or visit. The inhabitants are fun loving, and the temperate climate is exceptionally beneficial to one's health. Spanish culture prevails, and there are oodles of taco shops offering tasty menus of spicy, stuffed-tortilla delights.

The majority of San Diego's citizens migrated from other states or nations looking for a better way of life. During a vacation near Balboa Park in the early '90s, I saw the light. Two years later, I crammed all my possessions into a Toyota Celica and journeyed cross-country to take root at a campground in Santee, California. After three glorious months living in a well-equipped tent, I managed to kick off a new career in Information Technology—*and move indoors.*

Many of the characters in this work of fiction are based upon actual settlers who walked the Earth in the nineteenth century. These pioneers were true innovators who used sweat and sheer perseverance to mold this fledgling city out of the shifting desert dust.

As I researched historical material relevant to this story, my appreciation for these original Californians increased exponentially. I wish I could meet each of these fascinating personalities, especially the Father of San Diego, Alonzo Horton; industrious saloon owner, Tillman Burnes; multi-faceted genius, Jesse Shepard; and of course, Bum, the irrepressible Saint Bernard.

Chapter One

AS I STEPPED INTO THE GIANT WAVE, a leopard shark twisted into the translucent sea. A crab broke free from its jaw before the dappled creature vanished over the crest. I dove below the foam. The undertow snatched and then tumbled me in a froth of sand and crushed shells onto the bank. The beach shimmered, as deserted as the sky was devoid of clouds.

Seated upon barnacled debris from a wrecked brig, I looped a cord through the yellowfin croaker's gasping mouth and out the gills. I tied the fish to the stringer and grabbed my bamboo fishing pole. Three halibut and the heavy croaker fetched a couple of dollars at the market.

I retraced my footprints past the buzzing kelp and bleached driftwood to the path zigzagging up the orange cliffs. High above the sandy embankment, I supped from the canteen, stretched my leg, and scanned the coast. Up north, smoke spiraled skyward from Kumeyaay huts as children chased a dancing goat. To the south, the rocky shores of La Jolla glimmered.

After a productive morning, I pondered how the afternoon might fare. For now, I had to return to town and sell the fish before they fried in the noonday sun. Clive waited, tethered to a windblown Torrey pine. Irritable, the mule chomped the reddish bark off the trunk. I took a gulp before pouring the last of the water reserve down his throat. Clive whimpered, wanting more.

With the fish wrapped in damp burlap, we climbed up and beyond the ridge. On a cliff overlooking the Bay of San Diego, I stopped to gnaw on day-old bread and salted mutton. In the distance, I distinguished the red roofs of the Hotel del Coronado. Not that long ago, I hunted jackrabbits and quail on that barren, tick-infested expanse of sand. I could not believe the hotel's grand opening was in a fortnight. As I questioned what wealthy aristocrats might sojourn at the opulent beach resort, my eyes tracked the wake of a single-stacked ship approaching Ballast Point. Vivid pennants flapped from the rigging of the paddle steamer *Ancon*. Two years prior, I gained passage from San Francisco to Southern California on her sister side-wheeler, the *Orizaba*.

Eighteen hundred eighty-eight has just begun. I am Henry Gates, or Hank, as my few friends call me. Born in 1842, I grew up on a five hundred-acre tobacco plantation in Buzzard Roost, Alabama. Owned by my father, John Gates, Cedar Hall was the family's estate.

My schoolmates ached to fight the Yankees. Raring to help the cause, I, too, signed up with Jeff Davis' Confederate artillery unit in 1861. Our division lost no time leaving Selma and headed east. We attached to Jubal Early's Brigade in Virginia.

On account that I completed several semesters of college education, the Army promoted me to lieutenant. I commanded a battery of six twelve-pound Howitzers. I saw the elephant—meaning military engagement—at Seven Pines, Mechanicsville, Cold Harbor, Boonesboro, Sharpsburg, Fredericksburg, Chancellorsville, Gettysburg, Bristoe, Bealeton, and finally Spotsylvania. I remember them all, but Gettysburg left the worst mental scars.

At Sharpsburg in 1862, I received physical pain and injuries—shrapnel in my right thigh. I rehabilitated without amputation—honestly, this was purely the result of desperate pleading with the inexperienced surgeon. Most days, I do my best to mask the limp by smiling instead of grimacing.

At the end, Billy Yank charged our company at Spotsylvania, and I survived the balance of the war in a Maryland prison camp. Located in Saint Mary's County, Point Lookout was a living hell—full of despair and death—yet somehow safer than the slaughter-grounds of the battlefields.

Eager to get to food and water, Clive pawed the gravel. My gum crammed with Bull Durham, I let the mule find his way to the main trail and onto the Roseville road leading to New Town.

I passed south of Market Street into the eight-block district pigeonholed as Chinatown. The court teemed with young boys and old men pushing handcarts or herding farm animals. Dickering women sold vegetables and abalone from canopied stalls. Ah Wo Sue sat on the front stoop of his spic-and-span cabin.

"What have you got for me today, Mr. Gates?" the fisherman asked, filling a worn clay pipe with nutmeg.

"Just the usual, Wo Sue," I replied, unwrapping the package and dropping the fish on the narrow porch. The exclusion laws prevented the Chinese from trolling the ocean, and they longed for any seafood bigger than ear shells.

He puffed the woody spice and questioned, "How much for these small fry, Mr. Gates?" To frustrate the swarming flies, he protected the catch with the coarse fabric.

"You're a funny fellow, Wo Sue. This fresh fish will sell for four times what I'm seeking. The deal is fifty cents and a little information."

The lean man stoked his wispy beard. "What can I possibly know, Mr. Gates? They don't tell us anything down here."

Expression impenetrable, he peered from beneath the coolie hat.

"I've property in Horton's Addition, and shall buy more if I can negotiate the price. Wo Sue, I'm merely requesting that you keep your ears open for any good deals." I put out my hand.

"Sure, Mr. Gates. The real estate market is dead, but I'll do my best." Ah Wo Sue released coins into my waiting fingers.

"Where's Bum?" I inquired, noticing the unfilled water and food bowls. "Did that dog up and leave you again?" Last summer, at the Santa Fe Depot, a switch engine ran over the Saint Bernard during a fierce skirmish with a bulldog. Losing a right forepaw and part of his bushy tail, Bum had been nursed back to life by Ah Wo Sue. The lesser canine ended up in a waste bin.

The Chinaman laughed loudly. "Bum comes and goes, mostly goes. He's a thankless cur that won't be tamed by any man."

"If I see that Bum, I'll tell him to run on home," I promised, undoing Clive. "I'll be by in a few days to learn what you found out." As I rode off, Wo Sue's wife gave me the stink eye from a strip of tomato plants in the garden.

After returning Clive to Ernie Smoke's stables, I walked to a sunbaked canvas tent on an unimproved fifty-foot-wide by one hundred-foot-long lot. On Fourth and Beech Streets, my tract stood within a stone's throw from the undeveloped fourteen hundred acres designated as City Park. Only a month had elapsed since I made the purchase face-to-face from Alonzo Horton. The marking stakes and connecting strings still bordered the parcel.

On nearby lots, other speculators lived in similar conditions, or worse. Many families slept on the cold ground sheltered by striped Mexican blankets. There were solitary structures here and there standing up like defenseless pawns on a titan's chessboard. With the income from my mining claim in Julian, I hoped to be surrounded by solid walls before the flea season.

At the building once promoted as the Western White House, I paused to chat with Andy the Anteater. The menagerie fronted the Acme Saloon and Billiard Academy. There was a surplus of ants and termites in the sandy till of Fifth Street. The mammal's protracting tongue resembled a thin worm as it flicked at the columns of insects marching across the twelve-foot-wide wooden sidewalk. I fended off Bruin, the restless, chained brown bear, and elbowed through the tall doors—advertising the "Finest Brands of Liquors and Cigars"—into the poorly lit interior. A handful of old-timers slumped on benches; otherwise, the alehouse wanted for paying customers. The proprietor's son busied himself sweeping caked mud into tidy piles.

"Where's your father?" I asked. Inhaling, I shot tobacco juice at a brass spittoon strategically positioned at the midpoint of the floor. Some of the chew dribbled in.

"Jeez, Lieutenant Gates, your aim gets poorer every day," Tillman Jr. reprimanded, grabbing a mop. "No wonder the Yanks were victorious."

Tilly, as everybody called him, was a hardworking lad who enjoyed pulling my good leg, so I let the wisecrack go, but not before nailing the cuspidor dead center. "Bull's-eye," I chuckled.

The lanky youth snapped his heels and saluted. "You're my hero, Lieutenant Gates." He pointed with the mop handle to the rear of the tavern.

Perched on a stool, an elderly Chinaman guarded the entrance to the back room. He grasped a cord wound around an index finger that in the event of a raid could latch the door from the inside. I pressed one of Wo Sue's dimes into his palm and entered the gambling parlor.

Sufficiently livelier than the front of the house, the smoky chamber contained four poker tables occupied by raucous sea dogs. Brilliant three-mantle gas lamps kept the play fair. Tillman Augustus Burnes stood in a corner watching the fast-moving action. Short and thickset, the forty-year-old Irishman had piercing brown eyes and a bulbous nose. The vest of the owner's bedraggled suit was covered with stains from working in the kitchen.

"What a way to make a living," Till complained. He rested his forearm on the butt of a large-caliber British Bull Dog—the same type of gun Charles Guiteau used to murder President Garfield.

"What does Mary think of this?" I questioned. Recent hearsay claimed the government had the Acme under surveillance.

"My wife is quiet when finances are concerned. She's been hintin' about a family vacation to Hawaii for a while. That costs a pretty penny. Besides, you see how empty the bar is." He looked at my hands. "Hank, take yourself, you ain't even drinking."

"My doctor has me on the temperance diet. It's very popular with the Christian ladies."

Till chortled. He knew of my issues with alcohol, and I respected him for not browbeating me to death.

I changed the subject. "At least you're not running whores." I racked my brains for a diplomatic way of telling my friend that with the City Council's current crackdown on immorality, now might be the perfect time to quit the gaming and lie low. Wisely staying out of a man's livelihood, I inquired, "Any idea where I can find a bargain on lumber? Straight planks, not the scrap that's going up in most places."

"Are ya puttin' down roots?" Till asked. "Such a rarity for a well-heeled, Southern gentleman to live in a Yankee town. What did you pay for that patch of weeds?"

"Enough," I replied. In December, I shelled out eight hundred dollars for Lot 201 C. In the present-day bear market, plots on the next block advertised prices half that. "And I'm formerly well-heeled thanks to your Mr. Lincoln—God rest his soul. I don't have much to spend, though I need to nail something together before the gallinippers eat me alive."

"There is a guy at the wharf who will help—Joe Higgs. You've probably seen that Johnny Reb in here?" Till fidgeted with a gold timepiece. "Tell him I sent you."

"I'm acquainted with Higgs. Just because we're both from Alabama, it doesn't imply we are compatriots. That war ended long ago, and I'm trying to put those memories far behind me."

"Good luck with that, brother," Till snorted. He passed the pistol over to his son. "Adios. I gotta go feed the bear."

Chapter Two

AS USUAL, I AWOKE AT TWO-THIRTY A.M. In the starlight, I irrigated my kingdom of dirt. Once an erstwhile companion, since the war, restful slumber tarried far from reach. Specters governed my dreams, the undead arising from shallow graves to challenge why I wasn't also roasting in Hell. The wind snuck through the seams of my wool coat as I hooked the sword onto my belt. On most nights, to keep the repetitive nightmares treed, I roamed "Sailor Town," more widely known as the "Stingaree." Although treacherous, this nocturnal routine triumphed as much healthier than the countless years I threw away drinking myself into a stupor.

Resembling the Barbary Coast of San Francisco, San Diego's politicians overlooked the saloons, gambling parlors, bawdy houses, and opium dens proliferating throughout the "restricted" territories west of Fifth Street and south of H Street. Tantamount to the ocean's stingray, visitors were cautioned to avoid the Stingaree's long-reaching, poisonous tail or surely be stung. The Board of Trustees used the blighted area to corral the city's outcasts: vagrants, prostitutes, pimps, cardsharps, drug dealers, and the mentally ill. In addition, as a result of city planning, this rattrap imprisoned working-class citizens and Chinese immigrants.

I carried a modified Model 1850 Foot Officer's Sword. Lightened by eight ounces, a skilled smith shortened the razor-sharp blade to twenty-seven inches. Other artillerymen ridiculed my alterations to what was essentially a dress sword. This effective weapon had saved me in close combat situations when the instinct to live overrode any thoughts of reloading a rifle or revolver.

Wandering ten blocks south, I contemplated the past, present, and future. The past prompted a numbing depression—feelings of intimate loss and failure to safeguard my family. The present: a reclusive man eluding the naturalness of sleep by walking the lonely avenues. I harbored plans for the future, but didn't possess the vigor or willpower to act on these vague notions.

Extinguished after midnight to economize, clusters of arc lamps loomed high above hushed tenements. The taut cables reinforcing the one hundred thirty-foot steel light poles resembled monstrous spider webs. Tended by fellow insomniacs, a few candles or lanterns flickered behind shutters. I followed shadowy routes on a haphazard course to nowhere—the Stingaree.

On the north side of J Street, gambling halls resounded with the booze-fueled roars of winners and the angry expletives of losers. Wyatt Earp's famous Oyster Bar, situated in the Louis Bank of Commerce on Fifth Street, was remarkably lively this evening. Drunken buffoons loitered on the corners, the minority standing, while the majority sprawled in gutters or store doorways. In public houses, off-key voices chanted ribald lyrics accompanied by strummed banjos, plucked fiddles, and hammered pianos.

On Third and I Streets, the peculiar, sweet fragrance of opium wafted from the back rooms of Chinese establishments. Barefooted women huddling over whiskey barrels scraped the

"Yen Shee" from the blackened bowls of long-stemmed pipes. These dregs, mixed with raw opiate, gave a second chance to dull the senses. Hundreds of Asian Americans, along with adventurous Westerners, frequented the unmapped labyrinths of subterranean tunnels. As oblivious addicts clutched the shafts of bamboo pipes before the oil lamps used to vaporize the drug, hours, days, or weeks unreeled from abbreviated lifespans. I never entered these accursed dens, aware I didn't have the grit to escape.

From the endless rows of windowless shacks, a party of buttoned-up gentlemen exited, hurriedly dissolving into the mist, their passions temporarily slaked. Counterfeit climaxes moaned from the Lilliputian "cribs" as spiritless "China Dolls" grinded for piddling cuts of fifty cents.

At some juncture each eventide, I deliberated my purpose traversing these sinful byways and garbage-filled alleyways, always observing vice from a safe distance and in skulking secret. Occasionally, I overheard news or gossip that might be employed to my advantage. When agitated or lonesome, prowling the outskirts of civilization muffled the profane sermons preached by blue and gray-uniformed apparitions. Indeed, the titillation of watching other men and women succumb to their base desires became a habit-forming diversion.

Joe Higgs and a colored man loaded a wagon with boards at the lowest point of Fifth Street. A scattering of timber vessels with Northwest registries docked at the Pacific Mail Wharf.

Higgs swept stringy locks from his brow. "If it isn't my old friend Lieutenant Gates. Are you here to get your hands dirty? I thought the top brass always sat to the rear, brewin' English tea under frilly parasols and hopin' that whatever was happening at the front lines stayed out of earshot."

Swimmy-headed from the night before, I craved a cup of potent tea to push the blood through my anemic veins. I ignored the sarcastic criticisms and stated, "Till Burnes said you could assist with building supplies."

"Ah. I knew you were here for something and not solely payin' a social call to another Allerbammer Yellowhammer." The burly laborer spat into his callused palms and resumed talking. "Look who that mealy-mouthed foreman's got me workin' with. This black son of a bitch is the laziest fool I ever seen. Ought to be breakin' his back on your daddy's plantation. The slaves were happiest in the cotton fields where they had no time to think about takin' a white man's job."

The African American's eyes hardened; nonetheless, he continued stacking the planks.

"Joe, are you going to help me out or what? I want five hundred-feet of framing lumber to start and will need more in short order."

The docker leaned into my ear. "Meet me at the Pacific Coast Steamship Company when you hear the flour mill's whistle. Your cost is ten bucks. Do you own a horse?"

"A john mule," I responded.

"Well, he better be strong and quiet." Before turning away, Higgs added, "And bring a sheet of canvas to hide it."

At the Samuel Gordon Ingle Company, I acquired a sturdy pickaxe and shovel, besides putting aside a box of tenpenny nails and a claw hammer. I had distinct misgivings in dealing with Joe Higgs, yet had learned from experience that shady transactions were normal behavior in San Diego.

A friendly neighbor loaned me a handcart to truck off the rocks and brush covering my slice of Heaven. The owners or illegal tenants of the opposite plot left for greener pastures, but not before discarding all their litter on my property. It took multiple trips to clear the bulk of the dross onto a vacant tract. The terrain pitched gently to the sea. A haggard eucalyptus tree clung to life in the hardscrabble backyard. Twelve blocks west, the San Diego Bay gleamed through a coal smoke haze. I hadn't paid for an ocean view and often regretted this decision.

After removing the marking stakes and drooping cords circumscribing the land, stepping from the curb on Fourth Street, I counted off twenty feet to the imaginary porch. I used a brick as a mallet to reposition the sticks and string. The forty-foot-wide by fifty-foot-long rectangle outlined a two-story residence. Proud of my effort, I relaxed on the cart and visualized my home. Horton had pledged water and sewer lines within the coming months, once the thirty-five-mile redwood flume was coupled to the Cuyamaca Dam. Until then, I'd hump buckets from the artesian well by the Horton House Hotel and bury my scat under the only tree.

I cinched the canvas to the cantle of Clive's saddle as the mill's whistle shrilled doubly. At five-thirty p.m., an eerie twilight bathed the thoroughfares, thanks to the arrangement of sizzling artificial moons fastened to the tops of colossal electrical towers.

At this hour, the port remained idle; its longshoremen busy raising five-cent schooners at Snug Harbor, or any number of other convenient watering holes. The mule's hoofs clattered across the slippery cobblestones, the arc lights not striking this section of the wharf. Not trusting Joe Higgs in the least, I carried the sword in my jacket.

Dismounted, I tucked the payment into a carton of fishing tackle for security. As I stealthily advanced to the warehouses of the Pacific Coast Steamship Company, a hunched silhouette passed before the filmy panes of a lit window. The shape was slimmer than Higgs and crouched as a cat may stalk a mouse. Spooked, Clive clacked his metal shoes, distracting me for a moment. When my attention returned to the sheds, the figure could no longer be seen. I crept closer, ducking below the lumber-filled buckboard I hoped would soon be mine.

The tremors of shuffling boots resulted in a gurgling gasp and groan. This violent turbulence led to a thud that jolted the wagon. I crawled by the steering axle, extracted my knife, and slithered into the shroud of darkness. A wiry man rode Joe Higgs' back, arms wrapped around the massive neck. A raging bull, the docker attempted to shake his assailant free, but as he kicked and bucked, the assassin executed the *estocada,* impaling Joe's fat throat with a lengthy dagger. Higgs fell to his knees and flopped facedown into a puddle, sputtering as he drowned in an inch of muck.

The killer stooped and lifted Joe's head by the hair. Surgically slicing at the top of the spine, the murderer peeled the skin over the ears.

"Hepekwii it!" I yelled in Kumeyaay. "Stop!" Rushing forward, my sword swooshed the air as the Indian rolled, and still gripping the scalp, sprinted along the dock. I gave pursuit on the main rail spur, circumventing oil drums and dangling winching equipment. My dodgy leg lagged well behind the heels of an athlete who raced two hundred feet ahead. Near the terminus, he faded from sight at the long coal bins. By the time I arrived at the edge of the pilings, the blood-drenched heathen was far away, swiftly rowing a skiff. Seeing me, the man let go of an oar and waved goodbye.

Chapter Three

THE ASCENDING SUN THAWED MY BACKSIDES and shrank my shadow. The past evening had been a disaster. Not only did I lose my connection to a resource for cheap building supplies, circumstances linked me, though innocently, to a felony. I tried my best to stop the perpetrator. Despite this factor, I lay awake, fearing that someone saw me at the wharf. Who in their right mind would bid adieu after performing such a vicious act? Till had guided me to Joe Higgs. *What might he think or do now?* I contemplated telling the barman what had transpired, deciding to see if the newspaper had anything to report.

A boy on a milk crate sold pink copies of the San Diego Union. He took my change, bemoaning the ongoing white paper shortage. Page two posted a brief article on the murder.

Ghastly Find at Harbor

> SAN DIEGO, Jan. 29.—A doctor taking in the morning air, discovered a male with his neck slashed on the docks near the Pacific Coast Steamship Company. The severe trauma suggests the victim put up a formidable struggle before gasping his final breaths. Dr. Gregory Leeds furthermore stated that the unidentified man lost his scalp. District constables are actively

> interrogating the Indian populations. In our fine city, this atrocity is the 18th recorded homicide since ringing in the New Year.

Not inclined to become involved, I hadn't contacted a marshal. I never cared much for Joe Higgs and suffered no loss in his passing.

Till Burnes set a plate of fish and vegetables on the polished oak. He asked, "Did you get a chance to speak to Joe Higgs?" Motionless as a statue, the bartender watched me eat the flavorless rockfish.

I speared a soggy artichoke and replied, "You may say, I came late to the dance." In the mirror set above the bar, I inventoried the room. "What have you heard?"

"Jus' that they imagine an Injun carried out the crime 'cause of the brutality. Joe had coins in his pocket, which I assume you'd steal if you'd done the deed." Burnes winked conspiratorially. "Oh, and a lumber shipment has walked off."

"I didn't filch the wood. A man stabbed Higgs, ran to the end of the dock, and jumped in a boat. Can't swear the cutthroat was an Indian. Seeing Joe's tight haircut, I reckoned he could be."

"A customer said lawmen beat a confession from an old Injun campin' on the waterfront. The poor fella will be hangin' from a lamppost by sundown." Till scowled to himself and moved off to pour thirsty ranchers another round.

Unable to fall asleep, I trod the squalid passageways of the Stingaree. The aromas of fried meats, onions, garlic, and swill exhaled from open doorways. Tonight, danger lurked everywhere. Gunshots, accompanied by screams, reflected off ramshackle structures. Curious, I snaked past a chain of cribs toward the reports. Without forewarning, the door of a shanty burst wide, spilling a female and two males into the gully. The taller man leapt upon the woman's chest and pinned her wrists. The other trembled as if unsure what to do.

"Help!" she shouted, raking fingernails over the jowls of her assailant. "Ray! Ray!"

The lout's head jerked backwards, and I used this instant to snap the flat edge of my sword against his temple. He fell sideways, lying spread-eagle on his rump. The tempered steel emitted a metallic ringing as the hilt vibrated in my palm. Coming to his senses, the accomplice scurried away and sharply rounded the corner.

"Is this degenerate Ray?" I questioned, checking if the swine still had a pulse. The beast wheezed, although even in the weak lighting, I could see his scratched mug swelling. Chafed at the man's disrespect for womankind, I grazed the blade across his Adam's apple.

"No, Ray's my lover," she answered, alluding to her pimp. Rising and rearranging her clothing, the prostitute brushed off the filth and grumbled in exasperation, "Ray's worthless. He takes it all, leaving a meager pittance. You'd hope that in a nasty scrape such as this, he might be of *some* use."

I held my tongue. Normally, my experiences with panderers were limited to paying for services rendered.

"My name is Margaret Doyle," the blond revealed, offering her hand. "Or Molly if you like." I returned her firm grip. "Sir, I appreciate your assistance in this matter. A gentleman is impossible to find at this hour, and you certainly came by at the right moment." Hearing a moan, her countenance soured as she spun to stomp the horizontal man in the face.

"Hold up, miss," I admonished, pulling her off. "What will this Ray do when he sees that his client has been slapped around?"

Molly frowned. "Perhaps, you'll teach him a lesson in manners?"

"I'm finished here," I responded. "Was passing through, and now I shall be on my way. The smart move is to clear out."

"Easier said than done," she sighed. "Tell me your name, angel."

I hesitated before replying.

"Hank, stop by anytime, and you'll get a ride you won't soon forget," Molly Doyle whispered coyly before shutting and bolting the door.

Hooves clomped outside the tent, joined by the rattling of wooden wheels. Bleary-eyed, I gathered the flap, annoyed to view a red buckboard on my property. As the dust settled, the driver ordered, "Stand," swung off the spring-supported seat, and unhooked the bridle.

Yanking up my pants, I confronted, "What do you want?" As he edged closer, I recognized him as the colored man who worked with Joe Higgs. I seized my scabbard.

"No need for that, mister," he said, raising his arms. "I brought your lumber. Don't want nothin' for it—jus' makin' a delivery."

Fully dressed, I felt irritation veer toward animosity. Sword unsheathed, I approached the man tying the horse to my favorite gum tree. "I said boy, what are you up to?" Youthful, he stood shorter than I, yet more muscular and walked with a fluid grace. The boggling part—under the straw sailor hat, he wore an impertinent grin, the same smirk as the impenitent fellow who butchered Joe Higgs.

"May I sit?" the man inquired, already hovering over a box. When I yielded this concession, he said, "Let's be quick. I'd hate for the law to bag us with pinched timber."

"How did you manage to find me?"

"I've seen you around town, Mr. Gates. And you're listed in the City Directory," he responded as if that explained everything.

"Is the mare also stolen?" I asked.

"No Mr. Gates. Cherika is mine. The cart is bought and paid for. When I'm not at the docks, I take jobs haulin' freight for whoever is willin' to bear the cost."

"Why did you slit Higgs' throat?" I sat on my only chair, still clasping the sword.

"The less you know the better. Let's simply say, the bastard had it comin'."

I glowered. "To delay me from getting a sheriff, you *shall* provide a compelling reason."

"Got any family, Mr. Gates?" The man's fingers balled into fists as he waited for my response.

"Not anymore," I replied, seeing my wife's face and wondering where this conversation was going.

"You heard of the massacre at Thibodaux last November?"

"Just what I read in the papers," I answered. A founding member of the Knights of the White Camellia had organized the bloodbath.

"Dad worked like an animal on a plantation in Lafourche Parish. The laborers went on strike for higher wages and to be compensated in real currency, not the pasteboard tickets that could only be cashed at the company store. My parents were at the dinner table when Judge Beattie's Peace and Order Committee dragged them from their own house and shot both on the front lawn." Fuming, the man stood and paced. "My brother was close to home and hid in the bushes. Martin marked your pal Joe Higgs as one of the killers. Of the three vigilantes, Marty took care of the other two in Louisiana."

I had caught distasteful scuttlebutt concerning Higgs and believed the world would truly be improved without him pissing in the water. "What's your name?" I inquired.

"Kitch Cane. Catchy, isn't it?"

Inquisitive, I asked, "Is that your slave name?" With Cane for a surname, he probably lived on a sugar plantation.

"Yes, Mr. Gates. My father and I cultivated the cane fields until I left for San Diego. Mass'r Bragg was too damn lazy to label us something besides 'Cane.' I'm thinkin' of changin' it, maybe to Jefferson or Washington," he said sardonically.

"Well, Kitch Cane, that does have a ring to it. I'd leave your name alone. Let's unload these boards and get you out of here."

As we stacked the wood, Kitch floored me with the question, "Did you ever own slaves, Mr. Gates?"

"Less than fifty," I answered, reminiscing on the bucolic days before the Civil War. "My father regarded them as family," I lied, recalling the flagellations the overseer or headman meted out for transgressions as petty as stealing a peach. I grew up playing with the slave children on our plantation, but as an adult, I never accepted them as equals. The wagon was empty. "I suppose you consider this donation a bribe to keep my mouth shut?"

Kitch smiled and led Cherika to the buckboard. While harnessing the mare, he cockily responded, "I'd rather call it a business deal. Mr. Gates, you need my help to build this cottage. Ten dollars a week to start. I'm askin' half the salary of a carpenter. You've saved the money Joe Higgs wanted. That gives you seven days of my time."

I weighed my options and then—against good judgment—shook his hand.

Fig trees enveloped the rectangular garden behind Ah Wo Sue's house. The straight furrows were amazingly arable. I admired the thriving tomatoes, onions, peppers, and string beans. The varieties of cabbages were foreign, possibly Asian strains. Bent at the waist, the Chinaman hoed weeds that were choking plants resembling celery stalks.

"You must have a green thumb. What are those leafy things?" I inquired.

Upright and flexing his back, Wo Sue replied, "Bok choy." He dug a spade into a ripe heap of pig manure and mixed the brown glop into the red clay. "There are two corner lots on B and Sixth Streets that might interest you. The B Street School is scheduled to be completed by the end of this year, and the surrounding land will gain value with young families wishing to live nearby. The buyer left town and defaulted on the loan. Alonzo Horton re-purchased both parcels, almost for nothing. From what I've determined, he is short on cash. Many of his holdings are foreclosing due to delinquent taxes. You should go talk to him. I think Father Horton is shrewd but also quite practical."

"Thanks for the tip. Did Bum ever find his way home?" On numerous outings, I noticed the big dog riding an omnibus around town. Shop-owners always contributed treats to the Saint Bernard. With so much loving attention, Bum seemed honored to be San Diego's official mascot.

"Every once in a blue moon he stops by to sleep. I worry about him," Wo Sue answered, tossing an invasive snail into the adjacent yard. On the roadway, I heard more coiled shells smash against the rocks.

Chapter Four

UPON ARRIVING IN SAN DIEGO, I worked nine months at the Stonewall Jackson Mine, living in the company town of Stratton with a thousand other greedy miners. I had sweat bullets for twelve weeks double-jacking: swinging an eight-pound hammer, while my partner, Daniel Judge, hand-drilled into quartz and granite deposits. Once dynamite plugged the holes, and the slow-burning fuses were lit, thirty tons of mountain thundered to the ground. A tiny percentage of the unrefined earth contained flecks of gold. The muckers then loaded the boulders into one-ton cars to be propelled to the gargantuan mill. There, six hundred and fifty-pound stamps pulverized the ore. Governor Robert Waterman, the new titleholder of the mine, learned of my engineering classes at the East Alabama Male College, and saw fit to assign me the responsibility of installing and maintaining the state-of-the-art Corliss steam engine used to run the sixty-foot-tall hoist.

On the side, Daniel and I owned a mineral title in the hills south of Julian. Although we mined copper, gold flakes were an incidental product. There had been unsettling chatter around camp of the Stonewall Mine drying up and the Governor searching for a purchaser. Judge and I quit to work full-time on our claim. There wasn't enough of the reddish-brown metal to retire; still, a man could live on the proceeds and put a little savings aside.

An unfamiliar secretary ushered me into Alonzo Erastus Horton's cramped office in the Wells Fargo Express Company building on Sixth Street. Regrettably, Horton's former confidential assistant had died a few months earlier of acute pneumonia. Through the open window on the lower floor, sunlight slanted across the deeds and charts strewn on the mahogany desk. A toppled stack of shiny gold coins captured my attention. I guessed the Double Eagles might be props used to doctor up the sickly state of the real estate industry. As Horton peered up from a journal, he noted my gaze and stood. At seventy-five years old, the stout, balding man radiated exuberance.

He offered the robust handshake of an ex-champion boxer. "Mr. Gates, what a nice diversion from trying to manage my accounts. Please sit. Can I get Mr. Sledge to bring you something?"

"No thank you, Mr. Horton." I lowered to the "buyers beware" chair and deliberately packed a pipe with Kentucky Club. At this level, his authority became elevated—a judge on a bench. I struck a Lucifer on my heel and blew the smoke toward the pressed tin ceiling. "The other day, I looked at property on B and Sixth Streets."

The perpetual salesman moved to peruse a map of Horton's Addition pinned to the wall. With an index finger, he tapped twice. "Block Nineteen, Lots A and L? Not too far from your place on Fourth Street?"

"That's right," I puffed. "I understand they foreclosed."

"Buyer's remorse," Horton chuckled. "Luckily, I rebought them for less than my original selling price. And as a bonus, the Copperheads graded the slope before heading back East. But, I shouldn't be telling you all that. Why so interested? Is it the new grammar school?" Seated again, he stroked his chinstrap beard.

"What are you asking for the two plots? There's plenty of empty acreage in that area."

Horton's brow squinched as he thumbed pages in an accounting ledger. "Last month, you bought Lot 201 C for eight hundred. I recently noticed construction supplies on your premises." He smiled. "I'm elated to see another house going up in your neighborhood. Do you have architectural plans?"

"Yes. I am using the Queen Anne drawings from a Palliser planbook. I've obtained the required permits and shall commence work shortly."

Horton's eyes bore into me as he questioned, "Your copper mine with Daniel Judge, is it profitable?"

Astonished by his omnipotence, I answered, "At thirteen cents a pound, we'll never be rich." I knew that he had previous experience in various trades, mining being one.

We haggled until lunch before agreeing on the price of thirteen hundred, with the stipulation that I had to erect buildings on both parcels within six months.

As I left, Horton inquired, "Henry, are you attending the Hotel del Coronado's grand opening?"

As an introvert, I hadn't planned to go. "Why?"

"This event is an ideal venue to meet and greet. The whole town will be there. Since you're buying up land, it may be worthwhile to fraternize with the upper-crust."

"I'll write the date on my calendar, Mr. Horton."

"Call me Alonzo," he proposed and closed the gate.

I waited by the tent relishing the first smoke of the day. The nippy air refreshed on this cloudless morning. Kitch Cane arrived at sunup atop Cherika bearing breakfast: eggs, ham, and hot coffee. "What do I owe you?" I asked, accepting half and handing him a fork.

Kitch flashed even teeth. "The next time it's on you, boss." He stretched and surveyed the site as if measuring distances. "Where do we begin?"

I retrieved the *Palliser Model Homes* book and leafed to "Plate III," depicting the "Cottage at West Stratford, Connecticut." The detailed diagram illustrated a two-story house with steep, gabled roofs topped with a central chimney. Eighteen windows facilitated cross-ventilation and a cozy porch, labeled "Piazza" in the layout, led to the front door. The lower level accommodated a parlor, dining room, and kitchen, while the upstairs had three chambers to be utilized as bedrooms. A spacious attic could be converted to additional rooms if necessary. Collectively, the dwelling built in West Stratford was well designed.

Kitch studied the etching and floor plans, re-reading the description. "Says here, the cost is fourteen hundred and sixty bucks. You got that *and* enough to pay me?"

I admired that the man demonstrated literacy, yet remained unaccustomed and perturbed by his directness. "Your concern over my finances is duly noted. Are you capable of building this cottage or not?"

Cane gobbled the slab of the ham. "I'm ready to start. We'll need eighty to one hundred cubic feet of masonry for the foundation. No cellar, right?"

"Do you feel like digging a hole?"

He scratched the hard turf with a toe. "Nope, not if you don't."

Limestone quarries north of Pine Valley furnished materials for the construction of the Stonewall Gold Mine. "Can we use your wagon? Do you have tack to add my mule?"

"That's a heavy load. What of that new rail line?" Kitch mused. "I heard she's runnin' a regular schedule."

The San Diego and Cuyamaca Eastern Railroad was Governor Waterman's pet project. The track connected the city to the rural towns spreading east, terminating somewhere past Lakeside. I read of a quarry in Santee. Maybe they delivered—a sensible solution.

At the booking office in the Santa Fe Depot, I paid for a pair of round trip tickets to Santee. As Kitch sauntered off to the Jim Crow car, I snagged a used newspaper and boarded the train. During this time of day, the coach held locals or tourists exploring the backwoods towns along the latest rail line.

The paper's real estate section ballooned with grand advertisements by two hundred agents vying for sales. An announcement for the inaugural opening of the Hotel del Coronado dominated a page. Marketers billed the lodging as "The largest and most elegant all-the-year-round seaside resort in the World." Eye witnessing the incandescent electric lights, hydraulic elevators, and other newfangled marvels might be worth a day trip.

While we detrained at Santee, the conductor gave me directions to the Simpson-Pirnie Granite Company. He indicated the diggings were four miles away on the outskirts of town.

"A fellow on the trip said I'd get lynched out here." Kitch squinted at the lack of scenery and fixed his hat to block the glare.

"Not if you keep your mouth shut and you stay far away from trees," I advised, tilting my brim to the same angle. Those simple tasks should be easy for both of us to accomplish, as I wasn't in the mood to talk, and in this arid region, any vegetation higher than my waist had shriveled up. I yearned for the shadowy, humid forests of Alabama. With the "devil winds" blowing in from the east, the temperatures rose above normal. Chapped, my lips begged for moisture. I sucked on a pebble. "That must be it." Up ahead, a vortex of dust swirled from a jagged cleft in the hillside.

At the quarry, rock-splitters used feather and wedging techniques to break granite slabs from the cliff face. A few stony characters took a breather from hand-drilling or compressing curved metal feathers into the perforations to watch us pass.

Ambitious for new business, James Simpson tendered dimension stone at reasonable prices that included shipping. These smaller igneous chunks were adequate for construction. Simpson guaranteed that the order would arrive in two days.

On the way back to the station, a tarantula snared a dozing horned lizard. Watching the hairy spider crush the struggling reptile with its powerful fangs, Kitch questioned if I had given any more thought to turning him in for murdering Joe Higgs.

"Not 'til the house is done," I answered.

Through wavy glass, I saw a lantern ignite and heard a male and female arguing. I knocked on the building that Molly Doyle had entered after our chance meeting. A squat, swarthy man palming a blackjack opened the door. Sullen, he looked past me and demanded what I wanted.

"Are you Ray?" I inquired, pushing by. Molly sat on the bed without acknowledging me. Even in the gloom, I discerned the ugly marks bruising her cheeks.

"Who needs to know?" the pimp responded, riled that I filled the shabby hovel.

"Did he do that?" I asked. Closemouthed, she backed into a corner.

Nimble as a weasel, Ray lunged, brandishing the leather-covered truncheon. Instead of retreating, I stepped forward and raised my knee to his groin while blocking with an elbow. As the flesh-peddler fell, I cracked the nape of his neck with clubbed hands.

"Have you lost your mind?" Molly squawked. She stood atop the unconscious panderer. "What did you do?"

"He hit you," I replied, bewildered by her anger. "I couldn't let—"

"There are worse ogres than Ray Diamond running around. Are you taking over his job?"

"No, no, of course not. I actually stopped by to see if you left town." I rolled Ray and rifled his pockets, finding fifteen dollars.

"Ha! That's rich! You came to cash in on my proposition for a free lay. Hank, or whatever your name is, you have a violent disposition. That doesn't make you any better than the other miscreants in Stingaree Town. What's more, you don't consider the consequences of your impulsive actions."

I possessed a temper, occasionally uncontrollable, but I usually concluded that my morality abided on God's side of right and wrong. "I'm not like them and besides, I protected you."

"The last time, you warded off thieving rapists. This night, you'll get me killed."

"Sorry," I mumbled and passed the money.

"It's okay, angel," Molly said, taking my wrist. We stepped over Ray to the warmth of her sheets.

Chapter Five

IT BECAME EVIDENT that Kitch knew his job as far as construction. The stone arrived without delay, and within days, we dug and filled a trench for the foundation.

One afternoon, we worked at building the stem wall to raise the structure off the earth. After tightening the mason's strings sagging between the stakes marking the first floor, I stood back and smiled. Bit by bit, the house was taking shape.

Till Burnes rode up on a black filly with a crescent moon blaze on her forehead. "Who's your man?" he asked, gauging the property and our progress.

I had no clues to what pickles Cane might be in and considered making up a fictitious name.

My laborer wedged home a square piece of granite, and replied, "Kitch Cane."

"Sugar plantation?" Till questioned, ambling to the stack of timber. The bartender lifted a board and sighted along the edge for warpage. Nodding favorably, he let the plank drop with a clatter.

"Yes sir, Mr. Burnes," Cane answered. "The Acadia in Lafourche Parish."

"How'd you get my name?" the Irishman inquired.

"On Sundays, I walk my boy over to the Acme. We watch the animals at your menagerie. Aaron is partial to that cranky bear."

Burnes chuckled. "Bruin's wild! Don't let the wee one stray too close."

This was valuable advice. A few years ago, a constable allowed the shaggy beast to lick honey off his face. Deputy Wilbur now had an enlarged opening to his sinuses.

"Hank, the next time I stop by, we'll be sippin' fancy cocktails on your new porch." Mounting his horse, Till said to Kitch, "Somebody from Arizona brought in a Gila monster. I'm almost done knockin' together a cage. Bring the kid by, and I'll let him feed bird eggs to the god-awful creature." With a tip of his cap, the barkeep returned to the saloon.

"Mr. Burnes is sure interested in the wood," Cane noted. He frowned and tugged on his leather gloves.

"Till's all right and won't be a complication." I hadn't bothered quizzing Kitch about his private life, surprised to learn he had a son. "Are you married?"

Kitch grinned. "Six years and counting. Minnie is her name. She taught me everything I know. So far, we only have the one child. Aaron's three and never sleeps."

"Where do you live?" The majority of the African Americans who had migrated to San Diego from the southern states lived in agrarian areas, such as Julian, or below the city.

"Down south with the other brown-skinned folks. There ain't a lot of us—more since the last census. If things don't pan out for me here, maybe I'll move the family up to Los Angeles."

I mixed mortar and carried the bucket to the wall. Kitch loaded a trowel and buttered the stone for the subsequent row.

"Tell me if anyone gives you cause for concern," I offered. I recalled how Cane had slit Higgs' neck and reckoned he could take care of himself.

"Thanks," Kitch said earnestly. "You're already helpin' me out with this job. Minnie's grateful for the extra wages. She applied for work teachin' the neighborhood children." He paused and set the tool in the pail. "Mr. Gates, can I ask you something?"

"Quit with the Mr. Gates. Just call me Hank." Leg aching from kneeling, I sat against the blocks to rub my thigh.

Kitch smirked. "You're not trickin' me into usin' your given name. That ain't gonna happen, Mr. Gates."

"Fine, what's your question?" I turned and registered the misery etched around his eyes.

"I'm assumin' you slew Yankees in the war?" When there was no answer, he continued. "Puttin' Joe Higgs down should have been easier. He murdered my parents and destroyed my family. Expected to feel good afterwards—you know—retribution, justice. For months, I toiled side by side with the man while plannin' his execution. The anger became so intense some days I nearly burst. I prayed to hide my rage. There were times I thought he saw inside my schemin' head, or caught me starin' at him the wrong way. Higgs was hateful and I'm relieved he is dead, but now I see his face everyplace. Unable to stop broodin' on it."

I used a pocketknife to peel the cake from the bowl of my pipe. "First life you ever took?"

"Guess so. On the way up here, I scuffled with a highwayman who tried to swipe our stuff. Minnie smacked his noggin with a branch. We rolled him in an arroyo. The robber was still alive when we got going." Kitch inspected his fingers and bit a hangnail. "To be honest, I didn't check him up close. We kept movin'."

"Sometimes, it's best not to know. Holding onto that sliver of uncertainty lets you get on with life." I tamped in the springy tobacco and lit the pipe with a crooked match. "At Seven Pines, my first battle, I commanded my artillery troop to target a farmhouse used by the Federals. The lead shell landed short by fifty yards. The gunners raised the barrel and fired again—this projectile a direct hit. Our observer later reported seeing women and children running out of the building right before the second munition exploded. Remembering the almighty size of the blast, I fear they didn't find refuge."

"It troubles you? You stew over it?" Kitch inquired.

"After the war, I hit the bottle pretty hard, tramping the back roads, trying to forget everything. One chilly night, a farmer found me hibernating in his hog pen. Rather than sticking me with a pitchfork, Oscar Peterson took pity and put me to work. I lived there for a couple of years until the world started turning again."

"How are you doin' nowadays? Do the bad memories eventually fade?"

I shook my head dolefully. "There will come a day, Mr. Cane, when you suddenly realize a minute has passed without thinking of Higgs. You'll rejoice that it is possible—a few moments to breathe easy and stand straight. May I add my two cent's worth?"

"Sure, Mr. Gates."

"Don't confess to anyone else what you did. Not your brother, not your wife, not anybody. That's between you, God, and undoubtedly—the ghosts of the men you've killed."

The top-heavy boat plowed a furrow through the choppy water. In my best duds, I ferried across the harbor to Coronado Island with hundreds of enthusiastic San Diego residents and visiting dignitaries itching to see and be seen at the launch of the Hotel del Coronado. I skirted the weekend throngs at the wharf waiting to be shuttled to the event via railway cars. As an alternative, I walked among twin rows of citrus trees along Orange Avenue, away from the bay and toward the glittering Pacific.

During the early weeks of February, the Coronado Beach Company undertook a valiant effort to make the sandbar appear inhabitable by laying out tree-lined lanes, most still marked off with temporary signs. Past half-completed cottages, the red-shingled, coned roofs of the modern resort soared into the azure sky. Bordered with dazzling sand, the gigantic white castle and immaculate gardens created a fairyland in the midst of what had been sagebrush-covered hunting grounds.

Below the bay windows of the circular Crown Room, I merged into a column of guests ascending the steps to the main entrance. In the richly-textured lobby, I admired the lofty, coffered ceilings and drew in the vapors of the oiled wood paneling. I heard the echoes of music down the hall. In a voluminous space, an enthralled audience ringed a lanky, handsome man seated before a glossy grand piano. I recognized the musician with the handlebar mustache as the Spiritualist, Jesse Shepard, from a photograph in the newspaper. The unique range of the pianist's intonations splendidly accompanied the sublime melody.

I ambled into the central courtyard. Shaded by palm trees and vine-wrapped arches of blooming morning glory, I identified several local celebrities, including Wyatt Earp and his spouse Josephine. A cement stairwell cascaded to a panoramic view of the ocean. To the south, resembling broken shark's teeth, the steep peaks of the four desolate Coronado islands rose off the coast of Mexico. Northward, the cliffs of Point Loma plunged into the crashing surf. On the seaside patio, the City Guard Band played up-tempo John Philip Sousa marches as waiters delivered cooling refreshments to men and women in formal attire.

A gruff voice spoke by my shoulder. "Henry, glad you made it." I turned to regard Alonzo Horton and his wife escorting a younger woman. He wore a top hat and clutched a cane capped with a silver elephant handgrip. Mrs. Horton smiled from underneath a fringed parasol.

"Wouldn't miss it for anything," I agreed, appreciating their companion. Statuesque, she presented a curvy contour in a brown velveteen and copper silk bustle dress. Hatless, her shiny chestnut tresses swept up to the top of her crown.

"Henry, I'm pleased to introduce my lovely wife Sarah and Miss Mills, a classmate of my niece. Laura came all the way from Philadelphia to stay with us. Unfortunately, Gracie felt under the weather and remained at home."

Shaking my hand, Laura's blue eyes narrowed as she appraised my dusty morning coat and untrimmed Van Dyke. I could only imagine her thoughts after discovering I lived in a tent. The band switched to the cadence of an even louder march. "Is this your first time out West, Miss Mills?" I shouted.

"Yes. It differs significantly from what I pictured." In the high sun of noon, perspiration beaded her brow.

"How?"

"The scenery is so diverse, so dry, and the population is very—"

"Ignorant, uncultured?"

"I've met a medley of stimulating personalities," she laughed while batting away a fly. "From your accent, I detect you're originally from a more humid climate?"

"If you're asking if I served in the Confederate States Army, the answer is yes. I was born and raised in Buzzard Roost, Alabama. In '86, I moved to San Diego. California takes getting used to, but living in the Golden State has many advantages.

Mr. Horton is doing his best to establish our growing city on the international stage."

Sarah Horton held the sunshade over Laura's head. "Mr. Gates, we are hosting a small dinner gathering on Wednesday evening at our residence. Alonzo and I shall be honored if you'll be our guest."

With a short bow, I replied, "I'd be delighted, Mrs. Horton,"

"Wonderful!" Alonzo exclaimed. "We'll look forward to seeing you then."

Chapter Six

EARLY MONDAY MORNING, I AWOKE TO A BEATING—someone caving in my skull. Blind with blood, I strove to block the angry blows. Twisting, I wrapped my arms around my assailant and pulled him near. The goon grunted, ineffectively swinging his fists. I moved closer, biting at flesh tasting of sweat. Screams filled the tent as I gnawed into his windpipe. My mouth brimmed with hot juice and, in the end, his ragged breath.

Ray Diamond lay upon his back, blinking rapidly as his shredded jugular spurted life. As I drew my sword, his eyeballs bulged in apprehension. I aligned, and then slipped the thorn between the heaving ribs, slowly puncturing his depraved heart.

Outdoors, I spilled a pail of frigid water over my head. With coppery tongue and pounding brain, I collapsed and gagged against the house's foundation. Once again, I had stuck my—now tender—nose someplace it didn't belong. I crawled inside and, dripping, stared at Ray. The pimp gazed upwards, perhaps contemplating his future—except for the obvious fact that a silver shaft protruded from his chest. I wiped my face and threw the rag on his. Neighbors must have heard the ruckus, yet no one stirred. *How can I get rid of the body?*

Eager for freedom, Clive whinnied as we walked from Ernie Smoke's stables. I aimed southeast to a nameless section of town rarely frequented. The African Americans lived in a three-block stretch abutting Chollas Creek. Populated with a few dozen buildings, I picked out a red wagon parked by a shed. Kitch will help—*he's got to.*

I fastened a feedbag under Clive's snout and opened a gate in the whitewashed picket fence. The well-kept, one-story home was nicer than I had imagined. A mechanical click stopped me cold.

A husky voice advanced from behind me. "Don't move, mister. What're you doin' here?" With hands lifted, I swiveled to see a middle-aged colored man aiming a new John Browning lever-action shotgun.

Impressed, I queried, "Model 1887?" Gratified that I approved, he shoved the muzzle in my gut.

"Sir, I po-litely asked you a question." The gunman skimmed the trees to confirm that I arrived alone. "Why're you snoopin' about?"

"I'm looking for Kitch Cane. He's not expecting me but is acquainted with who I am. Mr. Cane is currently in my employ."

"And you came here like a thief in the night? That don't seem right, does it?" he hissed, spitting into the poison ivy.

Across the way, two juveniles hurried into the lane. One swung a machete, the other a club. From a backyard, an agitated hound started baying.

"Go find him," I said. "Say Henry Gates requests his assistance."

The man nudged his chin at the shorter of the adolescents. "Basil, fetch Kitch," he ordered. The remaining older youth removed my sword, swooshed it to show off, and jabbed the barb in my backbone.

As Basil thumped the doorframe, my stomach dropped, realizing that now was the perfect time and place for Cane to eliminate the only living witness to Higgs' murder.

A kerosene lantern illuminated a window, and a door creaked. After a brief conversation, Kitch uttered something into the house before leaping onto the lawn.

"Mourning, he's okay," Cane told the owner of the shotgun. "Thanks for keeping an eye open. Mero, give the gentleman his sword."

Mero retreated, feigned a stabbing thrust, and flipping the weapon, passed me the grip. "Blade's sticky," he remarked with a sly smile.

As the boys returned to their abode, Kitch called, "On Friday and Saturday, I have a job packin' oranges from Escondido. Let your mother know I'll need your strong backs." Basil and Mero waved goodbye and went indoors.

"May I?" I indicated the Model 1887. Mourning shrugged and conveyed the Winchester. "This is quite a piece of handiwork." I handed over the scattergun and inquired, "Ten-gauge?"

Nodding, he responded, "I use it for huntin'. There's too many critters on the other side of the creek."

"You never can tell what's out there," I concurred.

"Come on up for coffee," Kitch beckoned.

We entered the modest front room. He carried the light to a square table and offered a chair. "Sit a spell, Mr. Gates. I'm sure whatever is wrong can be fixed."

As I sat, a female asked, "Is this the Confederate you've been working for?"

With elbows folded, a petite, yet sturdy woman stood in the doorway of what I deduced was the bedroom. A child arose from the darkness and clasped an arm around her leg. Busily sucking his thumb, the curious tot tracked every move I made.

"Yes, Minnie. This is Mr. Gates. Please fix us a pot of coffee?"

"Ma'am, you don't have to go to the inconvenience. Sorry for disturbing your family."

"No worries," Minnie said. "We'd be getting up soon anyways." In the kitchen, she stoked a fire in the potbelly stove. The toddler presented me with a miniature train.

I lifted the wooden locomotive up to the flame and admired the intricate whittling. "Did you carve this?"

Kitch laughed. "No. Mourning gave that to Aaron. My neighbor is always makin' playthings for the kids." He became earnest. "Due to the earliness of the hour and the dried blood on your face, I assume you're here on urgent business. What happened?"

Minnie set boiling tin cups of coffee between us. "I'll let you men talk," she said softly, and withdrew to the bedroom.

Aaron chuffed, "Choo-choo" and rolled the toy on the uneven planking.

The bold, aromatic bean grinds energized me. I described my initial encounter with Molly Doyle and the later meetings with Ray Diamond, leaving out that I had slept with the prostitute.

"This Ray, he's still in your tent?" Cane cranked the knob to lower the lantern's wick. "It's almost daylight."

"Must be five o'clock. I thought we'd load him in your wagon and take a trip to South Bay."

"Can we scalp him first?" Kitch questioned, half-jokingly. "I mean, did anyone see you?"

"Not that I could tell," I answered. "We should get moving." I drained my mug and rose.

"And you think I'm obliged to help because of what you know?" Kitch lingered, obstinately drinking the brew.

"That has crossed my mind."

"So when this errand is done, we'll be even?"

"Kitch, it's not like that. I'm not forcing you to come, but I'm in a bind."

"Go," Minnie said from the bedroom doorway. "Mr. Gates rode all the way to Chollas. Sounds to me, you're the single friend he can run to, or maybe, the only one he's got left."

"Was intendin' to, Minnie. Jus' wanted Mr. Gates to understand that I don't have to."

Warning us to be careful, Cane's wife led Clive to the outbuilding. Aaron watched from the stoop.

"Why do you wander the Stingaree after dark?" Kitch inquired as Cherika pulled us toward the city. "What are you looking for?" The eastern sky brightened from black to indigo.

"That's a good question, which doesn't have a good answer. Sleep is hard to come by. When the war ended, the Yanks released us from Point Lookout. That's a Union prison in Maryland. The armies ceased exchanging prisoners, so before long, the encampment overcrowded—twenty thousand men striving to survive." The wagon jounced on the rutted course. "Bunked in tents or shebangs if we patched together enough canvas. If not, we lay in the freezing rain. Most detainees perished from starvation and disease. We ate rats and snails, slurping water from puddles tainted by overflowing latrines. The colored pickets who patrolled the tops of the fourteen-foot high parapets loved to shoot Rebs. The only way to escape the penitentiary was by dying. On many days, a bullet in the brainpan struck me as a valid option."

"I'd a given you what you wished for," Kitch asserted. "Shot you right in that pasty melon."

"That's a relief," I chuckled. "When the bloodshed ended, the guards let the captives free. Not the whole camp at once—in bunches. The Federals assumed the men would continue fighting or ransack the countryside. There wasn't any resistance residing in any of us. We longed to return to our families. I headed southwest with a gang of veterans. In Charlottesville, an old lady saw my blistered toes and donated her late husband's shoes. Walked for eight hundred miles through Virginia and Tennessee. We scrounged for food and foraged when necessary. No chicken coop remained safe from our scrawny band of misfits. The group condensed as we diverged. Some went to the Carolinas. Others kept on to Texas. A great number had soldier's heart and fell to the side of the trail—too mentally played-out to carry on. Nothing we said could make those fellas budge, so we abandoned them. A few rotten apples roughed up the native women. We had—"

Kitch interrupted, "Then you stroll in the front door of your mansion and what, your daddy's mad that you lost the war? Papa sent you on up to your room 'cause he had to set the cotton-pickers free and then burn his cash crop?"

"My father succumbed to dropsy after I enlisted, and the slaves let themselves go. Our plantation grew tobacco, not cotton." The mare plodded up Fourth Street, two blocks away from my parcel.

"Sorry, Mr. Gates. Sometimes I get worked up on the matter."

"Granted, but the war is ancient history," I placated, hopping to the roadway. "I'll check on things. Sit tight! If I'm gone over five minutes—vamoose."

The sky glowed dullish red as I cut crosswise to Sixth Street and hunkered in the dense scrub of the City Park. From this distance, my lot appeared vacant. I emerged from the tumbleweeds and froze—*just the wind wiggling the tent flap.* Inside the canvas cocoon, Ray waited patiently, stiffening and stinking up the tent with his vile excretions.

I rolled the flesh-peddler in a blanket and trimmed lengths of rope as Kitch cantered up on Cherika. Blood seeped through the thin material.

"Didn't I tell you to stay put 'til I came back?" I scolded, threading sections of cord under the dead man.

Cane tied up the bundle. "I got edgy," he responded. "How do I know who's swathed up in this fleece?"

"Can you account for everyone you care about?" I asked, seizing the loop knotted at the ankles and dragging the hustler from the tent. Snagged wads of my wardrobe adhered to the mess.

"I suppose. Everybody I hold dear is at Chollas Creek." He grasped the other end and counting to three, we heaved Ray into the wagon bed.

"Before we dump him in the water, you may take a peek. *Ugh!* These clothes need to be thrown away," I growled, poking at my soiled possessions.

"Bring them with us. Minnie uses borax for tough stains, and with Aaron, there's always mounds of dirty diapers."

I collected the garments and slung the haversack on the seat. *What a bad way to start the day.* I directed to a heap of rubbish in a neighboring yard. "Grab the reins and stop there." We hid the secret and turned south.

Satisfied that Ray was off my property and on his way to a watery grave; I prepared my pipe and massaged inflamed muscles. Lumps covered my crown and my left eye swelled half-shut. Tomorrow, I would look and feel worse.

Cane saw me probing my gums for loose teeth and questioned, "Do you think the pimp has any chums comin' to seek him out, *or you?*"

"Hope not," I mumbled. "I've enough problems getting any rest. Once the house is built, I'll be under lock and key." Entering *Rancho de la Nacion,* Cherika tread up a meandering lane bisecting a Chula Vista lemon grove. As the clouds parted, the morning dew glistened on the yellowing fruit.

"You never finished your story," Kitch prodded, steering the horse and cart over a clogged irrigation channel. "Before, you were tellin' me the men got fresh with the locals."

"That's putting it mildly. In the Kentucky woods, the Shawnee caught five members of our troop assaulting their squaws. The chief's son held us all responsible. As a former lieutenant, the men still treated me as the ranking officer. While I negotiated with Tonomo for the hostages' lives, our guys went on a rescue mission."

Cane scowled. "You saved rapists? Why?"

As the buckboard crested a sandy knoll, the southern point of the San Diego Bay came into view. "At nightfall, we strung up and gutted the guilty from trees outside our camp. It wasn't right to let the Indians administer the punishment. They were ours."

"What did Tonomo do?" Kitch inquired, braking in a clump of manzanita. "He must not have been thrilled."

We dismounted and congregated at the tail of the wagon. As I slid the carcass from the trash, Ray's head hit the ground with a thud.

"Same as now, Tonomo and his father, Big Jim, had their own set of disputes dealing with the U.S. Government. After I clarified our intentions and expressed remorse, he let us go." I rolled Ray onto his back.

Cane hitched a rope to the stiff's ankles, and we towed the burden through the pickleweed and cordgrass. Our boots submerged into the brackish marsh as the corpse sailed into deeper water. I carried rocks from shore and with the waves lapping our necks, we forced the weights into the pleats of the bedspread. Bubbles and blood mixed as Molly's pimp sank into the murk.

On the bank, we sat on a log to dry in the warm sun. I ached for a tin of Dr. Mettaur's Headache Pills to quash the throbbing behind my forehead. "That bastard better stay put," I grumbled.

"The fish will eat him," Kitch declared, using fingers to squeegee his trousers. "Or the bugs."

"Lobsters?"

"Yes, lobsters," he shuddered.

"When I arrived home, the place was deserted." I watched a pelican dive into the shallows and surface with a fin twitching from its pouch.

"What?" Kitch muttered. Maybe he fantasized of a swarm of spiny crustaceans besieging Ray, quivering antennae bent forward in voracious anticipation.

"Cedar Hall burned to the foundation. My wife, two children, mother, sister—everyone missing. A nearby farmer, who observed smoke a few months earlier, investigated but couldn't find any evidence in the rubble. The neighbors surmised that following the emancipation, the household vacated, incapable of managing the plantation without my father or the slaves. That was decades ago. I spent years searching Alabama, Mississippi, Georgia—most of the lower states. At each town that published a newspaper, I posted notices to contact me with information. No one had seen my kin or heard of them. I finally traveled north, until, as I told you before, Oscar Peterson found me in his piggery lying in a puddle of puke."

"That's rough," Cane commiserated. "What do you suspect took place?"

"To begin with, I blamed the Unionists. The damn Yankees had half of Alabama blockaded. The Loyalists raided regional farms and towns to resupply the Northern effort, however there were no indications that Federalist troops had been to Colbert County in recent months."

"Do you trust the neighbors who said your people picked up and left?"

"At first I did. On Allsboro Road, a covered bridge crosses Buzzard Roost Creek. There, I spotted my name and a set of peculiar characters carved on the railing." With a twig, I scraped a two-pronged pitchfork surrounded by a circle in the mud. Like the word "Croatoan" scratched into a tree by the Lost Colony on Roanoke Island, I never figured out its significance or who made the engraving. "One of my family members may have drawn it for fun or they attempted to make known where they went. During the last twenty years, I've shown this bident symbol to hundreds of individuals without any luck."

Kitch rasped his stubble. "Looks to be a cattle brand."

I traced the image, digging farther into the grooves. "Yup, I went to all the ranches. Nobody had ever seen that stamp."

"That's why you walk the Stingaree? You're unable to relax for vexin' about your folk?"

I nodded and erased the sketch with my heel. We listened to amorous great blue herons croaking in the copse of tall trees.

"Hey!" Kitch blurted. "Hank, you forgot to let me see the face of the man we jus' buried."

"Oh, now you want to call me Hank? Not Mr. Gates?"

"After today, we're even," he grinned. "In public—so I don't get a beat down—you're still Mr. Gates."

"Are you really going to fish for him on the bottom? Ray's coated with crabs and God knows what other horrors by now."

Cane clawed at his arms and around his throat. Shaking his head, Kitch moaned, "Hell no. Let him—whoever he is—be bug food!"

Chapter Seven

PAST A MATCHING SET OF GRANITE LION HEADS, a tuxedoed servant permitted entrance to Alonzo Horton's twelve-room mansion on 1929 First Street. A familiar piano melody drifted from the clerestory atrium—*Chopin.* I had heard this dramatic piece in the lobby of the Hotel del Coronado. In the vestibule, harmonious notes melted into an airy fantasia by Thalberg, or was this symphonic poem penned by the Hungarian virtuoso, Franz Liszt?

In full feather, Horton's two dozen guests huddled around a gleaming Steinway. Jesse Shepard's huge hands flew over the keys, his dexterous fingers covering all octaves at once. Still, it was Shepard's voice that astounded, ostensibly singing in bass and soprano simultaneously. Appearing on my elbow, Laura Mills smiled upward before returning her attention to the concert. The mellow radiance of the candelabras enhanced her rosy cheeks. Again, she met my gaze, irises shifting from emerald to sapphire. Her dilated pupils drew me into a magical world. Laura either didn't notice or chose to ignore my blackened eye and flattened nose.

The buoyant strain climaxed as the pianist transfused the very essence of Mozart. As the sound waves of the Baroque symphony rippled like water from the curly redwood-paneled walls, the final chord reverberated for a heartbeat before the euphoric audience burst into applause. Shepard slid back the bench and addressed his admirers. Bowing from the waist, Jesse's arm swept high reveling in the adulation. Sarah Horton embraced the musician and herded the assembly to the dining room.

Using the gold-bound place cards for guidance, I found myself planted beside Laura at the long table overlaid with white linen. Opposite us, Jesse Shepard sat with a younger, similarly mustached man introduced as his secretary, Lawrence Tonner. A waiter filled our crystal goblets with red wine. Too embarrassed to explain my difficulties with alcohol, and anxious to fit in, I pretended to savor the Inglenook.

Shepard seemed to register the fixed level of wine in my glass. Deadpan, with traces of an English inflection, he asked, "Mr. Gates, don't take offence, but did a drunken tumble off your horse create those abundant abrasions, contusions, and welts?"

Tonner waggled his head, habituated to his boss's unsparing observations. "Mr. Gates, I beg pardon for my employer's lack of subtlety. Jesse meant no disrespect."

"None taken. I own an ornery mule, although Clive is not responsible for this particular trauma." Laura and the other diners awaited my comeback. "These bumps resulted from a dispute with a jack rabbit whose burrow also resides in Horton's Addition. Evidently, I provoked Miss Hare by moving onto her ancestral territory."

Shepard broke into deep and resonant laughter, supplemented by Tonner and company. Laura choked on the wine and, giggling, clutched a napkin to her lips. Proud of my successful repartee, I gently patted her on the back. Partaking of another mock sip, I realized the clever musician saw through my charade.

"How coincidental," Alonzo guffawed, "seeing that rabbit stew is our second course." That prompted further levity and jovial exchanges which continued for the remainder of the meal.

After dinner, the women went to the parlor to gossip while the men stationed themselves on the rear veranda to sample snifters of brandy and gripe about skyrocketing taxes. It had been ages since I mixed with so many aristocrats. On the hill overlooking the terraced terrain and Horton's town, I leaned over the railing. Mute marble sentinels watched as I poured my pear-shaped glass and sprinkled the caramel-colored wine onto shrubbery.

The dialog turned to a dynamic analysis of the lackluster state of physical education throughout the city's school systems. I moved closer when Captain Conrad Wiedemann mentioned the Concordia Turnverein, a gymnastics club based downtown. A German-American group, the "Turners," used dumbbells, batons, and calisthenics as forms of exercise. A giant of a man, and an expert in boxing and fencing, he served as the lead instructor for the Turnverein. At the Acme, I overheard discussions of a matchup between Captain Wiedemann and *La Jaguarina,* an actress famous for besting Sergeant Owen Davis in a mounted broadsword contest a year ago in San Francisco. If her manager, Fred Engelhard, made it happen, the duel could be the bout of the century. Rumors implied that the master-at-arms refused to battle a woman.

To liven up the conversation, I questioned, "Captain, I hear you are scheduled to clash with *La Jaguarina* this fall at the Pacific Beach race-track?"

Amused, Wiedemann answered with a slight Germanic accent, "Lieutenant, I understand you saw action in the War of Separation, thus you're proficient with sharp-edged weapons. Would *you* dare challenge the 'Ideal Amazon of the Age'?"

"I should never endeavor to provoke the Fates," I chuckled. "As I age, my fencing skills grow rusty."

"Ah, I can assist with that," Wiedemann promised. "I tutor weekly classes at the Turnverein for men intent on maintaining or broadening mastery of the foil, épée, or sabre. Even if you're not interested in competition, the comprehensive program is guaranteed to increase stamina and renew vitality."

"Captain, I'm afraid my parents were not of German descent."

He grinned. "No matter, we accept most nationalities. Our goal is to expand membership."

"Then I may be inclined to take you up on that offer."

"We'll make a Turner out of you yet, Lieutenant Gates. Drop by when you get a chance, and I'll provide a tour of the facilities."

As the witching hour passed, the Horton's callers bid their farewells, thanking the couple for the delicious dinner. I converged again with Laura descending the steps. At the base, Jesse Shepard and Lawrence Tonner waited.

"Mr. Gates, Miss Mills, Lawrence and I are entertaining at my home this evening. We'd be pleased to invite you both." Shepard inquired, "Might you join us?"

"It's approaching daybreak, Mr. Shepard," I responded, noting the waxing Snow Moon. A blizzard had to be blowing somewhere at loftier elevations. "I must rise early if I'm ever to move into my house before the turn of the century." Kitch and I had made perceptible progress over the last few days. Despite my aching knees, we succeeded in laying the oak parquet flooring on the lower level and sawing much of the timber for framing.

"Is it a séance?" Laura asked, curiosity brightening her eyes.

Charmed, Shepard replied, "You know of my passion for Spiritualism? While roaming the wilds of Russia, in Saint Petersburg I became consumed with the possibilities of communicating with familiars who transitioned behind the veil. General Jourafsky himself trained me in the art of conducting the elaborate ritual. Upon returning to the United States, I studied with Madame Blavatsky, the founder of Theosophy."

The papers often reviewed Shepard, either as a genius or a quack. I questioned, "I read you denounced Spiritualism and have gravitated to the Catholic faith?"

"'Denounced' is too forceful a word. As an instrument of Providence, my musical improvisations manifest from the inspirational works of artists who came and went before me. Candidly, I do not fully fathom the nature of the physical and mental states that envelope me whilst I am before a piano. Intelligence and self-culture are persuasive motivations. My immediate goal is to pursue a literary career under the nom de plume of Francis Grierson."

"Why a different name?" Laura inquired.

"Grierson was my mother's maiden name. Publishing houses won't take a medium seriously; therefore, a pseudonym establishes my identity as a new author."

The front door clacked shut, and Mrs. Horton cautiously negotiated the curving steps. "Jesse, I'm ready!" she announced, the prospect of adventure removing years from her rounded features. Sarah smiled and said to us, "I'm overjoyed that both of you will come. It shall be such fun!"

I turned to Laura, who pivoted as a vehicle rounded the bend and halted before the retaining wall. In the welcoming brilliance of the carriage lights, the coachman helped the ladies into the plush seats.

Laura's shoulder pressed against mine as the ironclad wheels bounced on winter's ruts. "That long scar marking your jaw is hidden by your beard, but the rest of your face has endured a drubbing. I sincerely doubt a cute little bunny instigated such mischief. Mr. Gates, what exactly caused those injuries?"

"May I call you Laura?"

"Please," Miss Mills allowed.

"And you must use Hank."

"Hank," she murmured, trying the shortened word on for size. "I'd prefer Henry."

"Henry it is. Laura, I'd love to share with you what occurred. In spite of that desire, our friendship germinates from infancy. I believe that at least for today, it's best to let these wounds heal, and together, we can move toward an optimistic tomorrow. Is that palatable?"

Brows knit, she questioned, "Are you always this reticent?"

"I didn't use to be," I said, staring at the rows of shuttered houses facing the boulevard. There was so much I couldn't tell her. "Most of my evasiveness is to insulate myself, some to shield others." Forever and a day had passed since I felt comfortable trusting anyone.

"Henry, I ought to ask, was the altercation over a woman?"

The coach rushed east to the straightaway of J Street. I hesitated before replying. "Yes, while not in the way you might think."

Laura remained closemouthed as we arrived in Sherman Heights. A magnificent Queen Anne mansion loomed ahead on K Street. In the crisp stillness, the Villa Montezuma held her breath, a carnivorous beast crouching in ambush on a sloping hillside. A winged serpent clung to the mast of the Arabesque dome, screeching heavenward to galaxies of distant immortals. Omnivorous dragons and toothy gargoyles glared from roof peaks and rain gutters. In the pre-dawn fog, the green shingles coating the sides resembled the horny plates armoring a dinosaur surging from a swamp. The fiery eyes of red-tinted windows watched us trespass onto the estate.

A pointy-eared Abyssinian cat scampered out the door as we followed Jesse and Lawrence into the grand foyer. Resolved to bring arts and culture to San Diego, the wealthy High brothers had financed the construction of the Villa Montezuma. Alonzo Horton's uptown mansion dominated as larger and exceedingly refined, whereas this whimsical, knickknack-cluttered house won as considerably more remarkable. Exotic flowers blossomed everywhere, exquisite tile fireplaces embellished each room, and handmade Persian rugs preserved the European hardwood flooring. Through ruby-stained glass, the moonlight ignited the lyrical Greek poet Sappho and her writhing female confidantes.

Lawrence guided us along a corridor, stopping before a gilded painting of dreary Roman ruins. With a dramatic flourish, he pushed an indentation in the fluted molding. A seam widened as the walnut wainscoting parted to reveal a passageway. The secretary proceeded into the enfolding shadows holding a single candle. Clustered by anxiety, we stood in the epicenter of a vast expanse. The walls, if any existed, were unreflective, the disorientating effect a result of ebony-dyed velvet. Shepard used this clandestine space for séances.

Armchairs formed a semi-circle around a grand piano. Previously situated, six masked men and women sat silently. I expected Jesse to walk forward, but he didn't accompany us.

"Ladies and gentlemen please be seated," Tonner stage whispered and shepherded us to our places. "The entertainment will begin momentarily." Without advance notification, he extinguished the taper. Laura gasped and latched onto my hand. The vault remained pitch-dark and soundless as a crypt, except for the forced respirations of its jumpy inhabitants.

Sixty steady beats of a metronome later, a dyad of sconces flared, extending above the etched glass before settling to a dull glimmer. Jesse Shepard sat on a stool before the piano, fingers resting on the black and white keys. Something way beyond the ordinary was about to transpire.

The pianist inhaled and began. Gusts of Siberian air synchronized with a quartette of angelic vocalizations floating over an extraordinary melody, eclectic renditions that circumnavigated the globe and spanned the centuries. Fairy lights capered and danced across the ceiling. I predicted a phantasmagoria, yet could not detect any concealed projection devices. Percussive instruments, bells, tambourines, and trumpets resounded from the corners of the chamber as Shepard channeled the famous composers of the past. Strange, sweet arias upon the piano, harp, and guitar sailed through the zephyr from ear to ear. Throats of ethereal beings, no longer able to sing for themselves, forged a direct pathway to our dimension.

Evocatively primitive, the maverick concluded the recital with the "Grand Egyptian March." Stomps of parading armies, blaring horns, rhythmic drums, and cannon shots filled the room. The cabalistic fantasy ended the same way it had started, with the lamps extinguishing. In seclusion we applauded, skeptics and disciples alike. Genuine psychic or unsanctified charlatan, Jesse Shepard had a miraculous gift which he conveyed to us—an awakening that kindled the heart and uplifted the soul.

As the lone candle flickered once more, Lawrence raised Mrs. Horton to her feet and led us into the hallway. Sarah dabbed her eyes, wanting to congratulate the maestro. Tonner expressed regret and expounded on how these performances exhausted Mr. Shepard, who had retired to his bedroom. He thanked everyone for visiting and escorted the guests to the coach. I never discovered the identities of the veiled spectators.

Chapter Eight

MY FITFUL DREAM-SWEATS ENDED with me hearing Kitch, Basil, and Mero reviewing the floor plan beside the tent. At the bucket, I scooped out the drowning stink beetle and splashed water upon my face. The dusk to dawn affair had sapped me. The sun shined excessively bright, but I had to confess, these sensations of fatigue outranked a crippling hangover. Also perplexing, I wasn't angry at Cane for bringing his uninvited neighbors.

"Mr. Gates, last night must have been wearisome. I could put my lunch in those bags under your eyes," Cane quipped. Basil sniggered until Mero cuffed his head.

"I went to a dinner party at Alonzo Horton's residence and afterward attended a séance. Both were very entertaining and enlightening."

"Hobnobbin' with the bigwigs? Did Father Horton serve fricasseed squirrels? I heard about those delicacies from a friend who worked at the mansion. And you went to a dance? Mr. Gates, I can't picture you doin' the polka." Basil giggled and Mero again advised silence with the back of his hand.

"You're sort of right. The chef prepared platters of tiny birds—stuffed quail and lima beans. I'm still hungry."

Kitch tossed a packet. Within were warm slices of cornbread and hard-boiled eggs. "Minnie," he mouthed.

"Thank her." I tapped the shell against the foundation and peeled off the covering. "And it wasn't a dance; I said séance. I don't polka, waltz, or frolic in any manner that requires grace."

Mero spoke up. "You mean where a shaman talks to dead folks? Everybody sits around a table until someone jabbers they're a murdered uncle or Julius Caesar?"

"You're close. This was a mite unusual. A man played a piano, exceptionally well actually. Have you ever gone to one?"

Basil grinned. "We got something like that down in the bottoms. Pastor Richards calls it the sermon!" After the delivery of the punch line, the youth bowed.

Laughing, the crumbly bread stuck in my throat. I gulped water to melt the blockage and waved Cane over. "You want me to compensate these boys for working here? There's just enough for you."

"Ten more bucks a week. That's nothin' for another three laborers. Hank, we'll finish your house lickety-split."

"*Three* more?"

"Mourning's on his way. He's not known as an early riser, all the same, once he gets rollin'—that man is a mover and shaker."

"Are any of them skilled in construction?"

"Mourning is. He held a job with a gang of Chinese at the hotel on Coronado, and he has his own kit of tools. Mero and Basil are fast learners. They'll saw and carry the wood while we hammer it together. Please, Mr. Gates, it's a great idea!" Kitch implored.

Cantankerous, I answered, "Fine. It shall be your responsibility to keep them in line. If I don't think you are making continuous headway, every one of you will be without a job. I'll twice-check everything you do and won't put up with shoddy workmanship."

Offended, Cane rebutted, "That's not going to happen. We'll get the job done right."

Mourning approached on the lane, the dust from his boots swirling eastward. The man wore a straw sombrero and toted a canvas pack on his back. The wind conveyed the whistle of a somber tune.

"Let's talk," I said softening. We met beneath the thickening shade of the eucalyptus. With frequent watering, green shoots sprouted from limbs I assumed were long dead. "Kitch, I'm confident you'll do a first-rate job. If this pans out, I'll have additional work for you and your friends. I procured a double-lot where the city is building the B Street School. It might be feasible to fit six or eight small apartments on that land. I already foresee you as the foreman on that venture, depending on how you handle this project." Mourning had rallied the kids and tidied up the site. "You can still run your freight business. Just be sure the tasks are completed here."

Cane revolved to regard his neighbors. Mero seized one end of a heavy plank as Basil struggled to raise the other side. The younger boy tripped, and the board banged to the ground spilling over a box of nails. Basil stood with outstretched arms. Mero shouted, "Pick it up!" Embarrassed, my new supervisor sighed and kicked a stone.

I said, "In the war I led an artillery detachment of a hundred men. There were many sorts of people to prepare for battle. Most wandered in straight off the farm. Up 'til then, the only ones who told them what to do had been their ma and pa. Some shirkers liked to play around and slack off. Others considered it a right to bully the inexperienced or less fit. A couple went balmy. One way or another, I had to forge an alliance, or else we'd die at the hands of the Yanks."

"How did you do that? What made the soldiers behave?"

"Still haven't figured it out," I responded. "Not that I didn't try. All you can do is mentor your men and attempt to determine their motivations. A number in my command perished because I couldn't inspire the crew to row in unison and in the same direction."

"Were you in the Navy?"

"No. The Army. It's a metaphor—or analogy. I forget which." I snapped a leafless branch off the tree.

"Basil and Mero never met their father. Mourning felt bad for Mrs. Ivy's children and took them under his wing."

"Who gave Mourning that name?" I once knew an individual—a gunner—who referred to himself in the third person as "Doom."

"You'll have to ask him," Cane replied.

When we returned, Mourning and the boys were busy fabricating a set of sawhorses. While assessing the brothers, I noticed that when Basil squatted, his bare heels were visible through the soles of his shoes, and Mero's knees poked from the tears in his trousers. They stopped and turned, worried expressions tensing their faces.

"Kitch is in charge," I said. "Do what he tells you. I don't want to hear of any grief. Mourning earns six dollars a week. You two take home three to split. I'll spring for the midday meal. If it rains, sorry, you're out of luck. Any questions?" Reassured, they shook their heads. "I'll be back." Nodding to Cane, I walked toward Samuel Gordon Ingle's Hardware.

Similar to a general store, Ingle sold diverse varieties of merchandise. The brick building smelled of varnish, potatoes, and an unidentifiable odor. I grabbed five sets of gloves and a pair of dungarees for Mero. At the counter, I shoveled a pound of candy corn into a sack and queried the shopkeeper on boots to fit a fourteen-year-old.

"Buy 'em large. Size nine should do with room to grow. I got stockings for sale," Samuel added, maneuvering me to a barrel in the corner. I bought wool socks for everyone, including myself. In the near future, I would have to spend time with Daniel Judge at our mine to restore my waning finances.

Satisfied with my investments, I exited to find Molly Doyle gliding along the sidewalk. I sidestepped inside again, but it was too late—*she had seen me.*

"Hank!" she yelled into the dim interior. "Hank, I see you behind that shelf!"

"Miss Doyle," I said, drawing her indoors. I couldn't be caught on the street with a prostitute. "How are you?"

"Without security," she responded. "Do you know what became of Ray Diamond?"

"Can't say I do. Is he not taking care of business?"

"No he's not," Molly replied. "Haven't seen Ray in days. I fear something awful has taken place."

"What a shame if that maggot left town. Perhaps now is an excuse to change careers?" There was a chance I'd be able to talk Till Burnes into hiring another barmaid. He owed me a favor. "Are you open to a new path in the service industry?"

"Possibly," she answered, lifting a maul from the floor to test its heaviness. She let the tool drop with a thud. "Does it pay as well as lying on my back doing absolutely nothing?"

I had to crack a smile. "Doubt it. You'll need to work."

"Guess this gal's getting a might long in the tooth for the sporting life, don't you agree?" Impatient, Molly waited for my contradictory response.

"Not at all. You're still extremely alluring; however, your current profession often leads to poor health and sometimes ends in untimely death."

"Hank, it sounds like you care about me! Ray had a doc examine me once a month. I've never been ill a day in my life." She blessed herself twice with the sign of the cross.

"Good to know!" I exclaimed, recollecting our energetic evening together. "I'll keep you apprised of any more suitable jobs."

Tipping my fedora, I ducked out the door and hurried to my lot. The sawhorses were sturdy and in use. The brothers switched places, one cutting lumber while the other steadied the plank.

Basil's eyelashes fluttered as I offered the footwear. "For me?" he inquired, sniffing the lining.

"Son, I won't tolerate hobos on my estate," I responded, passing Mero the blue jeans and the sweets. "Divide these between your coworkers."

Mourning accepted the leather gloves and tried them on, flexing his fingers. He dipped his head and picked up a tool.

Kitch took his set. "Thanks, Mr. Gates. We're framin' the walls. Shall you be breakin' your tail with the help today, or are you rushin' uptown to waltz with your rich, white cronies?"

"I'll watch over you fellows and make sure nobody's napping or stealing my things."

"So that's how it's going to be," Kitch Cane beamed, handing me a hammer and a fistful of nails.

Chapter Nine

I MET DANIEL JUDGE AT THE ACME FOR DRINKS. Brand-name whiskey for my business partner and black coffee for me. Till wasn't around to pester regarding employment for Molly Doyle. Tilly said his dad had left to "cool off."

Several weeks had run by since we last worked our claim. Daniel had a full-time job replacing batteries and fixing electric lines for the telegraph company. He also delivered block ice on the weekends. I occupied myself building the cottage and embarking upon a real estate career in a sinking market.

"We need help at the mine," I grumbled as Till's son deposited uninviting plates of indigestible fried mutton. I liberally frosted the prehistoric sheep flesh with salt from a Mason jar that had holes punctured in the lid.

"All our gravy, what little there is, shall go to wages," Daniel cautioned. Judge was a sizable man with a potbelly that mismatched his thin frame. Prematurely gray, my partner looked older than his forty years.

"Well, claim-jumpers will take the land if we're not there." I spat out a solid piece and rolled the round object in my palm.

Judge scowled at the shotgun pellet. Forcefully stabbing the stringy meat, he threatened, "Like to watch them try. Suppose a limited income beats nothing. Do you know anyone who is trustworthy?"

No one living came to mind. "I'll ruminate on it."

"There's a guy at Western Union whose brother is seeking work. I met him. Seems decent. And there's a fella on my ice route—huge—that can easily handle an eight-pound hammer for hours."

Till entered the front, slamming the glass-paneled door. The barman lumbered over to us. "Somebody's blabbin' to the law about the back room," he hissed through gritted teeth. "You boys got an opinion on who that is?"

"Nope. Might be any of the boozehounds or hustlers that patronize your lovely establishment," Daniel replied. "You should shut down the action. And what's with this fat?" Disgusted, he dropped the fork.

"They're after me," Burnes moaned, ignoring the criticism. He glared at the snoozing Chinese watchman. "I'm tryin' to keep my damn head above water—jus' one bill on top of the next."

"Judge is right," I acknowledged. "For a family man, it's not worth a trip to the lockup. Till, I have a special request."

Burnes ceased pacing as he remembered his debt. "Special? What now?"

Last fall, a robber held up Tillman Jr. as he closed the saloon. Tillman Sr. heard a noise and, coming downstairs, reacted as any father would by defending his son. The "gun" that the hooligan flashed turned out to be a mechanical pencil pistol. For obvious motives, Till couldn't fancy seeing the bad publicity in the papers and petitioned my assistance to sweep away the mess. I happened to be available.

"Don't have a stroke," I answered. "There's a woman in the Stingaree who desires a different occupation. Something more reputable if you catch my drift. Molly's a knockout and will draw in new customers, which—I don't need to spell this out—is profitable to you."

"Hank, you slept with her, didn't you?" I shrugged. "I knew it! Fine, send her by," Burnes muttered and flung a nasty rag at me. "You tell her, I ain't runnin' no whore house." Still grouching, he fled into the relative serenity of the kitchen.

Daniel and I made plans to rendezvous at cockcrow and go to the claim.

We assembled at the Robinson Restaurant and Bakery in the mountain community of Julian. Judge and two men crammed into a booth by the window. My friend had understated Claude Horrigan's stature. Not merely broad-shouldered, the Irishman was a goliath with John Henry-sized biceps. The barbarian towered over Javier Rivera, a Mexican national of normal height and weight. Javier appeared average in every way except for his set of perfect teeth. They made an odd combination, yet as of now, the duo got along. Rivera poked fun at Horrigan's flowing blond locks and Horrigan ribbed Rivera with, "Are those paws even capable of holding a three-pound drill?"

After reading the bakery's chalkboard menu, Javier inquired, "Don't wanna be rude, but is one of you paying?" From a pocket, he fished out an arrowhead, a quarter, and a worn penny. "Times are tough with everybody leaving town. I appreciate the chance you're giving me."

"Sure Javier, order whatever you want," I responded. "You too, Claude."

We dined on crispy bacon and moist scrambled eggs. Our conversation stayed light, discussing unscrupulous businessmen and politicians or the unending losing streak of the Shamrocks semi-pro baseball club. Judge steered the talk to the men's personal histories, and I learned that both had basic mining experience.

Outside in private, Judge and I decided to hire the laborers, cutting them a fair percentage of all revenue. We would take turns monitoring their performance. Claude and Javier agreed to the terms, and a handshake sealed the deal.

This morning, I had ridden Clive through the backcountry while the others had taken the stagecoach from San Diego. Southward, I led the mule along the steep footpath to Orinoco Creek.

Daniel and I had bought the mineral title from a crusty old miner named Peabody. A small cabin that could be used for sleeping quarters, a portable steam-powered stamp mill, and a primitive smelter had been included with the unimaginatively titled Peabody Mine.

Near the waterfalls, we forded the stream and stopped on a wooded shelf overlooking our camp. Smoke wafted from the shelter's chimney.

"Well, if that don't grab the rag off the bush," Judge murmured, fists clenching. "Just what I was afraid of—*claim-jumpers!*"

As he edged toward the slope, I snagged an arm. "Wait! Let's see who's there first."

Daniel shook off my grip and dashed down the hill, trampling the brush. I hastily tethered Clive to a tree, clasped my sword, and pursued. A beefy man in a discolored union suit shuffled from the shack to stretch and pass gas. For a moment, he goggled at us, then, diving within, resurfaced with a shotgun and shouted. A pair of prospectors trudged from the mineshaft, sooty and shouldering picks. In a frontal offensive, Claude and Javier, who screamed Spanish obscenities, charged past Judge. The surprised trespassers must have perceived our lot as a smaller, unhorsed, and ultimately luckier version of Lord Cardigan's Light Brigade. Stunned, they pitched their weapons and hightailed into the backcountry.

Judge lifted up the Remington and discharged both barrels into the treetops. "Victory!" he hurrahed, twirling the gun overhead.

On my stinging knees and panting, I broke into relieved laughter as Horrigan and Rivera searched the grounds and mine entrance.

A wheelbarrow rattled from the darkness, muscled by the big man. "You're not going to believe this!" Claude exclaimed. "There's heaps of ore in there. Those jumpers finished the work for us!"

"Does that count if me and Claude didn't dig it up ourselves?" Javier asked, nodding affirmatively.

Daniel replied, "You still have to extract the copper and cart it to town. But yes, it's a good head start." He smiled and tossed Javier the firearm. "Make sure those thieves don't return!"

No longer a chaotic jumble of lumber, the escalating construction resembled a real cottage. Ready for a break, I took the afternoon off and went to Turner Hall on Eighth and G Streets. I'd been inside gymnasiums in San Francisco, and the humid lobby of the Concordia Turnverein likewise smelled of mildew and sweat. After hanging up my coat, I sought the echoes of activity, squeezing by a clique of ruddy gentlemen on their way to an alcove furnished as a lounge. Double doors parted as more men surged forth, the illumination from a large chamber highlighting the trophy cases lining the corridor. A boxing ring dominated the lively arena where fierce opponents jabbed and dodged. I spotted a set of parallel bars, though the majority of the exercise equipment remained a mystery.

Captain Conrad Wiedemann and his students were off to the side honing their fencing moves. I sat on a stool to watch. The class had pupils of varying ages, sizes, and proficiency levels. The instructor demonstrated the deadly riposte, a counter-attack following a successful defensive parry. Graceful and athletic, the master-at-arms exhibited excellent technical abilities. I knew in an authentic melee, I could take him. That is, without my bum leg.

Wiedemann summoned me. I hobbled over and clasped his hand.

"Welcome Lieutenant Gates! I'm so happy you've accepted my invitation." The teacher told the fencers to "Carry on" and led me on a tour. Racks of wooden Indian clubs and dumbbells covered the walls. Snarling pugilists battered unfeeling punching bags. "Our club is the *Eintracht,* which in English translates to 'harmony' or 'concord.'" The captain pointed out rowing machines, high bars, standard rings, and a pommel horse before pausing in front of a row of apparatuses resembling stylish torture devices.

"What are these?" I questioned. "This one resembles a medieval rack." I reminisced of the rustic days when human beings naturally grew strong by tilling the soil or chopping firewood to stay alive in the great outdoors.

Tucking thumbs in his waist, Wiedemann answered, "This, my friend, is the Sargent Combination Pulley Weight. If a householder doesn't have adequate room for separate equipment, this setup does the whole shooting match: chest weights, intercostal or upper trunk expansion, and as a bonus, a folding row-slide. It's a component of the Dudley Allen Sargent health machine system. Harvard University uses these in their exercise programs." With gusto, he described the functions of the other contraptions.

"Impressive," I allowed, as he wrapped up the sales pitch. "I've come to realize that I've neglected my overall fitness with inadequate diet and constant lethargy."

"Henry, we'll strengthen you mentally and physically with nutritional counseling and a strict regimen of regular daily exertion. Earlier, I noticed you observing my students. I teach intermediate and advanced swordsmanship lessons on Tuesdays and Thursdays. The Turnverein has protective masks to borrow, although you must supply a fencing outfit and foil. How about it? Will you sign up?"

Intrigued, I responded, "By all means. It sounds like fun."

I returned from the Peabody Mine dog-tired yet encouraged with the rapid pace of our newly hired hands. They worked well as a team: Horrigan swinging the heavy hammer and Rivera precisely placing the drill bit. Once enough metalliferous earth had been accumulated, the crushed and smelted matte was sold to the Stonewall Jackson Mine for final refinement. Ironically, Claude became both the brains and the beast in the operation. Javier made the drudgery more enjoyable by serving as the clowning amigo. Both valued the bonuses added to their allowances.

The rafters supported Kitch as he framed around the single brick chimney. Boston-made windows leaned against the first floor, and piles of cedar roof shingles filled the yard. "How did it go?" he asked, perspiration dripping down his face.

"It was a long day," I replied. "You're making good progress. Where are your guys?"

"I sent Mourning to fetch the lath and plaster. Basil and Mero are in class. They can be here the entire weekend."

I recalled that his wife accepted the grant to found a school for the colored children. For an instant, I felt annoyed learning the brothers were not on the job sawing wood. My father hadn't considered education for his slaves, deeming literacy a wasted or dangerous effort. Even twenty years later, I bore some of the same views. Resentful, I contemplated reducing their salaries.

When Mourning arrived atop Cane's wagon, I unloaded the bundles of slim, white, pine strips, and sacks of gypsum powder. I questioned how he received the melancholic name.

Mourning grimaced and answered mechanically, "Mama died alone when she pushed me into this world. Mass'r Nelson said, 'that pickaninny born in blood and mourning,' so that's what he called me, and every person since."

"You got a last name?"

He responded proudly, "Dew."

"Really? Are you serious?"

"Friends started it as a jape, but I now use Mourning Dew when makin' my mark."

I nodded and we kept stacking the raw materials. "Tell those boys not to come here on the weekend. I'm sure Mrs. Ivy has chores for them to do, plus Mero and Basil should have homework."

"The family needs the money, Mr. Gates. I do what I can, still, it ain't enough. Those young men could eat a horse and their ma's been ailin'."

"Understood. They will get it, no strings attached. The kids work hard when they're here."

Mourning glanced sideways, disbelief rising and suspicion lowering his eyebrows. With a grunt, he went to shield the plaster with a tarp.

Chapter Ten

I LAY ON THE FLOOR, gingerly rubbing a thumb over my eye socket and cheeks. No severe discomfort. The last time I checked in a mirror, the shiner had dulled to a bluish-yellow, and the nicks had healed to inconspicuous scars. In the clammy chill of predawn, I fixated on the midpoint of the ceiling.

The house was coming along nicely: roof watertight, exterior encased in clapboard, and most of the windows were installed. Soon, the doors could be hung, and the interior lathed, plastered, and painted.

As the copper vein deepened, Daniel optimistically advised hiring additional miners at the Peabody Mine. Eventually, I'd amass enough capital to snatch up surplus real estate.

I counted another promising aspect. Molly Doyle, enthusiastic to be labeled a respectable woman, had smoothly transitioned from feisty harlot to feisty barmaid. Till was very pleased with her conduct.

Still, I felt anxious. The papers hadn't published anything else relating to the murder of Joe Higgs, and the "disappearance" of Ray Diamond, the whoremonger, never became a story. Violent crimes had become too common for the provincial constables to solve.

Even though Laura and I saw each other at a few memorable events, my feelings for her remained conflicted.

There was always the dull pang that pressed my soul when contemplating the plights of Elizabeth and the children. My son and daughter had been born during the months I bivouacked in Auburn. Alice must be twenty-seven years old by now and Robert twenty-eight. Not seeing them since they were toddlers, I doubted I would be able to identify their adult faces.

I dressed quickly casting off the heartache and general sense of malaise. Outside, I washed and racked wood for the stove. In the makeshift kitchen, my mood lifted as the sun soared above the Laguna Mountains. A brisk draft streamed past my shoulders and whisked any lingering depressing notions out the empty window frame. In a ceramic bowl, I beat the eggs, water, salt, and pepper for the omelets.

I always heard their banter before the wagon rolled into view: Basil telling a joke and Mero attempting to top it with a yarn all the more outlandish. Kitch gripped the reins as Mourning's hunched torso swayed with every bump of the uneven terrain. Cherika, also yearning to dine, picked up her gate. The brothers hurdled from the back and zigzagged toward me yelling. Cane yawned as Mourning led the horse to the haystack and water trough. A sizzling spinach omelet slid from the iron skillet onto a plate.

Kitch hopped upon the porch and rapped on the doorframe. "Tax collector!" he called. "Get your wallet!" The planking squeaked as he moved into the hallway, stopping at intervals to inspect a test coat of plaster. "It's hard as your head. Guess what I got?"

"Apple pie?"

"Cherry," Kitch joshed, placing the daily portion of cornbread on the table. "I understand the City Council is talkin' of creatin' a police department." He seasoned the hot food with chili powder. "With your years of experience, they should appoint you chief."

"Take these, funnyman," I said, dispensing dishes. "Combating crime and corruption is a job for a man with Wyatt Earp's qualifications. On second thought, gambling and prostitution is his bread and butter, and shutting down Stingaree Town is on top of the conservatives' lists."

With the first meal of the day on our laps and legs hanging over the lip of the porch, we watched the mare chew her fodder. Carts and carriages clogged the arteries as the boom town awakened. Much of the flock flew the coop during the recession. Sooner or later, the chickens would return. Now was a splendid opportunity to buy extra land.

On a bench, I unstrapped the meshed mask and shed the padded jacket. I gasped for oxygen, swabbing my face with a towel.

"You're improving!" Walter Werner complimented. He sat next to me and coached, "You need to be on the offensive. And try to keep that left arm up!"

I chuckled. "That's as high as it goes." We sat in quietude as Captain Wiedemann stabbed a cocksure attorney in the bony chest. Walt had joined the class a few days after me. He was good, and we became fencing partners.

"Hank, I've been meaning to ask you something. Concerned citizens have weekly get-togethers to discuss methods of curbing neighborhood crime and violence. There's a meeting tonight. Might you be interested in going?"

"Vigilantes?" Civic outrage over unusually odious crimes incited "popular justice." Mob lynchings proved to be the public's favored alternative to drawn-out court trials. I had witnessed enough violence before, during, and after the war to detest the actions of bloodthirsty gangs.

Walt snickered as the skewered lawyer walked off in disgrace. "No, no. Nothing of that nature. You read in the newspapers about the possibility of forming a police force? Our organization assists the city's understaffed constabulary."

"By patrolling?"

"That's our primary role. We also collaborate with the detectives on unsolved cases. Our members often maintain personal contacts unavailable to the sheriffs."

"Who are these members?" I envisioned a tribunal comparable to the Knights of the White Camellia decreeing imprisonment or death upon hapless African Americans, Indians, Asians, and Hispanics.

"All persuasions. A handful from the Concordia Turnverein. Doctors, judges, businessmen, politicians, veterans—folks like us who are morally obligated to lower the crime rate. Augmenting the arm of the law is vital to the continuing prosperity of San Diego."

"And why should these representatives of the topmost echelon admit me into their fold?"

"Hank, I've vouched for you. I'm certain of your integrity and convinced that you are better with a sword then you let on." Walt, awaiting a response, combed fingers through thinning red bristles.

"What do you fellows call this secret society?"

With a straight face, the accountant replied, "The High Order of the Missing Enchilada."

"You're kidding, right?" I conjured the ridiculous image of a maize tortilla hotfooting for Tijuana.

Werner tittered. "The group originated in the fall, and we haven't finalized a name yet. Since I've only attended the last two months, I get little say in the matter."

I weighed the pros and cons of his invitation. On the positive side, I had already made the rounds of the Stingaree, occasionally aiding someone in distress. It seemed healthier to perform this duty in the legitimacy of a structured association.

Alonzo Horton recommended the advantages of fraternizing with San Diego's upper class for business considerations—mingling with the wealthy may hasten that. Being restricted by the accountability of a committee? *Definitely a negative.* Enticed by the concept, I wanted to learn more.

"Count me in," I said, rising to go home.

He grinned. "That's outstanding! Hank, one further thing before we leave. Just to let you know, there is an initiation ceremony."

In a part of town where the arc lamps never touched, I waited near a modest-sized factory. A modern red safety bicycle swung from a sign advertising "injury-free" transportation. This was a bustling industrial block in the daytime, but once the workers closed up shop, the only hoots came from roosting owls or the tortured shrieks of hallucinating vagrants. I sealed my collar against the cold and inhaled hot nicotine. A slender physique elongated from the shadows.

"Care for a nip of Tanglefoot?" Walter Werner offered a brown bottle. Not hearing an answer, he suckled the glass teat and pocketed the rotgut. The accountant wiped runny nostrils and sighed, "Okay then."

I trailed Werner along an alley congested with lobster traps, in and out of a foul-smelling stockyard, and over a stagnant drainage ditch, before halting at a dilapidated warehouse. Male voices and golden light leaked through gaps in the siding.

"This is it," Walt said, a hand upon the entryway latch. "We'll sit in the back. After the call to order and the invocation, you'll be introduced as a prospective member. The president gives the new people a chance to talk about themselves and lets the room pose a few questions. Don't worry, you'll do fine." He took an extra sip and pushed the door.

Bales of wool and bolts of fabric lined the whitewashed storeroom. The center was cleared, and the dirt floor swept spotless of textile fibers. Planks suspended between crates accommodated the two dozen men facing the low platform. Similar to a playhouse, a row of lanterns acted as footlights on the rim of the stage. Curtains hid the back. On top, a set of chairs were positioned adjacent to a blackboard. A map of San Diego gridded into sectors covered half of the slate. Printed in bold letters, "Liberty Equals Free Enterprise," filled the other side.

We sat behind a foursome of animated gentlemen debating the spiraling prices and decreasing quality of corn. From somewhere in the wings a boy came and turned up the lights' wicks until oily fumes belched from the globes. The staging completed, two men outfitted in formal attire and one wearing ecclesiastical vestments ascended the scaffolding, stopping before the seats.

The imposing man in the middle spoke in a clipped Germanic cadence. "Good evening! Prayer at the commencement of a meeting is a perfect way to remind ourselves that God is here. He is the reason for everything we do, and with His help, the cause of our triumph. Reverend Glazkov shall deliver the blessing."

The assemblage stood, hats removed and heads bowed. A scraggly-bearded cleric stationed on the left of who I now inferred was the person in charge intoned in a Slavic accent, "Dear Father, we thank You for all who have gathered here. We trust in You wholly and surrender ourselves to Your grace. We pray that Your Holy Spirit inspires our hearts and strengthens our bodies to obliterate the insidious pestilence spreading like a fungus across these United States. Your humble servants beseech Your glory and praise. Amen."

The congregation parroted "Amen" and sat.

The tall man remained upright and scanned the audience. "Divinely put, Reverend! I see some new faces out there. Welcome! I ask that you stand with your sponsors."

Walt and I rose with the other pairs.

The leader thumbed his lapels and rocked on the soles of his boots. "Very well! First, let me introduce myself. I am Heinrich Braun, the interim president of our band of merry men." Smiling to the baldheaded man on his right, he announced, "This is my brother, Wilhelm, who is the acting vice-president." The sibling waved a hand and simpered sheepishly. Wilhelm did not resemble Heinrich, being corpulent and of a lighter complexion. "This arrangement will change once our constitution and by-laws are ratified and a vote can be cast by ballot." The president's roving gaze zeroed in on a dapper chap with a monocle. "We'll begin with you sir. Kindly tell us your full name, where you hail from, and your current profession."

Alfred Blume stated that he came from Kansas and was a practicing physician. The medical practitioner moreover specified that he was fluent in both Spanish and Mandarin. A businessman with a swollen jaw inquired if he pulled teeth. Blume responded, "No, I'm a doctor" and referred a "painless" dentist.

"Glad you are with us, *Herr Doktor.* A man with your intellect and skills shall come in handy," Heinrich flattered.

Next to disclose his identity was a rancher who had moved to "civilization" thinking the city as "much healthier" and "culturally beneficial" for his wife and girls. The cattleman had migrated from the Midwest, and when somebody loudly sneezed, I missed his name.

Half-listening to a legal query regarding grazing rights on open land, I concentrated on the president. Apish brows met overtop a penetrating stare that, at this moment, bore upon me. Braun nodded for me to speak.

"Hello. My name is Henry Gates. I was born in Buzzard Roost, Alabama, and have lived in San Diego for several years. I'm building a residence by the City Park and am dabbling in a couple of new ventures, such as real estate and mining." No one had questions for me.

"Thank you for participating! We have achieved a significant milestone. It's March, and tonight is our sixth official meeting. I'll bet many of you are as thrilled as I to see our ranks expanding at such a fast rate." As Heinrich laughed, the mirth never thawed his eyes.

Engrossed, I studied the speaker. Squashed flat, his hair shined black, the pomade-soaked locks coiling on a wide forehead. Bushy sideburns wrapped the tapered, pockmarked profile. Long and sharp-edged, the man's nose slanted over a well-groomed, waxed mustache that curved upwards, resembling the angry horns of a bull. Again, I reread his eyes—obsidian and insensate as a crocodile's.

"We are still seeking a name for our organization and will consider any suggestions. A member proposed the 'Knights of Columbus,' which I adore; however, the Catholics reserved that superb moniker. And the 'Hermetic Order of the Purple Turnip' doesn't accurately state our intentions, don't you agree?" Winking at Walt, Braun proceeded. "What *is* our purpose? What *is* our mission? Our motto is *'To Serve and Protect.'* To *serve* our constables and marshals by fighting crime and therefore *protect* the citizens of this fine city. How do we—?"

Gently patting Heinrich's elbow, Reverend Glazkov leaned close and whispered in his ear.

Head bobbing, the president apologized, "Ah yes, Reverend. I forgot to mention, starting this month, we have tea and coffee available for those drowsy from my endless prattle." Braun emanated hospitality as he pointed to a sideboard manned by the same lad who regulated the lighting.

Quite a few people got in line. Somnolent, I deliberated loading up on caffeine, but didn't want to draw unnecessary scrutiny.

Irked by the interruption, Heinrich resumed, "*Serve and protect*. How do we accomplish this crucial task? With the help of Constable Hurley." A rotund officer waddled to the foot of the stage and stood at attention. I had noticed this mutton-chopped man once or twice in restaurants on Market Street. "Carl is here as an emissary of law enforcement. He will alert us to any issues in which we can provide aid. The main undertaking for our fledgling organization is to stand up for the men, women, and children of San Diego by coordinating citizen patrols." At the chalkboard, Braun tapped a finger on the map of the city. A bold letter labeled each of the twelve sections. "Following the meeting, I urge everyone to grab a buddy and sign up for a patrol route. We'll do our utmost to assign you a geographical region near your lodging."

Walt asked excitedly, "Let's partner up. You and me! Sound good?"

"Sure." I only knew Werner from the gymnasium. The bookkeeper appeared suitable and as worthy a partner as any.

"Herr Doktor Blume, Sam Wheeler, and Henry Gates, come forth." Amongst the smoking lanterns, Heinrich stood on the fringe of the dais, arms unfolded to his flock. I glanced at Walt, who blinked twice and fell behind the others walking up the aisle. The president hoisted me upon the podium. "Please face forward." The three of us fanned out across the stage. "After becoming acquainted with the motto and mission of our association, are you willing to take the vow of membership?"

As one, we answered, *"Yea!"*

"Then recite this oath: I pledge myself in service to law enforcement in whatever capacity I may find and to guard those that are powerless to defend themselves."

I mumbled the verse.

"As acting president, I accept you into our organization with every right and privilege to which such membership entails. Turn around."

Satisfied the show had concluded I was exhausted and ready to leave. I slowly swiveled. In one flowing motion, Glazkov thrust a stag-handled saddle knife into my gut. With the heel of my left hand, I batted the blade away, the tip slashing my vest before clanging to the floor. Nodding in approval, the clergyman or whoever he might truly be, stepped backwards and retrieved the weapon.

Throughout this physical assault, my peripheral vision caught the agile doctor darting sideways, clutching his arm. Infuriated, he straddled Wilhelm Braun's rib cage, pressing a scalpel to the simpleton's pimply chin. The "reverend" charged to pull him loose. As blood stained Blume's sleeve, I prodded under my own shirt, revealing crimson digits. I had not captured what transpired with Sam Wheeler, but the cowboy no longer graced our presence.

"Well done, gentlemen! Two out of three's not bad! Not bad at all!" Cleaning a rusty fish filleter, the president congratulated, "I hereby proclaim you both initiated." In a mocking manner, Heinrich shaded his brow as if searching for the cowardly rancher. His left hand swished the air in an effeminate gesture.

At the blackboard, with an open palm, the president erased "Free Enterprise." On the smeared slate, after "Liberty Equals," he wrote "To Serve and Protect!" and underlined the phrase. Then he drew a menacing stick figure raising an exaggerated club over a smaller defenseless character whose chalked eyeballs were comical X's.

The leader bellowed as he whirled with arms extended, "United together as the Spear of Achilles, we shall reclaim the streets!" Clapping and cheering, the motivated crowd leapt on benches and pumped fists. Mesmerized, my jaw dropped seeing the tattoo inked on Heinrich Braun's ropy forearm. It was the same strange symbol I had seen incised beside my name on the bridge spanning Buzzard Roost Creek: *a two-pronged pitchfork ringed by a circle.*

Chapter Eleven

I ESCORTED LAURA TO THE PLAZA overlooking the Horton House. The hotel had a well-groomed park, the boundary hemmed in by a new picket fence and trimmed hedge. A five-tiered fountain gurgled at the heart of the square. Through opposite gates, the half block gradually filled with early birds alighting for the weekly concert. I reserved a green patch of grass and unfolded a sheet. From this position, we watched the City Guard set up their instruments on an eight-sided band shell. Laura opened a picnic basket and laid down a dish of cheese and crackers. As we toasted with goblets of apple cider, I questioned her beliefs on the temperance movement, mindful that she packed a non-alcoholic version on my account.

"My dad drank a lot," Laura answered. We leaned back on locked elbows and gazed at faraway constellations twinkling in the twilight. A fingernail Worm Moon climbed above the observatory perched upon the hotel's dormered roof. "Every day, he indulged from the crack of dawn until he fell into bed that night. Again and again, my mother got fed up and threatened to leave. Yet my father wasn't unlike any of the other men in our town. It's not as if Dad walked around knocking over china, and thankfully, he never hit us. He took good care of the family."

A gaggle of children galloped past, rolling hoops with sticks. Affectionate couples and boisterous families sat nearby, enjoying the festivities.

"How is your father? Does he often write you?"

"Henry, a mechanical twine binder, strangled him on our farm. He didn't come home for dinner. Mother rang the bell. His dog returned—alone—running in circles and highly agitated. In the light of lanterns, old Faithful led us to the fields. We found Dad bundled to a bale of wheat. The look on his face gave me nightmares for—"

Taken aback, I stiffened. "Laura, I'm so sorry to hear that. That's an awful memory to cope with."

Laura stared dolefully, then, powerless to contain herself, burst into giggles. "Henry, I was being facetious. My father is fine and owns a successful millinery shop in downtown Philadelphia."

Caught off guard by the fabrication, after a moment of registering her amusement, I joined the hilarity. Laura's effervescent temperament forced me to admit how humorless I had become and how distant from the merriment of my own youth. I made a mental note to laugh more.

Laura reached out to me. "The drinking part *is* true, and I wish he'd stop, but Lord, I won't hold my breath." Ravenous, she offered a serving of deviled eggs.

A man mounted the stage, and, following an energetic greeting, the band launched into an original number entitled the "San Diego March."

As the rousing music rose to a crescendo, I considered the marvelous time I was having with Laura, the rising walls of my house, and ultimately, the blue ink pricked into Heinrich Braun's muscled arm.

Molly slid a tray of beer mugs upon the bar. Tilly collected the dregs into a jug for those unwilling or unable to pay full price.

He plunged the glassware into a basin and scowled as the soupy water squirted onto his shirt.

"What can I do for you, angel?" Molly teased, placing a warm palm on my thigh. I brushed off the advance and examined her. Clad in a scandalously skintight, splashy skirt, the saloon girl's arms and shoulders were bare and the bodice cut low over her bosom. No longer blond, the raven-tinted dye intensified the blue of her eyes.

"How is the mid-day special?"

"The pork chops?"

I screwed up my face, not able to make out Till's chalkboard scribble. "If that's what it says."

She frowned. "That's the only thing he cooked today."

"And some English tea please."

"There's no commission on a cup of boiled water," Molly whined.

"Forgive me, but I'm assured you're doing well," I said, taking in the mobbed room, her silk stockings, and shiny kid boots. "So are you now a law-abiding woman?"

"Yes Daddy, I'm a 'good' girl," she leered and adjusted a small, jeweled dagger retained by her garter belt. "The Acme's clientele is similar to the scum in Stingaree Town. Once in a while, an old customer spots me. It's working out. I moved to a flat on Seventh Street. Nowadays, every cent goes to rent instead of Ray. Therefore, I'm still broke."

"Welcome to high society," I said, encouraged that Molly strove to stay upright.

As Tilly came near, she spouted, "Without delay, I must find a young, virile man to treat me with the respect I deserve. Nothing could please me more than a precious baby growing in my tummy."

The flushing adolescent delivered the steaming lunch plate and scooted off.

"Nicely played," I said, tapping my utensil on the swine's sliced vertebra. "Till won't relish you flirting with his boy." I remembered why I was there. "In your travels, did you ever hear of Heinrich Braun or his brother Wilhelm? German heritage though not recent arrivals on the boat."

"Nope," Molly responded. "Why? What do they look like?"

"Heinrich is tall with black hair and pocky skin. Wilhelm is short, bald, and, on one of his better days—a half-wit."

"That resembles all the men in here."

I sprinkled salt on the tabletop and spread the granules with my hand. With a finger, I traced the bident inside a ring. "How about this? It's a tattoo."

After viewing the drawing, Molly replied, "In my trade, I've seen lots of ink. This design isn't familiar. I'll speak to my ladies of the line and let you know." Canvassing the regulars, she adjusted the snug-fitting corset to flaunt an additional acre of flesh. "Time to brighten the lives of my sad, lonely souls. Most of these cowboys haven't been close to a two-legged female in months—I'm hoping." The barmaid hesitated. "My way of life is such that I don't get the chance to say thanks very often. Hank, I appreciate your efforts in landing me this job." She grinned and planted a sloppy kiss on my cheek before flitting off to wrangle tips.

I walked past the bar and into the kitchen. Normally—out of disgust—I avoid seeing where my food is prepared. Regardless, I had to smoke out Till. The sinew in the cook's forearms bunched as he butchered poultry into pieces on a central block. As not to startle a man wielding a Chinese cleaver, I coughed and moved to the table. Glancing at me, he tossed plucked necks into a crock.

"Not much goes to waste," I observed, noting the bowls of hearts and gizzards. Flies buzzed from pot to pan, sucking the sweet juices.

"You just ate that," the Irishman asserted. He danced a pair of amputated chicken feet across the slick surface. The macabre puppet show was unnerving.

"No, I had the pork chops." The ripe odor returned memories of the battlegrounds.

"Was it? Was it pork, Hank?"

Tilly nodded as he scooched by balancing a platter of fresh baked bread.

"Your kid's working hard," I remarked.

"He's a chip off the old block."

"Thank God he got his looks from your wife."

"Mary gave him the smarts, too," Till professed. "That woman told me years ago to get out of this business. Wants me to go back to engraving and open a print shop. Maintains that it's honest work." Blood and grease splattered the front of his once-white apron. Dejected, he stroked the rectangular blade on an oiled sharpening stone. "What're you doin' round here anyhow?"

"Do Heinrich and Wilhelm Braun ever frequent your establishment?"

The honed edge drifted near Burnes' thumb. "Say again?" he inquired in a low voice, laying the knife on the ledge.

"The Brauns. They're German immigrants. Are you acquainted with them?"

"Yep. They claim to be from the East Coast and have been rootin' around for a while." Till lobbed skin and bones into a pail for his animals. "I don't think Heinrich is someone you ought to meddle with."

"Why? What's he up to?"

"Him and his brother were here grillin' folks about local real estate deals. They badgered us, askin' who was ready to leave town now that the market is in the toilet—owners so down on their luck they might sell for cheap. Kind of pushy. I suspect he's a land-grabber." Till hacked legs off a duck.

"There's a bumper crop of crooks trying to seize property in unethical or illegal ways. What makes him that distinctive?"

With a whack, Burnes wedged the blade into the end of the cutting board. "Since you're in my kitchen questioning who they are, I assume you're already suspicious. What's your concern?"

"Heinrich Braun is the leader of a citizen's organization to which I'm affiliated." At the adjournment of the meeting, the president emphatically briefed us to keep our mouths shut.

"Is your club's goal to increase public sanitation awareness, or fatten up all those cute, homeless street urchins?"

"Their rallying cry is 'To Serve and Protect.'"

Till smirked. "That has the earmarks of a vigilante group." He seemed uneasy. "Hank, I'm not advising you what to do, and I reckon you can defend yourself in the worst of circumstances. But sometimes . . . sometimes, it's preferable to let Satan slip by in the cloak of darkness. The next man can take the heat."

"Heinrich's that wicked?"

"Over the years, I've watched droves of hard men walk through the doors of my tavern, and, to be fair, I've done my share of things I'm not proud of." Burnes crossed himself, murmuring a terse prayer. Raising his gaze, Till yanked the cleaver from the wood. "I'm guessin' you've seen what's in that man's eyes. Or . . . what's not."

I described Heinrich's tattoo, omitting my previous exposure to the symbol.

"Brother, that's Diablo's pitchfork. My sage advice—back off—don't get involved."

As I left by the rear gate, the pops of snapping ligaments bounced off the walls of the alleyway.

Walter Werner and I slunk along a path in the southwest corner of Stingaree Town. Wilhelm Braun assigned our patrol team "Section B," the three square blocks between I, K, First, and Third Streets, otherwise tagged as Chinatown. It felt weird making the rounds with a partner at my side, and I was jittery. At midnight, the uptown arc lights turned off to save wear on the carbon electrodes. Walt crouched at any noise and created a racket by bumping into trashcans. I couldn't blame him. After sundown, two people navigating the constricted passageways took more room than one. I didn't know exactly what we were searching for yet recognized this part of town as the right place for turmoil.

Walt shoved nuts into my fist. "Here," he whispered. "Let's have a snack."

Roasted in salt, the pecans made me thirsty. My patrol partner gulped a concoction reeking of perfume and petroleum. We crisscrossed back streets, passing flocks of scurrying men distinguishable as Chinese by their oversize jackets and long, braided queues. I steadied the three-pound sword hanging at my side.

By a utility shed, I casually probed Werner to find out what he knew of the Braun brothers.

He itched his side-whiskers and responded, "They're prominent land surveyors. As I said before, I've not been with the Sword of Achilles—" The man wavered as he guffawed. "Sorry, Spear of Achilles. The latest name for the organization tickles me. So serious! Reminds me of those pulp magazines my son reads. What again were you asking?"

"The brothers, what's their story?"

"Aye, the Braun boys," Walt replied, squeezing his jowls. "From what I've picked up, Heinrich, the older sibling, served as an officer in the Franco-Prussian war. Little Wilhelm idolizes Heinrich and chases him around like a puppy dog."

"Were they ever in the southern states, such as Alabama?"

My colleague took another swig of Red Eye and hawked, blotting his mouth on a sleeve. "When I first met Heinrich, he mentioned they came from New York City. Why are you interested?"

"Just curious," I answered. "Heinrich Braun's a captivating man."

Endeavoring to "let our presence be known," we kept policing, this time walking down the middle of Second Street. Without gas lines, the residents lit the main thoroughfare with colorful paper lanterns.

A female approached along a muddy rut slicing the center of the lane. Draped in a flowing Chinese tent-shaped dress, her stunted feet hovered over the ground on elevated shoes. I checked behind us seeing no one else.

"My baby hot," she said softly in a thick accent. The woman carried a straw bassinet, her alabaster visage as masked as a Chinese opera singer. Walt stopped. "Will you help my son?" At four a.m., this mother and child should be at home. *Something's wrong.* Again, I took stock of the neighborhood. Near enough for me to make out guttural breathing, her hand drew away the blanket. A mummified infant curled in the cradle, its pigmentation gray and mottled.

As I peered closer, she caressed a tuft of matted hair. Narrow-spaced eyes enlarged, multihued in the flickering lamplight. Thin lips opened, baring lengthy fangs gaping into a howl. Inhuman, the "baby" appeared to be an exotic species of monkey. Enraged, the hunched creature sprang and my world went black.

Chapter Twelve

"HANK," WALT COAXED. "HANK, WAKE UP!" My torso jounced, however my eyelids wouldn't unstick. "Let's go. Stand up!"

Stump liquor flooded my lips. I sat up sputtering, "Where are we?"

"Still in Chinatown. They robbed us and smacked you on the noggin."

I felt a gash over my ear and squished the flap of scalp back in place. Vivid white globes swam across my vision. Shaky, I fumbled for the sword and found it missing. The silver dollars in my pants—also gone. "Who were they?"

Werner squinted at the welts on my face. Blood smeared his chin, and his hand cupped a tooth. Tonguing his gum, my patrol partner tucked the canine in a shirt pocket, as if preserving an unusual souvenir. "Three men in black bushwhacked us. One flew through the air and flattened you. The others stole your weapon and my watch." Walt absently rubbed his wrist before tilting the flask.

Although I spit out the moonshine, the aftertaste coated my tongue. Essence of corn mash induced heavenly memories. "Where's the lady?"

"When the commotion got under way, she and that nasty critter melted into the mist."

I reached again for the 1850, unbelieving it lost. "I need my sword."

"Nothin' I'd like better than to catch those pagans. That can wait, 'cause now, I'm takin' you to a doctor to treat those cuts. A few look bad."

"Put the tooth in your cheek."

"Huh?"

"A doctor or dentist can replace a knocked out tooth, but it has to stay moist. More importantly, we have to get there soon."

Walt fished the cuspid from his overcoat, held it underneath his nose, and then making a wry grimace popped the ivory into his mouth. "Darn thing smells funny," he mumbled, hoisting me vertical.

Succeeding a rough trip crosstown, I braced against a hitching post while Werner rang the bell of a stately home by the harbor. Above, a lamp caught fire and progressed step by step downstairs. I checked twice when reading the plaque beside the entrance. "Dr. Gregory Leeds" was the same man who stumbled upon the body of Joe Higgs. My cranium hurt too much ascending the stairway to consider the fluke.

The doctor ushered us into a room cluttered with books and shiny instruments relating to medicine. He cranked up the lantern as Walt explained our situation.

The physician left and returned with milk. After scrutinizing the eyetooth with a magnifying lens, Leeds rinsed the bony object in the fatty cream. He instructed me to, "Keep the light steady," and pressed the "avulsed canine" into the cavity in Werner's gum. "Clamp firmly on this ball of cotton. Stop by in two days and we'll see if it took."

Walt gripped the arms of the chair and grunted acknowledgement.

"He said a monkey did this?" Leeds questioned. I nodded as the doctor sterilized the slashes with rubbing alcohol. "These are not as severe as they initially appeared—not bite marks. Be that as it may, I'm concerned the feral animal contracted rabies." He inspected the contusion on my forehead, "You received a slight concussion. Take it easy for the next week. In a French medical journal, I read that Louis Pasteur has identified a vaccination for madness. Alas, the discovery is too recent for the Emmett House in Old Town to store any vaccine. If you experience paralysis, paranoia, or difficulty consuming water, we must put you out of your misery." I hoped he was joking.

The doctor opened the glass doors of a cabinet and provided Werner fresh gauze. For my injuries, he passed a bottle of Sloan's Horse Liniment, assuring me the medicine was, "fit for man or beast." Our pockets empty, I swore payment for his services.

Walt and I parted by the seawall, each groaning ill-humored versions of goodbye.

Kitch watched from an upper window as I arrived home. Harsh sunlight flashed in my eyes as he lifted the sash. "We wondered when you might show. Thought you were on a sleepover." Cane's jaunty smile faded as I grew closer. On the front steps, he continued with alarm, "You're a wreck. Another one of your night walks?"

Spent, I raised a hand for silence and dragged myself upstairs to the bedroom. Kitch followed, persistent with his interrogation. "Why do you look shark bit?"

Sprawled on my bedroll, I recounted what had occurred, ending with, "It's imperative I regain my sword." Unable to relax, I pondered why the item seemed so essential.

"Hank, you need to find that Chinese lady. You never even saw the men."

"She had white paint on her face," I grumbled. "I didn't clearly see her either."

"What about the monkey? How many monkeys can there be?"

Mourning entered the room with a plate of runny eggs and scraps of burnt bacon. He astonished me by stating, "Eat some breakfast, Mr. Gates. Come nightfall, we'll get your sword."

"Are you proposing we go back to the Stingaree?" I inquired, feeling improved with hot coffee in my belly.

The man had a grumpy demeanor. "No one messes with *my* dinner." He took the dish and went downstairs.

A ringing filled my ears. "Did he say dinner?"

"Mourning takes things personally," Kitch whispered. "He counts on you for a regular salary, and, trust me, nobody wants to stand in the way of Mourning's wages."

"Ugh," I moaned, wearied again.

Mero and Basil scampered in, tailed by a frisky puppy. The speckled hound tugged my shoe from beneath a mound of clothes.

Basil cried out, "Mr. Gates, we brought you this dog! You've got yourself a buddy." He giggled and threw the footwear across the floor. The cocker spaniel trotted after the "toy."

"And someone to guard your belongings," Mero contributed. Noticing my lesions, he asked, "Are you alright, Mr. Gates?"

"I'm fantastic, Mero. Just cut myself shaving." As the boy shook his head in consternation, I questioned, "What's the pup's name?"

"Hector, of course," Basil, answered. "Same as the dog that lives at the White House."

"Of course," I repeated as Hector snuggled close and snored.

Loaded for bear, Kitch and Mourning arrived at dusk. Dew toted the prized John Browning shotgun on his shoulder. Cane carried an old Enfield Mark I revolver.

"What do *I* use for protection?" I inquired. "My noble features and charismatic personality?"

"You're a fine lookin' man," Kitch jested. "Ladies love a fella marred up with scars. Your job is to lead us to the place where you were robbed. We'll handle the rest."

I pried my duff off the porch and stretched my bruises. My skull throbbed, but the soothing jolts from the West's Electric Cure kept the pain manageable. Naked without my sword, I led the way to Second Street, taking a circuitous route on uncharted pathways and shady lanes.

"Let's find where the natives congregate," Kitch advised, "and ask who owns a monkey."

"They won't talk to us," I forewarned.

"Damn right they will," Mourning vowed.

The clacking of blocks resonated from gambling parlors on I Street. Resolute, Kitch charged into the nearest building with Mourning on his heels. Parties of four squatted at low tables clutching gaming pieces to their chests. The slapping of Chinese dominoes stilled at the disturbance.

"Gentlemen, excuse us!" Mourning said loudly. "We're seekin' a woman with a monkey."

The pai gow players returned blank stares, either not comprehending the question or choosing to ignore us. One skittish man dropped the white and red dotted blocks and grabbed a short stack of bills. Kitch snagged him by the collar.

"Where do you think you're going, amigo?" Cane boomed. He hauled the obese gambler from the game. The fellow kicked with his feet, sending the board, coins, and dominos flying. A lantern upended, spilling combustible oil on the ground. Fortunately, a quick-witted man used his jacket to smother the flames. In the bedlam, the struggling gamer rolled from Kitch's grasp and catapulted into a passage. Springing like cats, we pursued through the small opening.

Already dingy as a rat's nest, inward, the lack of ventilation stifled. Over the generations, Chinatown had evolved into a maze overseen by architects with haphazard senses of design. Built from the center out, rooms without windows connected more rooms without windows. Squeezed into an endless corridor, my knuckles scraped against the misshapen, rickety partitions. Impossible to see ahead, I sought the strained breathing and curses of my companions. In a separate chamber, with no roof to obscure the stars, men and women slept on planks cushioned by worn layers of matting. Angry glares wakened from wooden headrests as we rushed into the adjoining cubbyhole.

"This way!" Mourning bellowed, smashing a flimsy barrier. Cracks in the surrounding dens filtered the dusty light. In an alcove, a bowl and pitcher stood upon a stand. Bags of rice filled the corner, and neat rows of canned goods stocked the shelves. "Where'd he go?"

Kitch searched the storage area. "Has to be here someplace," he muttered, punching the containers.

"This way!" I exclaimed, pressing a finger to my lips and indicating a hatch in the floor leading to a root cellar. "He got away!" Leaving the storeroom, my allies remained on either edge of the doorway as I alone sustained the conversation while moving along the hall.

I slid down a panel and tallied my bumps. The blood had coagulated, forming a crusty scab that smarted when touched. I took out the cobalt-colored, electric cure bottle and attached the electrodes to my temples. The weak tingle signified a dying battery. I vigorously rubbed the vial to wake the genie.

The blows of a tussle forced me upright. I found Kitch wrestling with our fugitive. Mourning shoved the shotgun's muzzle into the folds of the Chinaman's neck.

I snatched the long pigtail and flipped the man onto his back. "What's your name?" I inquired, hurling the cap and twisting hair around my fist.

"Shiji," he snuffled.

"Shiji what?" I jammed a thumbnail into the pressure point behind his earlobe.

"Tan Shiji!"

"Where is the monkey lady?" I demanded. Mouth ajar and tongue protruding, he didn't reply.

"Hold him tight," Kitch directed. Gone momentarily, he now held a sack of imported rice, which, without preamble, he used to suffocate Shiji's face. Cane counted to ten as we listened to the muffled screams and watched the stubby legs jerk. He thrust the bag aside and roared, "My friend asked you a simple question!"

"Please, she'll kill me," Shiji whimpered. "There's no place for me to go."

"Not our burden," Mourning said. Impatient, he cocked a shell into the Browning. "I'm itchin' to see if my baby will blow your head clear off or jus' make you twice as ugly."

The bettor blurted in staccato, "Go to the boarding house on Third Street. It's called the 'Welcome.' There is a rooster on the sign. She's on the top level. Never lets me inside, so I don't know which room."

"Who is?" I inquired.

"Madame Kim. She's the one."

I let go of his queue and stood. "Were you the thug who robbed me?"

"No, I'm an accountant. I assist Madame Kim with her keno operation. Do I look like somebody that could attack you?"

"Certainly not," I responded. Smelling his fright, I pulled the bulky man straight, wiped off his robe, and pushed five notes into his hand. "There's a boat leaving for San Francisco at sunrise. Be sure to be on it."

Chapter Thirteen

A BANNER EXTENDED OVER THE TWO-STORY BUILDING. In purple letters, "Welcome Boarding House" translated the Chinese characters. Artwork illustrating a black and red crowing rooster hung under a lamp. Upscale for Chinatown, the tenement's windows were closed to the damp air.

Inside the vestibule, stairs led to the second floor. I bird-dogged Mourning and Kitch, wincing as the treads creaked with each step. On the landing, I counted four doorways.

"Which room?" Cane asked. Ambient light reflected off the barrel of his Enfield.

"We've got one chance in fo—" I halted at a noise in the frontward section. A grizzled man exited and yawned. Paying no attention to us, he shuffled past and descended the staircase, presumably to empty his bladder. Madame Kim would want a good view. "My guess is the other room by the court."

I advanced, stopping between the apartments. As I pressed an ear against the wall, a bell chimed from below. Outside peering up, the old-timer sounded the alarm. Door locked, I rammed against the wood. Shotgun gripped in both fists, Mourning booted the crossrail, splintering the doorframe. I tumbled inward, crashing into a dresser and sending up billows of cosmetic powder. A caged monkey whooped at a woman straddling the windowsill.

"Not this time, dear!" Kitch exclaimed, grabbing the flapping hem of her satin robe. Satisfied with his swift reaction, he sat the keno operator beside a desk strewn with dollar bills and Chinese lottery tickets. The imp yelped from the barred enclosure.

"Ma'am, do you remember who I am?" I questioned. In the hallway, a wide-eyed family huddled in an entryway while the elderly watchman stared from the stairwell. "You and your cohorts mugged my friend and me."

Free of the pancake makeup, Madame Kim appeared younger, somewhere in her early twenties. Apart from the insolent smirk and clenched hands, she might be considered pretty.

With a shrill command, the girl quieted the agitated primate. "How did you find me?"

"We followed you here. Give me my sword and the names of your accomplices. Did they coerce you to perform the sick baby hoax? Look at my face!" Searching the packed space for my weapon, I growled, "Don't tell me you already sold it."

Kitch and Mourning stood by the cage feeding the playful animal grapes. Scratching my lacerations, I flared, still mad at the ape.

"Your sword is fine," she assured, lighting a slender cigar. "The men? I can't tell you their names. They work for me, and I'd lose respect giving them up."

At the table, I sorted the singles. "There's two hundred here. Isn't what you earn from gambling enough? Why did you assault us?"

"Who are you to talk? You Americans burn Chinese houses and businesses, throwing hardworking people into the street," Kim hissed. "The United States pillaged whole villages in Africa and forced the inhabitants into slavery. Mother and Father sold their factory in the Kwangtung province. They sailed ten thousand miles hoping to find the 'Gold Mountain.' Now dead from your countless diseases, my parents rot in Mount Hope cemetery along with my sister and brother. I am saving what I can to send their bones to China for repatriation. There's no gold left in California, and the only mountains I've seen are made of horse dung."

Unqualified to refute her statement, I said, "There's a new organization lowering crime in the Stingaree. We'll be back, and next time, I won't fall for any of your tricks."

Madame Kim blew exhaust from the pursed corner of her mouth.

"Lady, I'm not leaving without what's mine."

Mourning came toward her, his sneer scaring me.

The girl muttered to herself and slid the monkey cage to the side. On hands and knees, she pried the planking out of the floor. From the hollow, Kim removed my long blade.

"The watch, too," I added. Expressionless, the thief surrendered the items. "And I'm acquainted with two boys whose *real* mother could use financial aid. Would you care to make a donation?"

Madam Kim exhaled and extinguished the cheroot. I departed from Chinatown with the winnings in my pocket and a sword by my side.

"Henry, I'm wondering who you really are," Laura groused as we tread a gravel path in City Park. A habitat for rattlesnakes, bobcats, and coyotes, the fourteen hundred scrub-filled acres overlooked downtown San Diego. "Whenever we meet, you're more the worse for wear." A flashy-feathered male quail topped with a stylish hat of erect plumes chased a squawking female over the footpath. "After so many months, I scarcely know you at all."

"What can I tell you?" I wished she'd seek a straightforward statistic, such as my middle name. That was easy. I did not have one.

The gears in Laura's head spun as she prioritized a limitless list of questions. "First off, what's going on with your face today?"

"I had an unpleasant encounter with a monkey."

Her cheeks turned pink. "First a bunny, then a monkey. That's exactly the lame answer I expected. How can you be so glib? I'm trying my best to trust you, Henry Gates, yet you baffle me."

"Laura, I'm a mystery, even to myself." As I hurried to keep up, I modified the theme of the discussion. "Are you interested in seeing my place? It's practically finished."

"Paid for with blood money, I suspect," Laura speculated, drawing to a stop.

"Every cent was justly earned." Not digging too far into the past, I acquiesced, "Most of it anyway."

A glimmering of amusement flickered as she tempered. "Thank you for clarifying that for me. Yes, I'd love to visit your home."

As we circled to civilization, the conversation shifted to entertaining anecdotes regarding her friend Gracie, and lavish details about the splendid living conditions at the Horton mansion. I smiled and nodded, doubting the wisdom of asking Laura to evaluate my cookie-cutter domicile, its design torn from a mass-produced planbook.

In any case, from the sidewalk on a gorgeous day, with the brightest of stars emphasizing the relief panels enhancing the asymmetrical façade, the house was spectacular. The Boston window factory had glazed the lower sashes with two panes of ordinary glass while the upper sashes combined white lights in the center with tinted lights on either side. A hood decorated with filigreed millwork shielded the four steps leading to the spindled, wrap-around veranda. The siding and trim still needed painting.

"Henry, it's very handsome," she commended, shading appraising eyes against the glare. "And you built this yourself?"

"With lots of help," I replied. "Some might express I'm in the way."

"What exterior colors are you using?"

The only color I could visualize was gray. "I'm counting on you to choose a pleasing scheme."

Laura blushed. "Venetian red is all the rage. I'll mull over the trim."

"That's ironic. The architects proposed that hue."

Mourning leveled the yard with a bow rake as I maneuvered her by a stubborn rock in the uneven walkway. Gaze downcast, he bowed as I introduced Miss Mills.

In the foyer, the stairway's stained glass radiated rainbows onto the white plaster.

"Charming! Pastel wallpaper goes well with dark molding," Laura suggested, gliding gloved fingers on the walnut bannister.

"Tremendous idea," I concurred. "Come on, I'll take you upstairs."

"Oh my! Will I be molested?"

"I think not," I answered, and grinned. "It'll be a challenge, but I shall be a perfect gentleman."

"Hmmm," she murmured, climbing the risers. "Perhaps I should have brought Gracie." Laura frowned at the disarray in the main bedroom. "That's your bed? You sleep on the floor?"

"It's so much softer than the ground," I responded and slammed the door.

Downstairs, I led her to the parlor and dining room, both wanting furnishings. Busy attaching shelves on the kitchen's rear wall, Kitch looked past his shoulder. "Mass'r Gates! Suh, if

I knowed dat you bringin' guests, the afternoon tea be ready an' on de table!"

Embarrassed by his exaggerated slave lingo, I stammered, "Knock it off, Kitch! This is my friend Laura Mills. Laura, this character is my foreman, Kitch Cane."

"Yassuh, Mr. Gates." Cane hopped off the ladder and bowed. "This must be the nice lady you babble on about. Are you showing Miss Mills where *she'll* be cooking and doing housework?"

Laura laughed and crossed to the nickel-plated Grand Quaker range. Impressed by the wicker-style base shaped to mimic a woven basket, she replied, "It is tempting." She asked me, "Are *you* well-versed in using this appliance?"

"Still learning. There's a pie puller here somewhere," I answered, twisting levers, opening compartments, and finally shrugging.

Flustered by Cane's brash comments, I guided her into the backyard. Basil and Mero played with Hector under the gum tree. The energetic puppy bounded after a stick as the boys threw the toy farther and farther. Seeing us, they dashed forward.

Basil pleaded, "Uncle Henry. Hector needs a collar. Can you get him one?" He held the squirming animal up for Laura's approval.

"Sure," I responded. "Patent leather with diamond-studs?" Basil nodded as the dog licked Laura's face.

Mero stood apart. "My mother said thanks for buying the books for our school. She's quilting you an eiderdown blanket to stay warm."

After setting the cocker spaniel in the dirt, the boys continued the game.

Watching them play, Laura chuckled. "Are you actually their uncle?"

"That's the first time they called me that. For your benefit, I reckon—kids fooling around."

"That colored man in the kitchen; you said he was your foreman? Where did you meet him?"

"Kitch? We ran into each other one night." I thought of Cane relieving Joe Higgs of his scalp.

"And you allow him to work unsupervised?" she questioned. "I understood you came from the Deep South."

"It took a while, but now I rely on him for everything." It felt strange coming to this realization—placing so much faith in an African American, a former slave. "My dad's probably rolling in his tomb."

"Are those his children, and is that old fellow his father?"

"No. Mourning is his neighbor on Chollas Creek, and those kids live there, too. Kitch's wife, Minnie, is a teacher. They have a son named Aaron."

"And what was that about the cooking and cleaning?"

Fazed by Cane's brazenness, I answered, "I don't know. Maybe he sees that I'm alone and wants to stir up the pot."

Laura turned and asked, "*Are* you lonely?"

A genuine response dishonored my family; nevertheless, I replied truthfully, "Less and less every day."

Chapter Fourteen

MOLLY CAME UP WITH AN ADDRESS FOR THE BRAUNS. Her circle of "fancy ladies" had more dirty laundry on San Diego citizens than the Pinkerton Detective Agency. Heinrich and Wilhelm lodged at the Cliff House in Ocean Beach. William Carson and Frank Higgins, the real estate promoters, set up a railroad to the coast using a borrowed locomotive. After hearing poor reviews on the intermittent transportation service, I rode Clive instead. It felt good to depart the city and inhale unsullied air. Happy to be far from the stables, the mule's ears flopped to the rhythm of his hooves.

The seven-mile trip allowed me occasion to think. I wasn't confident the tattoo on Heinrich Braun's arm matched the markings on the bridge arching over Buzzard Roost Creek or related in any way to my missing family. I hadn't learned scads about the brothers, other than they were new to town, from the Eastern Seaboard, and bought up as much land as they could—using any measures possible. Till Burnes warned of Heinrich's instability. This admonition came from a man launching an additional enterprise fittingly entitled the "Old Tub of Blood," an alehouse reserved exclusively for roughnecks thirsting to iron out opposing views. I was in concord with Burnes—Heinrich Braun oozed impiety.

On Niagara Avenue, the Cliff House lazed on a flat parcel by the sea. An octagonal observation tower—manned by an old salt using a brass telescope to scan the horizon for sailing ships—rose from the wide, three-story frame building. Recently constructed, the landscape surrounding the hotel remained bare of vegetation. By the water's edge, black horse carriages dotted the shore. Fully-clothed couples slogged through the sand or with trousers and skirts gathered high, fled the advancing tides. Originally named Mussel Beach, during the past summer, I attended a clam roast hosted by Carson and Higgins. On that sunny day, twenty-five hundred lots sold for sixty dollars each. Under the prevailing somber clouds and seeing the dense forest of "For Sale" signs, I was thankful that my bidding hand stayed on my lap. I conjectured when the owners would adopt the local custom of burning their idle residence to the foundation for the insurance money.

After leading Clive to a water trough, I entered the lobby by way of an arched balustrade. A sheaf of realty advertisements were arranged on a stand. Folded in half, I presented the leaflet to the receptionist and requested to leave a note for Heinrich Braun. The helpful man dropped the paper into slot 324 of the mailbox.

On the stairs leading to the third floor, I passed a white-aproned maid stuffing linen into a laundry chute. I softly tapped on the entryway of room 324, retreating around the corner. Nobody unbarred the door, so I rapped louder. More silence. I pushed the lock rail and slipped a knife into the frame, gently pressing the blade back and forth against the latch while pulling the knob. The portal sprang open.

Lace curtains waved in the ocean breezes. The chamber appeared unoccupied. Sheets stretched tight across the wrought iron bed. To the right, a doorway gave access to a separate room. A polished wardrobe mounted on a lion's paw base stood against the far wall. Suits sized for a large man hung from the rack in the top section, whereas the lower drawers stored shirts and underwear. A surveying tripod leaned against a dented canister protecting a tarnished level. The center tray in the Louis XVI-style desk held lists of names and addresses marked with real estate property prices.

With no ventilation, the connecting room smelled musty. Not as well-kempt, rumpled garments littered the rug of Wilhelm's accommodations. A formation of empty Old Overholt rye whiskey bottles—the purported libation of Abraham Lincoln—paraded over the windowsill.

I revisited Heinrich's quarters, noticing a leather trunk poking from underneath the mattress. Unlocked, the container sheltered a cherry wood box alongside stained photographic wet-plate holders and six chemical jars of collodion. I lifted the item by the handle and set it on the bed. The front unhinged to expose the twin Darlot brass lenses of a stereo camera. The back housed the tailboard: a sliding rectangle of frosted glass used to focus an image. An etched plaque stated the device had been manufactured in Paris. Scuffed by constant use, the Dubroni was old enough to be a Civil War relic.

There weren't any photographs in either bedroom, and I searched again, this time checking for secret stashes. Upon further examination of the chest, I discerned the interior to be smaller than the exterior. With the equipment removed, I located a release on the bottom. Concealed below the lid, a stack of 3-¼ by 4-¼ inch glass negatives filled the case. I unsuccessfully combed the area again for the resulting stereograph albumen prints. By raising the miniature black and white reversed-likenesses to the light, I squinted to make out their content. Without a stereo viewer, it was a laborious task. I flipped through the assortment of plates, realizing the left-eye/right-eye perspectives framed the same forbidding scenes—freshly-dug, unmarked graves.

Daniel Judge recommended meeting at the Acme to thank our employees for their progress at the Peabody Mine—and more quietly, a celebration to reward ourselves for the wealth we rapidly accumulated. Together, we hired three more miners to assist Claude Horrigan and Javier Rivera. Claude now acted as the copper mine's manager. To speed up productivity, Daniel arraigned for shipments of supplementary machinery to process the ore.

We comprised a diverse group: Judge and Horrigan were both Irish; Rivera was born in Sonora; Howka Cuero, a native of the Campo band of the Kumeyaay Nation; Alan Wu came with a positive endorsement from Bum's caretaker, Ah Wo Sue; and Archie Cohen, a Jewish deck hand. Plus me, a rebel from a Southern state still longing for its own sovereignty.

Till lined up seven jiggers of bourbon and a shot of tea for me. "You footin' the bill?" he questioned before touching the glass to his lips.

"Guess so," I answered as Judge draped an arm over Horrigan's neck. Both slurred the chorus of an Irish drinking song. Deep in their cups, they had started the party after lunch.

Burnes' gruff voice mixed with the off-key warbling, ". . . *Wipe the floor, your trotters shake. Isn't it the truth I told ya? Lots of fun at Finnegan's wake."* He leered and downed the top-shelf liquor. "Quite a mishmash you've assembled here. Ordinarily, I wouldn't let a Chinaman in the door. We rack up heaps of Mexicans and Injuns, but the Chinese always get folks riled. Glad he's dressed normal and not wearing red pajamas."

"The man's a hard worker."

"I'm sure he is. That there's the dilemma." Till dumped out an ashtray and inquired, "What's the matter, Hank? Are you bound up? You heard the saying, 'a pint a day keeps the doctor away.'"

I snorted. "Never had that digestive issue, even when I fell off the wagon." I gave an accounting of the unusual negatives hidden under Heinrich Braun's bed.

Till muttered something unintelligible and re-lit his stogie. "You showed pluck breakin' into that flannel mouth's hotel room. Why would anybody want to shoot pictures of burial sites? What's it mean, and did you take any?"

"I left the stereographs there. And no, I don't know their purpose. The images may have spanned many years."

"Anything else is in the photos? People or houses?"

"Nope," I responded. "It was difficult to view the negatives. I saw mounds of dirt, six-feet-long by two-feet-wide, and a few bigger—most likely mass graves. One plate revealed a shovel or pick lying on the ground. I got the impression after seeing multiple sets of footprints that several people were involved."

"What are you gonna do?" the saloon owner shouted above the increasing noise.

"Not much I can—" A sharp elbow jammed into my rib. *"Watch it!"* I swiveled to eye a twosome of strapping longshoremen grappling with Alan Wu.

"Jus' the headache I needed tonight," Burnes grumbled. He grabbed a truncheon and hustled past the long, narrow counter.

Ready to defend my laborer, I held back as Ah Wo Sue's nephew gained the upper hand. Javier tossed a billiards cue, and Alan used the pole to box the assailants' meaty heads. Then with a powerful boot, he sent the brawnier of the dockworkers flying over a table.

The inebriated crowd cheered encouragement as Till put the other fellow into a coma with one expeditious stroke of his baton. "Mop this up," he ordered, and stomped to his station at the bar.

Arms resting on the railing, Daniel asked, "Was that some kind of Oriental fighting?"

"Dunno. It was fun to see Alan kick his ass. The stevedores will go mad hearing a skinny Chinaman trounced their buddies."

My colleague agreed and gave his word to return Alan Wu to the mine by daybreak.

Incredulous, Kitch questioned, "You decided *I* should design the exterior *and* layout the floor plans?"

Under the noon sun, we stood on the eastern corner of Sixth and B Streets. Lots A and L of Block Nineteen lay beneath our toes in their fallow glory: rubble, chicken bones, and mountains of horse manure.

"I understood you could read and write? You had no trouble with the Palliser planbook." I tilted backwards to crack my spine. Although I now owned a conventional bed, my back ached from hauling furniture into my place. The paddle steamer *Ancon* had docked yesterday morning with my shipment from San Francisco.

Cane's lips parted to speak and then clamped shut. He targeted a crow with a rock. "What do you foresee?"

"The double plot is fifty by two hundred feet. I'd like to fit eight apartments into that section."

"One or two bedrooms?"

"Maybe half-and-half? Whatever is best. My goal is to maximize income and minimize maintenance. Keep them basic and use quality materials. With the school almost finished, families shall hanker to live nearby. And that brings in new commerce."

"It's a huge project," Kitch said, shoving hands into his pockets. "With the downturn in real estate, will anyone move here?"

"They'll come. Can you do it?" I inquired. Catching the glint in his eyes, I perceived he was becoming responsive to the concept.

Cane raked the whiskers on his chin. He looked up and met my gaze. "I'll require extra help."

"What are you and Mourning currently earning?"

"Hank, you know our earnings since you're the one payin' us."

"Double it."

"White man's wages ain't that high. Your copper mine is doin' that well?"

"Kitch, I'm not made of dough. Mines always peter out—that's a fact. Once you own land, as long as you keep up with the taxes, it's yours forever. This afternoon, I hope to buy these adjacent lots. Then you can put up another apartment building and be the superintendent of both."

"What about my freight business?"

"Delegate and take a cut."

Kitch's face split into a smile. "I want to do this. As I was sayin', I lack enough carpenters."

"Hire dependable men, from Chollas Creek, Tijuana, or wherever. Eventually, you should come to a point where your hammer spends the day in your belt. You'll just use it to knock slackers on the head. That's called managing. And as far as Basil and Mero are concerned, it's okay if they stop by after school or on the weekends to lend a hand. But make sure those boys keep up with their studies."

Brow creased, he pondered, "Hank, why are you bein' so good to us? Why not hire your light-skinned pals? Is this generosity reparation for whatever brutality took place twenty years ago on your daddy's plantation?"

I thought back to my father and how he had taught me to handle the slaves. I had plenty to atone for. "Those are logical questions. The answer is not that complicated. In January, you exhibited gumption by arriving at daybreak with a cartload of free timber. Then you had the arrogance to ask me for a job. The house was completed sooner than I expected and under budget."

Skeptical, Cane inquired, "That's it?"

"You need more?" I felt myself opening up. "To be honest, you don't rattle my nerves. That's rare. Mourning is moody and impossible to read, yet always puts in a full day. Your neighbor was also instrumental in retrieving my sword. You both proved your loyalty. Mero and Basil remind me of kids I grew up with at Cedar Hall. Does that resolve any issues you might have?"

Kitch stood at attention and snapped a lopsided salute. "Yassuh, Mr. Gates. I meant, *yes sir,* Lieutenant Gates!"

Laughing at his silly grin, I pressed an envelope containing an ounce of golden flakes into his fist. "That's worth twenty bucks. *Now* can you start?"

"Nice to see you again, Henry," Alonzo Horton greeted. "May I get you a drink? Water to wash down the grime or something harder to take the edge off?"

Parched, I responded, "Water's fine." Horton rang a bell, and Mr. Sledge slid from behind a lacquered screen with a pitcher and beakers. On my prior appointment, I hadn't spotted the private passageway.

After a sip, Alonzo said, "This week, I'm working with the City Council to pave or at least oil the midtown routes. With this eternal wind, I'm covered from head to foot in soot by noon. Evolution necessitates the patience of the Saints."

"And bundles of cash," I added, sweeping my pants with the duster.

"Yes, that too. Sometimes—" He rubbed his eyes. "Often, I think I'm wasting my breath trying to raise this city from the ashes."

"You're just overworked, Father Horton." I loaded my jaw with Bull Durham.

Alonzo chuckled at the moniker and nudged a spittoon fashioned into an overturned top hat. "You may be right. Mrs. Horton has been up late the last few evenings with her séances, so I haven't slept well."

"Jesse Shepard?"

"Yes. As a musician, he is a certified genius, but insomuch as the sorcery and hocus-pocus, I am not fully convinced. It's the infernal noise. An old man needs his rest." As if to labor the point, he yawned. "Excuse me. How can I be of service, Henry?"

"A couple months back, I bought two allotments on B Street. The property next door is available." Landholding papers in Heinrich Braun's desk had noted derelict tracts on Block Nineteen. "I hoped that you repossessed these units."

A dozing tiger, Horton's ears perked. "Let me take a look." Thoughtfully tugging his silver beard, he bent toward the wall to contemplate the map. "I remember these." Seated again, he submitted, "Henry, why don't you buy the entire block?"

About to expectorate brown juice into the cuspidor, I choked. My stomach churned as bits of tobacco trickled down my windpipe.

The real estate magnate prodded the stovepipe closer, and I spit the whole wad. I spluttered, "I'm afraid I haven't enough capital."

Alonzo scribbled a figure on a slice of letterhead and laid the proposal on the end of the desk.

"Are you mad?" I asked. *Five thousand dollars.* I could not afford that, still—*what an incredible deal!*

Teeth gleaming, he purred, "I'll loan the balance. How much are you able to scrape together?"

"Half that. Maybe three thousand."

"Will four percent interest do the trick?"

Suspicious of a trap, I questioned, "Why so low?"

"This town must be built. Most of what I sell returns foreclosed—always two steps forward, one step back. It's very tiresome for a seventy-five-year-old New Englander, even for a man as strong as an ox." He laughed self-deprecatingly. "Twenty years ago I bought Horton's Addition for thirty-three cents an acre. Everyone thinks I am rich—not anymore. Henry, I know you'll develop the land and not wind up on my stoop begging for a refund." Horton stuck out his sizable hand. "Shake on it, and after lunch we'll sign the paperwork."

Alonzo selected a fine restaurant downtown. Steak and potatoes were never so filling.

Chapter Fifteen

ON K STREET, I TARRIED ON A CASK outside Treacher's Barrel Factory. A post on the door announced the need for a "Reliable Cooper," and a sign on the window advertised "The Only Crozing Machine in San Diego."

In the loneliness of the wee hours, I waited for Walt Werner and chewed upon my latest real estate transactions. In addition to my house, I now owned twelve lots. Had my greed for land clouded my judgment? Time shall tell. In the meanwhile, I owed Alonzo Horton monthly payments. To add tension, after the midday meal, he interrogated me on my questionable relationship with his niece's classmate. Apparently, Gracie and Laura discussed me at the dinner table. I cited that by Alabama law, technically, I remained married. Nothing inappropriate had happened or could happen until I determined the whereabouts of my family. Understandably perturbed, Horton did not want Gracie's friend herded down an unknown path leading to certain disappointment. The awkward discourse ended with a commitment to disclose more of my past with Laura.

Internally rehearsing that ticklish conversation, I jumped as Walt drifted from the swirling fog, soothed to see the injured tooth still imbedded in his grin.

"Good as new!" Werner reassured, pulling up his lip to display the reinserted canine. "A bit rocky, but so far, the darn thing hasn't turned black or fallen into my soup. Sallie, she's my wife, never even noticed." He drank from his flask and coughed violently. "This Coffin Varnish prevents infection."

"Right," I conceded, curious if his doctor felt the same way. "I hope this patrol will be less eventful than the last." A boggy lane stank of carrion. We did an about-face and hurried in the opposite direction. My vision darkening from pinched nostrils, I gulped fresh air. "What *was* that?"

"Slaughter house," Walt whiffed. He pressed a thumb to the wobbly tooth and spat. "The Chinese save every scrap, 'cept the offal." With haste, my partner spun open the bottle for a taste. "Let's try H Street. Perhaps some greenies are in over their heads."

"Greenies" were travelers to San Diego looking for excitement or pleasure yet unfamiliar with the myriad hazards of the Stingaree. Gin mill bosses commissioned "steerers" to lure the feeble-minded or naive to their establishments. Once lassoed, the assisting bartender plied the chump with unlimited free tar water. Subsequently, in the alley, an upper-hook or billy club subdued the staggering greeny, enabling the steerer to strip the victim's pockets. Documented in daily newspaper articles, politicians unanimously deemed these robberies detrimental to the vital tourism trade. Often found without underdrawers, none of the saps had been eager to testify.

On the west side of Fifth Street, and cited as an institution where the barkeepers collaborated with steerers, McInerney's public house teemed with griping laborers and randy sailors. Walt pushed by the riffraff to buy beer as I grabbed a corner table. I checked out a contrasting combination: a gentleman attired in an expensive outfit jabbering to another fellow also dressed in a suit, its threadbare fabric wrinkled and patched.

Werner sat, sloshing foam as he slid the mug. "You ain't gargling with that, are you?" he shouted above the clamor.

My fingers unwrapped from the damp surface.

"You a bible-thumpin' Mormon or one a dem teetotallin' Sons of Temperance?" Not waiting for an answer, he chugged his suds and switched our glasses. "There you go. Now, nobody need think you're an altar boy."

"I'm none of those, but thanks for your concern."

Halfway through my malt liquor, Walt belched and again asked for clarification, shaking his head at my pithy explanation. "Never considered quitting, *not ever!* I drink to get drunk, jus' like me pappy, and his pappy 'fore him."

Pointing inconspicuously, I questioned, "What of those two? The secondhand jacket is plying the silk stockings from a bottomless cup."

"He *is* a dandy," Werner allowed as his deteriorating diction countrified. The accountant signaled the barmaid for ale and slapped her backside as she sashayed away. "Reminds me of Sallie's round bum when I first saw her in church." Shifting his contemplation to the mismatched pair, he said, "Let's jus' be patient. Nice to be indoors outta the cold, don't ya know?"

When one doesn't imbibe, it is easy to feel isolated in a room filled with shrieking laughter. At an ill-treated upright piano, a Navy seaman, flat hat canted at a rakish angle, pounded out a salty version of "Dinna forget yer mither, Sandie." At a square table, an impromptu card game began, each player reading their hand as if this deal held the meaning of life itself.

"Two o'clock," Walt informed, raising his timepiece to read the tiny dial. "Hank, I'm grateful you got back my watch. My wife'd tan me proper findin' it gone. 'Twas an anniversary gift, or maybe Christmas." Eyes shut; he wedged the chronometer to his ear.

At the circle of high rollers, an angry scuffle diverted my attention long enough for the suspected greeny and steerer to evaporate, leaving a spinning whiskey bottle.

Werner's peepers flickered as I coaxed, "Come on!" He floundered following me to the street. "Go that way," I whispered. He lurched to the left side of the building. To the right, I rushed along the byway between McInerney's and a half-done structure. I united with my partner by a pile of rubbish. "See anybody?"

"No." Humped and wheezing, Walt had the pallor of a man about to lose dinner and three gallons of sour beer.

"You alright?"

"Aye. Just give me a minute." He embraced the gate of the taproom's privy. "They must be here somewhere."

"Stay put, and I'll look around." Werner nodded and squeezed into the outhouse.

I reentered the construction site. On closer inspection, I realized the carpenters had laid down their tools ages ago. The framework was plundered of everything not nailed to the floor. I stepped through a gap in the rotting skeleton into a vaulted room. A moan rose from beyond a buildup of debris. Visible in the dull moonlight, the man of wealth crawled toward me, the crest of his crown darkly slick. I helped him to his feet.

A shadow sprang from the rafters onto my shoulders. Excruciating agony twisted my maimed leg as I crashed to my knees, then to my belly. After losing the sword to Madame Kim, tonight I carried only a bayonet—this easily wrenched from my grasp by the attacker. The pressure of his body squashed the wind from my lungs, and an arm across my throat kept oxygen from returning.

"Mister Busybody needs a lesson in butting out of other people's business." The steerer flashed the edge in my face and growled, "Using your own pig sticker, I'll cut off that meddling snout, and then slice off—"

The assailant's forehead struck mine as the greeny conked him with a brick.

"Get off, big fella," Walt persuaded, heaving the gorilla off my chest. As I sat against a wooden column, he delved into the thief's coat and presented the swag. "Sir are any of these yours?"

"This one," the man answered, taking the fattest wallet and removing two bills. "May I offer you both a reward for your efforts?"

"That's not necessary," Werner responded, unrolling a ball of twine from a pouch. Humming to himself, the accountant deftly trussed the mugger's limbs. "You *could* fork over the brand of that cologne you're marinated in. Now and then, my wife tells me I got the kick of ol' Mr. Crappie's barnyard." He cackled, "Sallie, she's a corker, that gal." My associate sobered. "Buddy, if you ever come back to San Diego, do us a favor and avoid the Stingaree."

Minnie ladled steaming soup into a bowl. In front, Kitch and Aaron played a lively game of pick-up sticks. "Anything else I can bring you, Mr. Gates?" she asked, pouring a cup of pink lemonade.

"No thanks, Minnie. This smells delicious." I dipped the toasted bread into the chunky broth and questioned, "How did you and Kitch get together?"

Ready for a joyful response, I felt puzzled as her posture stiffened. "What in particular do you need to know, Mr. Gates?" She sat across from me wringing a dishrag.

"Please refer to me as Henry or Hank. Mr. Gates is way too formal. I see that your marriage is solid and wondered how you met—that's all."

"Even though you're his boss, my husband calls you Hank. I keep telling Kitch to show more respect."

I spooned chicken from amongst the noodles and suggested, "You should sell this soup in cans. The public will love it."

Minnie beamed. "It's not bad, I must confess. Mourning gives me spicy herbs from his garden. That's what wets your appetite."

Aaron giggled and threw up his arms as the pyramid of rods toppled.

For a protracted moment, her eyelids closed as if evoking a stressful memory. "Kitch and I weren't from the same plantation in Lafourche Parish. When I turned fifteen, Mass'r Gillis said I had to be married and bear children. Tandel became my first husband. We had twin girls, Ruth and—"

Kitch sensed reticence and inquired with unease, "Minnie, you okay?"

"I'm fine," she responded. "Venus was my other daughter. An unending drought dried up the cotton and Mass'r Gillis had to sell a few of us to stay afloat. Being a woman, they sent me to an auction in Thibodaux. Before I left, Tandel said he would come for me, and we'd flee with the little ones. He never came." Her voice lowered. "In a pen with more slaves waiting to be sold, an African tried to lay hands on me. By chance, Kitch was in town running errands and heard my screams. He hurt the man while rescuing me. We ran off knowing we'd be punished."

Eels filled my bowels as I relived an exceptionally vicious beating at Cedar Hall. Getting whipped to the bone is a terrible way to die. "The owner chased you?"

"Mass'r Gillis sent Mr. Brooks, but he went the wrong way. At night, we took the back roads to Jackson. Kind folks put us on the freedom trail to Canada."

Aaron cried for his mother to join the fun. Minnie smiled sweetly, assuring the boy she'd be there soon. "Easy Joe, someone we traveled with and trusted, said Moses sent a message for runaway slaves to meet at the old Cherokee hunting grounds near Muscle Shoals."

Incredulous, I questioned, "Harriet Tubman?"

"That's what we thought. Easy got paid by a slave catcher to lead him to where we hid. Captain Garner captured us and three others taking refuge in a thicket. The captain couldn't watch everyone all the time, so Kitch hit him with a stick, and we dragged the body into a gulley and covered it with leaves."

I frowned, recalling Cane's similar story about a bandit on the journey to San Diego. He said Minnie knocked out the outlaw. "Dead?"

"Can't say, Mr. Gates. I pray that spiteful man still lives and ask God to save the soul of Easy Joe. We wandered by ourselves from then on, here and there, not too long in one place. After the war, we wound up in Chollas Creek. Kitch started the freight business with what he made on the docks. And now we have a sturdy roof overhead and a beautiful son."

"You *are* fortunate," I admitted. "Did he tell you we owned slaves on my father's plantation?"

"Yes, Mr. Gates. It's hard to believe a white man is sitting right here in my kitchen declaring he's keen for my soup."

"We'll look into finding you a canning machine," I said, finishing the fruit drink.

"I wish to express my gratitude," Minnie hesitated, "Mr. Gates, for giving my husband that job. He loves working with his hands. Comes home worn out, but contented. It's a blessing for our family."

"Kitch is a good man, Mrs. Cane."

Later on, alone in my empty house, I wondered what became of Minnie's daughters.

Chapter Sixteen

WALT CRACKED THE TOOTHY, MANIC GRIN OF A CHESHIRE CAT. Unable to control his elation, he bent forward and whispered, "Here we go!" My patrol partner pulled a flask from a pocket and uncorked the cap. So consumed with what was about to happen, he forgot to drink. Werner replaced the lid and slid the bark juice into his vest.

The audience faced the seven potential Spear of Achilles members. Spaced across a low platform, the men wore expressions ranging from apprehension to cocky self-confidence. For those of us who had formerly passed this baptism of blood, many found these moments of anticipation to be the best parts of the monthly meetings.

Heinrich Braun repeated the same lines he had last time, "As the acting president, I accept all of you into this organization with the rights and privileges to which this membership entails. Turn to me."

The engagements transpired abruptly, making it impossible to accurately chronicle the stages of each confrontation. My head spun, eyes glued to the Reverend Glazkov and President Braun.

Glazkov sucker-punched the steelworker from Pittsburgh whose iron jaw refused to dent. The reverend found himself locked in a chokehold gasping for breath. It took three men from the front row to subdue the raging metalworker.

Heinrich's initiate, August Hamey, a cabinetmaker from Kentucky, was not as lucky. I was unable to distinguish what befell Sam Wheeler, the rancher who had moved his clan to the city. During that induction, Walt fixated on me, likewise missing the movements Wheeler used to vacate posthaste. This time, I caught the whole interaction.

The president's instruction to turn signaled the start of the test. As Hamey swiveled, Heinrich slashed the greenhorn's breast with his corroded fish-gutting knife. He seized the collapsing cabinetmaker by the collar and sent the poor fool tumbling off the rear of the stage. When the leader hurried to assist Reverend Glazkov, powerful hands snatched the woodworker under the drapes and presumably out the back door. This well-practiced misdirection took effect in the blink of an eye—imperceptible to anyone distracted by the general mayhem.

A few scuffmarks were the only physical evidence that August Hamey had ever stepped into the textile depository.

Laura listened closely as I narrated the events in my life preceding the Civil War. These quaint antebellum stories were as faded from memory as the engineering texts I studied at the East Alabama College. The strain of battle had conditioned me in ways I could not justify to a civilian who had not experienced similar horrors. Losing my family crushed and numbed me. The result? Innumerable postwar years squandered searching a stitched up nation for a reason to live.

"What was she like?" Laura inquired. We sat on a padded wickerwork couch on Alonzo Horton's spacious patio. The help served tea and biscuits on silver trays as half-naked statues eavesdropped on our dialogue. "Your wife."

"We were too immature to get married," I responded, watching sailboats skim over the smooth harbor. Thinking hard, I failed to reconstruct Elizabeth's face, merely seeing flashes of light striking her blond hair. Through thick and thin, I carried a tintype of my wife and children, ultimately losing the treasured icon while fording a swollen stream in some godforsaken wilderness. "Beth enjoyed making people laugh." I touched my forehead as if manipulating my brain might conjure ancient visions.

"And?" Laura laid a reassuring palm on my arm. "What else?"

"News arrived of the Confederate attack on Fort Sumter. Then the Union organized extensive naval blockades to hamstring the Southern economy. My schoolmates chomped at the bit to join the Yellowhammers, and so did I. We laid down our books and picked up weapons in Selma. I crossed paths with a granger from—"

Laura cut me short. "Henry, you're not answering my question. That was the war. I wanted to hear more regarding Beth's personality. You told me how an aunt introduced you two at a church social, that you courted her for a year, and about your extravagant wedding. She had a splendid sense of humor. Is that all that comes to mind?"

"I loved her. That's what I remember most."

A seagull landed between us. "The ocean's that way," Laura directed, indicating due west.

I crumbled a cookie. The bird approached, curving its yellow beak to study us with one black eye. I tossed the bits on the deck and clucked. The gull hopped closer.

With the teacup to her lips, she asked, "Are we alike?"

"You and me? Sure. We both hold hot beverages and English crackers in high esteem."

Laura simplified, "Am *I* comparable to *your wife?*"

This question did not have a risk-free comeback. I stepped carefully into the minefield. "No, I've never met your equal. Miss Mills, you are unique in every way." The feathered creature hooked the largest morsel and flew away.

"You've got that right," she smiled, patting my wrist. "Thank you for sharing. I realize the past is difficult to relive."

"And what of you, Miss Mills? How in the world can you still be single? You must have had bounteous beaus."

"Me? My story is not as riveting." Laura stood to sweep the remaining pieces off the edge with her foot. Fingers gripping the rail, the woman gazed at the manicured gardens. "Believe it or not, several men proposed before I came out here."

"Only several? What happened?"

"Nothing happened. After graduating from Smith College, I wasn't ready for marriage. For a time, I helped at my father's millinery shop and then accepted a job as a clerical assistant at a law office in downtown Philly. My parents selected successful suitors, although none were particularly appealing. No spark—do you catch my meaning?" Laura swung to register my reaction.

"I understand exactly what you mean."

"Henry, I'm a borderline old maid, they call it—a spinster."

"That's funny," I said. "You're just a teeny, little baby. A highly educated baby."

"Don't mock me. I'm in my thirties. My mother sent me to San Diego to find a man."

"And did you?"

Laura smirked. "Yes, but alas, he's married."

Claude Horrigan sent a message from Julian. The telegraph read:

THE WESTERN UNION TELEGRAPH COMPANY.

17 S D 42 DH

RECEIVED at SAN DIEGO, CALIF. 2:10 PM APRIL 26TH, 1888

Dated JULIAN CALIF. 26

To MR H GATES

OUR FRIENDS RETURNED FOR DINNER. THEY ARE STAYING OVERNIGHT. PLEASE COME AND SAY HELLO. CLAUDE

I rounded up Daniel, and we rode to the Peabody Mine. Already dusk, Alan Wu and Archie Cohen sat by a fire pit. A whiff of venison stew drifted from the bubbling pot. Horrigan and Rivera appeared from behind a copse of ironwood, both bearing firearms.

"Jefe número uno! Jefe número dos!" Javier exclaimed, lowering the muzzle of his Remington. "We almost blasted you!"

"Thanks for keeping your finger off the trigger," Judge responded sarcastically. "Where are they?"

Claude pointed at the mine with his rifle. "Follow me, gentlemen." He lit a lantern and stooped into the entrance. "Howka Cuero's been guarding the prisoners."

Seventy-five feet down an isolated tunnel, we stopped at a barrier. Cuero rose from a crate and stood by the slats of the gate. The three banished claim-jumpers lay in the dirt glaring through puffy eyes. Red blemishes dotted their arms.

Disturbed by the blisters, I asked, "Are they diseased? Is that Saint Anthony's fire?"

Our manager unlocked the cage and dragged one of the men upright. "No, that's Saint Howka's fire. Archie saw this prig running off with our supplies. He tracked him to their camp and came back for us. Howka had the brilliant notion of flinging a pot of hot coals into their tent. It's a method the

Kumeyaay use to settle differences with opposing tribes. Watching these buffoons dance around, well, I all but wet myself."

The Indian waved and smiled widely.

Horrigan questioned, "What should we do with them?"

"String the bastards up," Daniel advocated. "Nothing worse than a thief."

I squatted on a boulder to massage my leg and inquired, "Did they steal anything of value?"

"Just cans of stewed tomatoes and two blankets," Claude responded. "Oh, and Rivera's soiled britches that were dangling on a branch to dry. The Mexican crapped himself."

Face reddening, Javier retorted, "Not true! Those are yours!" Horrigan laughed.

"Tie their hands and bring them out to the campfire," I ordered. "And get them something to eat."

I accompanied Judge to the ventilation shaft, where we discussed our options. On principle, I was against a hanging.

"Hank, I refuse to let those sneaks go!" my business partner argued. "Who can tell what they'll do next time?"

"Seems they only took enough to survive. We'll take them to Julian and let Captain Hopkins deal with it."

Daniel scoffed, "The law won't do a dammed thing. Hopkins will let those scoundrels loose to slay us in our sleep!"

This was a valid consideration, yet I had a better solution. "We can hire them."

"What?" Judge sputtered. "I don't trust those muggins!"

"From their previous illegal achievements here at the mine, we know they can excavate. Give them jobs."

He grumbled, "Hank, we ain't the Salvation Army."

"And we're not the Skeleton Army. Let's reason with them."

Rivera led us to the cabin used as bunkhouse. He forced the captives onto the floor against the beds.

I put a log in the stove and sat by the heat. Daniel paced the narrow expanse, wielding a double-barrel shotgun. "Who's the ringleader?" I asked. Two of the men glanced at their plump companion, the very fellow we had seen emerging from this shelter with the scattergun. "What's your name?"

Clothed in the same flannel union suit, armpits ringed with sweat, he mumbled, "Foghorn."

"Is that your real name or a nickname?" Judge challenged, thirsty for an excuse to slam the gunstock into their heads.

"My mother christened me Cecil. Now I go by Foghorn."

"Why's that?" Judge queried.

Cecil put the heels of his palms together and blew.

"And your friends," I questioned, "are they also privileged with amusing titles?"

Foghorn aimed his chin at a stumpy, bald man with a barrel chest who looked to possess superior upper body strength. "That there's the 'Mole' and the other feller is 'Roundhouse Mike.' Mike did a stint at the rail yards until he got himself crippled."

Roundhouse hoisted a gnarled arm. "A coal chute come apart and broke my wing. The company didn't set it right—sent me packin'."

"That geezer can still swing a pick," Mole said defensively. "The Creator works in mysterious ways."

"Amen," I concurred, kneading my sore calf.

Eyes closed, Mole shouted, "Praise the Almighty!"

Keeping to the decision I made in the mine, I said, "You gents have two choices. Be on your way, never to return to this neck of the woods, *or,* you can unite with us and earn an honest wage. It's your call."

Mole lifted his bound wrists in a pleading gesture. "Mister, with God as my witness, we meant you no disrespect—thought the claim was abandoned. We were starved, and Foghorn didn't have a bedroll." Rivera's—*or Horrigan's*—stained pants swaddled his bowed legs. "I'll muck for you, or do whatever has to be done."

"Foghorn's the best shot-firer there is. No mishaps, not one, if he's stuffin' your holes with gunpowder," Roundhouse extolled. "And me, I have a few useful years left. I'll dig with my fingernails if you tell me to."

"How about you, Cecil?" Daniel inquired. "You been quiet. Staying or going?"

Foghorn shoved out his limbs. "Untie us boss, we're sticking around. We won't do you no wrong."

I withdrew my sword and sliced the bindings. "If any of you steal from us again, Mr. Judge shall hang you from the nearest apple tree. If he's unavailable, I'll slit you all from stem to stern and wipe my blade on your shirts. That's a promise."

"Don't know if these scrawny trees will bear three full-grown men," Judge mused. He rubbed his paunch and sighed. "But Lordy, Margaret Robinson's apple pie sure is a treat."

On my freshly painted veranda, I watched the purple flowers of the crape myrtle tremble in the fluctuating air currents. The spade used to plant the tree was stuck in a mound of clay filling a wheelbarrow. I would use the excess to level low areas. Except for sundry odds and ends, to the extent I could be concerned, my home was finished. Laura kept insisting I throw a housewarming party. I continued to procrastinate.

Cane slipped through the front door carrying iced tea. Hector darted past his shins, running to me for attention. "Here you go chief," he said, setting down a glass. "I put a pound of sugar in there, jus' as you like."

"Ah. Sweet tea can't ever be too sweet." Satisfied with my most recent handiwork, I questioned, "Tell me, what you think?" I purchased the shrub from Kate Sessions at the San Diego Nursery.

Rooted in the matching rocking chair, he answered, "It's blockin' my view of the bay. Now you need public water. Any word on when the utility pipes shall be laid?"

"The papers report the project is lacking capital, and since the conduit passes over the Indian reservation, there are legal problems." A slimy puppy tongue licked my fingers. "The San Diego Flume Company is demanding that the government steps in."

"I am a slow walker, but I never walk back," Kitch said quietly. He focused on a solitary man in the other lot scraping out a trench.

"What's that you said?" I placed Hector on my lap. The dog reeked of the sheep manure the horticulturist had recommended as fertilizer.

"I'm a slow walker, but never walk back," he quoted. "Mr. Lincoln said that. The president was speakin' about perseverance." My exhausted neighbor dropped his shovel and used a stack of foundation blocks for support. A hunched woman brought a bucket of water. "Should we go help him?"

"These are my church duds. Maybe after I change." Dubious, Cane contemplated my scruffy jeans. "Plus my keester is killing me. That ground is tough as cement. Anyhow, an update on the status of our new apartments would be great. Did you receive everything you requisitioned?"

"Simpson is deliverin' a shipment of stone and mortar tomorrow. We cleared and leveled the block. The excavation for the footing is coming along, yet as you jus' said, the earth is unforgivin'."

"Keep the men on schedule. I went by the B Street School and noticed the outside is done. How is Roundhouse Mike doing?" Last week, I transferred the ex-thief from the mine to the carpentry team.

"Mike loves workin' for an African," Kitch responded caustically. Antsy, my foreman stood, and leaning against the milled porch post, stretched to swipe cobwebs from the attached fretwork. "In spite of the screwy flipper and big mouth, the man does his job. At any rate, my guys want him gone."

"If he gets under your skin, let him go," I advised.

"No way," Cane snorted. "That cracker ain't goin' nowhere. I didn't forget your speech on everyone rowin' together. Roundhouse Mike will be servin' *us* lunch soon enough." He set the empty cup on the table before clomping down the steps and heading next door to lend a hand. Hector and I napped in the onshore breezes as the two men toiled.

Right as I was planning to mosey over and introduce myself, Till Burnes dropped by on his dusky filly. "The original spaniel landed on the Mayflower," he educated while falling to his knees. Tail wagging, Hector ran into the yard and slobbered on the barkeeper's cheek. "Good dog, nice doggy!" With the puppy held in his arms, my friend claimed Kitch's relinquished seat. "That your man out yonder? Did you send him there to dig?"

"Nope. That's on his own time. Cane hasn't learned to take a breather."

The Irishman put his shoes on the railing and exhaled. "Won't let my wife see this place. Mary is tired of living above the saloon. She can't invite any ladies to visit, 'cause it stinks."

I shook with laughter. "Are you thirsty? Sorry, I don't have anything stronger than iced tea."

"Appreciate the offer," he replied, "but I'm not here on a social call. We need to talk. You asked about the Braun brothers. Yesterday, I overheard something unusual."

I sat up straight. "From who?"

"A carpetbagger rolled into the Acme for a slug. Sat at the bar and started gabbin' to another fella. Their conversation turned interestin', so I listened close. Do you recollect

Sherman's policy to leave a path of destruction across the South?"

"William Tecumseh Sherman, the Union general?"

"That's him. Crazy Uncle Billy," Till answered, setting Hector on his paws. "These rogues were Northern veterans, and the hefty one mentioned Major Henry Hitchcock—"

I interrupted, "Hitchcock came from Alabama. That traitor consorted with Sherman's staff and then demolished his own state." Outraged, I summoned memories of my own razed plantation and unaccounted for family. The general's "hard war"—meaning burning and pillaging—scorched the entire Southland. On frosty nights huddling in my trench, I smelled the bitter results from his unnecessary carnage and fantasized of revenge.

Burnes resumed, "From what I picked up, General Sherman assigned the major an elite squadron to impersonate Confederate infantry. My customer gloated that owing to his combative nature, Hitchcock recruited him to lead a unit. Outfitted in gray uniforms, him and his Yankee pals passed freely throughout the countryside, doin' whatsoever to whomsoever they pleased. Drunk on my liquor, the jackass rambled on tellin' long tales of arson, rape, and the piles of civilians he laid to waste. I nearly leapt over the bar and throttled the son of a bitch."

"Why didn't you?" I inquired, quaking with anger.

Till rolled up his shirtsleeve. With the nib of a knife, he traced the same tattoo that tinted Heinrich Braun's hide. "That's why." My friend's mouth distorted into a frightful grin. "Hank, I left the hellion in one piece so you could talk to him yourself."

Chapter Seventeen

LEVI NAUGHTON STRADDLED A SAWHORSE. I learned his name from one of the papers he carried—a document entitling the bearer to land on Coronado Island. To aid with balance, a cord tethered his thumbs to a rafter. In this configuration, Naughton's full weight rested upon his crotch. While imprisoned at Point Lookout, I witnessed the operation of a commensurate apparatus. Union guards nicknamed the punishing device "Mary the Marching Mule," after Robert E. Lee's spouse. This cruel method of torture often left soldiers incapable of walking for days—if ever.

Other than periodic salvos of profanity, my captive had yet to communicate.

Together, we occupied the Acme's cold room, an insulated space stacked with three hundred-pound cubes of artificial ice. Only God and I could hear my prisoner's cries for mercy.

I studied the middle-aged man, who, longing to liberate himself, or ease the suffering, lifted knee-high boots in painful attempts to contact the stand's center beam. With bricks hugging his calves, this proved to be a hopeless mission. Hatless, hairless, and jacketless, over the hours, the braggart's complexion blanched from a healthy pink to a waxen blue. Slate-shaded eyes blazed above the drooping walrus mustache hooding his entire mouth.

Our prey entered the refrigerator of his own volition, imagining that his overwhelming charisma had won him a steamy liaison with the alehouse's most vivacious barmaid. As substitutes for the warmhearted Molly Doyle, Levi Naughton encountered the unsympathetic saloon owner and his namesake waiting in the wintery darkness.

"Are you ready to talk?" I asked.

Powerless to mask the cramps wracking his thighs, Naughton rumbled, "I'll kill you. Then I'll shoot the bog-jumper and his potato-eatin' spawn."

"Seeing I'm here and you're there, that seems pretty unlikely." I rose from the carton of carrots. "Levi, tell me all I need to know and you'll be set free. You have my word." With my sword, I jabbed at the circled two-pronged fork imprinted on his arm. "What is that? Explain its meaning." He hacked up lung butter and spit.

"You're not helping," I snarled, swabbing the thick, yellow saliva from my cheek. I approached with more bricks, staying far from his thrashing extremities. "These blocks are heavy and will cause harm if we leave them on too long. We must be attentive to prevent permanent nerve damage. By now, you've concluded that we fought on opposite sides. Don't fret, I no longer hold a grudge. What's the point? In retrospect, Honest Abe was on the money when he wrote the Emancipation Proclamation. Let the historians sort out the politics."

"What's it to you?" Naughton hissed. Flushed from renewed exertion, bright splotches marbled his jowls.

I snagged his ankle with a looped rope and tied the twitching leg to the base. With both limbs secure, I attached the rectangles of sun-dried adobe.

As I released his appendages, the screaming began. "It's the Spear of Achilles. The major made us get tattoos."

"Major Hitchcock?" I quizzed.

"Yes," he answered.

"Why?"

"That's how we identified each other when—" The fever-pitched howls returned, every shriek separated by chest-bursting gasps for air. I hoped my prisoner would not faint from the seizures.

"Relax yourself. I'm taking off the bricks." As the burdens fell to the floor, blood rushed to his groin instigating new squeals. I pricked at the inked pitchfork with the sharp edge. "You were saying?" He coughed and requested water. "First describe the Spear of Achilles."

"Hitchcock sent us to terrorize the Southerners."

"The families of Confederate soldiers?"

"Everybody. He said General Sherman wanted the war settled, no matter the cost." The carpetbagger's torso rocked as he rode the sawhorse. "I don't feel my legs. Let me down." The man's fingers turned an unnatural shade of purple. He inhaled deeply. "Uncle Billy preached a load of crap about removing a bandage—hurts less if you tear it off fast."

Angry, I questioned, "How does torching a man's livelihood and cutting off his food supply benefit anyone?"

"Destroying all useful resources defeats the enemy."

"Your whole band of rabble-rousers received identical tattoos?"

Even in the chill, Levi's temples beaded with perspiration. "Yes. Hitchcock had us scratch in the ink. We made them ourselves." The crude emblem was indeed childlike.

"What were the major's orders for the Spear of Achilles?"

"We burned farms, dismantled railroads, and decimated livestock."

"Not civilians?" I inquired.

Eyelids fluttering, he answered, "Only if we were in jeopardy."

Till overheard him boasting of massacring townspeople. "Just how many women and children did you murder?"

His lips parted, and the response took too long. "None—no need."

"How many states did your gang frequent?"

Naughton replied, "Virginia, the Carolinas, Georgia, Tennessee—"

"Alabama?"

"No. Based in Kentucky, our unit remained east of Macon. I told you everything. Now, get me off of here."

I drank from the canteen. "Where did you find the Confederate uniforms?"

He taunted, "On dead Rebs. Had to sew up lots of holes."

"Are you associated with Heinrich Braun?" I questioned.

"Never heard of him." The man gazed upwards as if remembering something, a common tell for a liar.

Internally counting to thirty, I cautioned, "Don't make me strap these weights back on. I can tell that you've met Braun. What's your relationship?"

"There was a Lieutenant Herman Brown. He led the Spear of Achilles into Alabama and Mississippi."

I fixed the collar of my overcoat, and inquired, "A German?"

"Not that I recall. Had an East Coast accent. Said he moved to Kentucky from New York."

"Did he have a brother?"

He responded, "Herman spoke of somebody named William."

They had to be one and the same. "Give me a description of the lieutenant."

Naughton's depiction of Herman Brown matched Heinrich Braun to a tee.

"Levi, did you know him well?"

"At the encampment, the major put the men through training. He wrote up personal histories in order for us to fit in with the Reb soldiers. At night, Brown and I went out carousing. That mongrel was insane."

"More than you? How so?"

"Herman always talked about his hobby—photography. Wouldn't shut up. I'm no saint, but the pictures he took—they weren't normal."

Intrigued, I asked, "What do you mean?"

Naughton replied, "He had dozens of stereographs of folks in coffins. In the stereoscope viewer, those stiffs looked real—floating right in front of you. Some croaked regular, maybe old age, or disease came for them. Other photos were of wanted men propped up in wood boxes: bandits gunned down by the sheriff or bounty hunters for the reward. One time, Brown—drunk—showed me an item he was especially proud of."

I waited for him to continue. "And?"

"Herman said a local child got run over by a carriage. He gave me a print of the girl. Creepy—no coffin—the kid lying in a hollow. Dressed up nice and holding a bunch of posies. Except for the blood, she might be taking her afternoon nap."

"That's sick," I muttered.

"That's not the odd part."

"Tell me."

"Brown was fascinated by the afterlife—obsessed. He believed in Spiritualism and habitually attended séances. Herman thought if you captured the image of someone who just died—you could steal their soul."

Till Burnes collaborated with an amenable guano smuggler. As of sunup, Levi Naughton was conscripted as an able, if unwilling, crew member of a poaching schooner on course for the lower islands of California. Captain Moodlin assured us he had no plans to return anytime soon.

The page listed three names. Heinrich Braun or Herman Brown—his alias elsewhere—labeled them all as troublemakers.

Walt questioned, "Which one should we hit first?"

"Let's start at the nearest," I answered. "George Pomroy is a few blocks east. What did he do?"

"Thou shall not steal," Werner snickered. "Ol' Georgie stole a horse. There is also an adulterer and a drug dealer. It's not plain to me if hanky-panky is a crime or if the opium trade breaks a commandment? Perchance, 'thou shall have no other gods before me?'"

George Pomroy, the supposed thief, lived on G Street. Walt and I walked the neighborhood, eyeballing the building from every angle.

Heinrich's fleshy puppet, Constable Hurley, provided the names at the prior Spear of Achilles meeting.

Wilhelm Braun split the twenty-four addresses into individual lists of three to five suspects. "Happy hunting fellas!" he exclaimed. "We can't have these rascals spoiling our precious city. Send the dirty dogs up to Los Angeles!" With a yellow-toothed snigger, the younger brother unbuttoned his coat to expose a shoulder mounted Colt Peacemaker. "Go get 'em!"

A boy and girl played in the backyard as a woman scrubbed laundry in a tub. Once she clipped the shirts on a line to dry, the children were called inside.

"Walt, why are we snooping around here?" In the beginning, curiosity had drawn me into what I now considered a group of vigilantes. I felt awful persecuting this family. Did chance or destiny bring me to the man who arrogantly bore the exact symbol I saw by my surname on the Buzzard Roost Creek Bridge? *Was Heinrich Braun responsible for the disappearance of Beth and the kids?*

"Hank, your guess is as good as mine," he responded, climbing the stairs. Walt took a belt of Tarantula Juice and sniffled. "I got a headache. Let's wrap this up."

The same lady answered the knock. Her plucked eyebrows pinched as she questioned our purpose.

"Madam, is your husband home?" my partner asked.

"Mr. Pomroy," I added.

"Why?" she replied loudly.

"Just want to talk to him. Is he here?" I heard a shuffling noise in the front room.

A male gained substance from the shadows. "Can I help you?" he queried, opening the door. The slender man wore the attire of an office or bank clerk.

Walt inquired, "Are you George Pomroy?"

"That's me," he responded, stepping onto the stoop. Suspicious, his wife watched through the screen.

Werner rubbed the knot in his neck. "We need to speak to you."

"If you're here to make another bid on this place, I'm still not interested. As I stated to the other chaps, we have no intention to relocate."

"That's not why we're here," I said. "May I ask who they were?"

Pomroy patted his thinning scalp. "Germans. Possibly related. Hard to determine with foreigners."

"Those cheats wouldn't accept no for an answer," Mrs. Pomroy complained, tugging her sleeves. "They offered half of what we paid." She buckled her arms. "The taller one warned that we'd regret missing out on 'such an extraordinary opportunity.' I don't welcome veiled threats."

I questioned, "Did they give their names?"

"No! Not even when I said I'd call a constable!" she responded sharply.

"Sir, can we confer with you in private?" I asked. "On the lawn?"

George nodded at his spouse and accompanied us to the curb. The boy pressed his freckled nose against the window.

Embarrassed, I kicked a clump of dandelions growing in the sandy loam. "I have to inquire if you know anything about a lost horse?"

He tilted his head. "What? You're looking for a horse?"

"Yes," I responded. "Do you own one?"

Exasperated, Pomroy raised his hands. "Do you see any place to store an animal?"

"You must board it," Werner disputed. "There are many stables close by—or you sold it."

"Mister, I already told you, I never kept a horse. Are you accusing me of stealing?"

My partner moved forward. "Take it down a peg, pal."

"Who are you guys anyway? There are no animals here. I am employed as a specie clerk at the Consolidated Bank. The office isn't far—*I walk there!*"

Walt asked, "Species? You talkin' 'bout a paint or quarter horse?" I couldn't be positive if Werner was being serious or just kidding.

Pomroy stifled a laugh. "Specie denotes coins and has nothing to do with the equine species. My job is to deliver customer's drafts and checks to the banker's clearing house. They transfer the funds between financial institutions. The work is boring as heck. I don't care; it feeds my family."

"Georgie, I'm a bean counter myself," Werner confided. He adjusted the suspenders cinching up his high-cut trousers. "Might be easier addin' up all dem numbers if I went to school, but Pappy needed me pullin' stumps on the farm." Chummy now, he allowed the clerk a taste. "And multiplication is twice as—"

"George, it's dinnertime!" Mrs. Pomroy hollered from behind the varmint rifle.

We proceeded along Wilhelm's "troublemaker" list, unable to corral the two-timing Ralph Lorings. Julius DuCarmont was actually a licensed pharmacist, not a despicable opium peddler. Further questioning revealed that the Braun brothers had similarly accosted the pill pusher.

Over a late dinner, Walt and I discussed the results of our search. As members of the Spear of Achilles, we were unwittingly being used to strong-arm householders reluctant to sell to the aggressive land-grabbers. I suggested uncovering the outcome of Heinrich's vanishing initiates.

"The Brauns sometimes act a mite fishy," Werner agreed. He gorged on a plate of diamond turbot. "Definitely worth an investigation." Dark beer washed the flatfish downward. "That's up to you. I'm done—outta here."

"What are you implying?" I inquired. "You're not flying away, too?"

"Aye, Hank. Things are bad." He belched out, "very baaad," stretching the last bit of the phrase. "Instead of sinkin' with the ship, we're boardin' the next train to San Francisco."

"Walt, I'll miss you as a patrol partner." With the death of the real estate boom, everyone and his mother was leaving town. I worried about my own expenditures. "Is Sallie ready to move?"

"Her idea," he responded, picking his teeth with a slender bone. "Wife's got family up north. Claims I can find an accounting job anywhere."

"I'm confident you will. Wish you the best," I said, extending my palm.

"You too, buddy. Good luck with those shysters."

Chapter Eighteen

EARLY IN THE DAY, SOMEBODY RAPPED ON THE REAR DOOR. Persevering to hang a tricky sheet of wallpaper, I ignored the interruption. Louder blows propelled me off the stepladder. Impatient to resume my work before the paste dried, I hurried to the kitchen, finding Mourning Dew on the back stoop. Twisting his cap, the carpenter looked both embarrassed and nervous.

"Are you okay?" I asked. "Has something happened to Kitch or the boys?"

"No, Mr. Gates. They're alright. It's Mero and Basil's mom. Mrs. Ivy got sicker—spittin' up blood and such. Can't walk anymore."

"Sorry to hear that. Did you take her to the doctor?"

"There ain't no sawbones in Chollas Creek. I tried gettin' medical treatment in National City, but Doc Blume sent us away."

"Blume?" The name sounded familiar. I feared the worst. "Is it consumption? Are the kids healthy?"

He nodded. "Far as I know, Mero and Basil are well. Thought she was jus' fightin' the grippe."

"There is a doctor that may help. Where's Mrs. Ivy now?"

Mourning answered, "Out front in the wagon. Kitch's on the job and the boys are at school. Minnie said she'd bring 'em home afterwards."

The buckboard quaked with hawking as we rounded the corner. Rail-thin, Mrs. Ivy curled on a rug covered by an unfinished eiderdown quilt. Swollen fingers clutched a handkerchief saturated with red-tinged sputum to her lips. I hated the lies—gentle words of hope—I used to comfort the pitiable woman.

Doctor Leeds examined the cart's withering passenger and diagnosed the malady as advanced tuberculosis. He took us aside and grimly advised, "There's nothing I can do. Transport her to the sanatorium at the north end of Switzer Canyon. The nurses will tend to Mrs. Ivy's needs before she passes." As we altered course for the Pest House, Leeds bellowed, "Disinfect what she touched, and don't forget to incinerate her bed and clothing!"

"So this is the Acme!" Laura shouted above the din. "I've never been in a saloon!"

"There's a first time for everything!" I yelled as six rowdy shipmates jostled between the tables. "Are you having fun?"

Eyes dilating, she made a face at the impenetrable mass of cobwebs coating the ceiling. "Are those—?"

"Spiders," I responded. "Till imports the bugs from Brazil. Insists that they add atmosphere."

Laura quivered, moving her fashionable elbows off the tacky armrests. "It's disgusting." Edgy, she seemed ready to leave. The smelly menagerie outside hadn't impressed her either.

I stroked her sleeve, and said, "Think of the anecdotes you'll tell in Philadelphia."

She pulled apart, muttering, "Henry Gates, you're such an ass."

Suddenly at my side, Molly asked, "Who's this young lady?" Laura cringed as the barmaid reached to fondle her tresses. "Don't get in a huff. Just seeing if that's a wig."

"Laura, may I introduce Miss Doyle. Molly's an old—" I stopped speaking as Laura's chair tilted backwards and emptied.

"Hank, you're such a dunce," Molly confirmed. She sped after Laura, chuckling.

From the sidewalk, I watched the women jawing in the lane. Molly's animated gestures placated Laura. Biting my cheek, I anticipated her loathsome glare. The glance came, this more of a flash of sorrow, or worse—pity. Laura posed a few questions. The barmaid answered, and both laughed. Then arm in arm, they returned to the Acme. Molly smirked at me and then walked to the bar.

"What was all that about?" I inquired, not eager to receive an unrestrained summary of my failings.

"Your friend is exceptionally perceptive," Laura responded, accepting the "on the house" beer Molly delivered. She tipped the mug and guzzled half. "Henry, you must buy me something to eat. I'm famished."

"How much did she tell you?" I asked again.

"Molly said you ran her pimp out of town and then gave her this job."

"The latter part is true though Till is the one who hired her. I can't fathom what became of her panderer."

She consumed the ale and flagged for another round. Molly left a wet ring as she switched cups, taking no notice of the "she's cut off" motion I sliced across my neck.

Laura ordered the "Mediterranean Meal" and stared me down. "Molly is well-versed in the intricacies of the male mentality. Hank, you saddened me by insinuating that I would run to Philadelphia. Your flippant words made me wonder if our relationship means anything." Tilly clanked nearby, dumping brimming cuspidors into a pail. "You pretend to be courting me, yet I'm utterly bewildered by your motivations. What precisely do you want?"

"Laura, you know I'm married." Commitment—the perpetual argument.

"To a woman who's been gone for twenty-five years!" she exclaimed.

"Beth may still be alive. And there are my kids. . . ."

Her lips thinned. "Your children! Are we having an affair? That's how it feels to me, always hiding from a ghost."

I couldn't lose her, too. "Laura, I'm very fond of you and cherish our moments together."

She quaffed her second beer and sighed, "As do I."

"Please don't go back East."

"Molly told me that as a veteran, you've got major issues which will require a great deal of my patience." Without hesitation, she launched the ground assault I had not prepared for. "Have you even considered filing for a *divorce?*" The word hung in the air as if trapped by sticky strands of spider silk.

"Can you wait a little longer?" I queried.

"Yes, Henry," she answered, "although not forever."

Hector and I took our evening gallivant around the neighborhood. As the energetic cocker spaniel chased cottontails throughout lots overrun with pepperweed, I had time to meditate.

Pipe in hand, I ventured to strategize on how to confront Heinrich Braun, the man inexplicably coupled to the loss of my family. Nothing worthwhile developed.

Laura's frank analysis weighed upon me. She raised legitimate grievances. I had to choose between the freedom of a fruitful life with her and my current pathetic existence. Put so simply, with the sun quietly kissing the bay, the choice was obvious.

A magnificent cottage soared into view as I rounded the block—*my home.* The sight always thrilled me: rocking chairs on the piazza, three floors of windows, and the steep, gabled roof crowned with an ornate brick chimney. Yet it was the striking colors that caught my attention. Laura had selected these sanguine hues as if foreseeing that she might someday have to live with the results.

Hector raced forward, and I trotted to keep up. Aroused by a noise, he scampered across a field of tall lavender, barking. I tagged along, watchful for stinging nettles, rattlesnakes, and other sharp objects God devised to inflict misfortune.

The dog circled an excavation, stopping to sniff a human-shaped package. My neighbor, the one who Kitch had befriended, leaned on a shovel. Behind him, the house's foundation surrounded a forlorn tent. A single lantern gained dominance as the sunlight faded. The grave was half finished.

"Come here, boy!" I called. "Hector!"

"Always impulsive, that Carrie," the man mumbled, wiping his eyes. "She wanted us to move here. Said the climate would *improve* her constitution. *Jesus!*" The widower looked up from the pit. "I've seen you around. My name's Luther."

"You can't bury her within city limits," I said. "There's a cemetery—Mount Hope."

"Can't afford it, and I need her near." Luther tossed me a pick. "Don't just stand there. Be of some use."

I spent the day at the construction site. The framing for the initial apartments approached completion. Passing a board to Kitch on the upper story, I inquired how Basil and Mero fared without their mother. While I had not visited them in a few weeks, I knew the brothers lived under Mourning's roof.

"They're jus' kids," he responded. "Basil thinks his mom's at a hospital and has faith she'll be comin' home soon. Mero, he knows better and doesn't say much."

"How is Mrs. Ivy?"

"We rode out to the Pest House on the weekend. They're takin' proper care of her. On the day we were there, Mrs. Ivy felt fine, able to sit up and chat with her boys. The nurse said the infection can subside and the lungs may heal."

"She's out of the woods?"

"Doubtful," Cane replied, lining up a nail. With hard blows, he hammered the fastener into the stud. "It spread to her blood—won't be long now. Hold still. Slide up that end."

Kitch hired residents from Chollas Creek to increase the team to six full-time carpenters and helpers. On normal days, the laborers bantered good-humoredly or sang African American work songs, the humorous ditties modified to the tasks at hand. Today, I only perceived grumbling.

"What's going on?" I questioned. "Everyone's in a crummy mood." Below, Mourning reset the sombrero on his forehead and bowed to saw a plank.

He clawed out a bent nail, and answered, "The men are vexed."

"At me?"

"No," Cane responded. "You treat them square. Yesterday, a pair of lawyers rode into Chollas Creek tellin' us to get lost. They produced papers statin' the government owns our land."

"A judge will not allow that. You have the property deeds?"

Cane smiled cheerlessly. "Almost all of us been livin' there over ten years. Nobody remembers how our settlement started. When I arrived in San Diego, I learned that Chollas Creek is where the coloreds lived, and that's the place I built my house. There's nothing written down. We own no rightful claim."

"You're squatting?"

He didn't reply.

"What shall I do?" I asked. "There must be legal recourse."

Kitch frowned. "You've done enough. But I'll tell ya, Mr. Gates, we'll burn the whole lot to ashes before we let anyone drive us from our homes."

Chapter Nineteen

I CROUCHED BEHIND THE TEXTILE WAREHOUSE. Indoors, the Braun brothers conducted the May Spear of Achilles meeting. Concealed by long wooden spools, I waited to establish what happened to Heinrich's initiation victims. Maybe the stunts were hoaxes, and the newcomers weren't actually injured. The bloody stabbings certainly looked authentic, and I had a scar on my chest to prove it.

A match flickered in the shadows, illuminating three profiles. The tobacco glowed as a cigar went from mouth to mouth. Annoyed that I had not detected company and sensing a sneeze building, I pushed a finger under my nose as the skunky vapor drifted my way.

After the last assembly, I checked the newspaper for homicides or missing person's posts. The rancher declared he had a family, and the cabinetmaker worked with his brother. Surely, a friend or relative cared if these two didn't come home. Nothing.

Here as an observer, I had no intention of stepping in. Tense, my palm slid to the sword's hilt as a silhouette rose and walked to the shed, exchanging faint words with an obscure figure. As the man passed to reconvene with his gang, I saw a patch over his right eye. He brandished a club, and whispered, "It's time. Get ready."

The threesome sauntered toward the building, one sneering as he pounded his fist. They entered the room. I crept close and spied the hoodlums huddling below the stage. Heinrich Braun's voice boomed within the storehouse, "As the president, I accept—"

"Hank, turn around—slowly." I followed the pistol's barrel to the owner's steady hands, then up to his face. *Walt Werner!* "When you didn't show, I knew you'd be near. Remove the sword."

He appeared and sounded clear-headed. I surrendered my only weapon and said, "I understood you left town."

"Not yet."

"Are you conspiring with Braun?"

"I've been his accountant for fifteen years. Heinrich pays me handsomely, and I'll go wherever he sends me. He ordered me to monitor your actions." Werner snatched the scabbard and designated an alleyway. "This way."

"Why is Braun so intrigued by me?"

Blade unsheathed, he answered, "We keep an eye on all new members."

"If you don't trust me, why did you ask me to take part in your fake vigilante group?"

"Heinrich is seeking able men to expand his enterprise. As a disgruntled ex-Confederate, I took it for granted that you'd fit in with the other misfits. Never thought you'd be such a spoilsport."

Now was not the occasion to reproach myself for falling into a quagmire. If I kept Werner talking, I might delay the inevitable. "What are they doing to that man?"

"No more questions. You should worry for yourself," he hissed. Onwards, I recognized the same stockyard drainage trench we crossed on the evening of the original gathering. I recalled that the rickety board used as a bridge was unstable.

"Walt, I haven't told anyone about the Brauns' real estate schemes. Honestly, I have no problem with what he's up to—merely interested." I forced a laugh. "You must admit, the initiation ceremony is unorthodox."

"You go first," he commanded, directing with the sword.

Leg dragging, I overemphasized the limp to delay our progress. "Is Sallie real? *Are* you married?"

"Course I am. That gal tickles me. Stand straight, shut your yap, and get moving."

The soggy lumber bowed under my weight as I shifted my hips to maintain equilibrium. Cubed cracks textured the pine as it yielded to brown rot. Polluted by the herd, the stagnant water smelled awful.

"Where are we going?" I squinted at the cattle pens hazarding to guess at whom or what waited ahead. "Are you meeting someone?"

At the end, I turned as Werner walked onto the mossy strip. Eyes earthward, he clasped the sword in his right hand and the gun in the other. As the red-headed man reached the center, both arms lifted for balance. At that vulnerable instant, I jumped upon the plank.

The timber held, springing us upward. My heel clipped the beam, and I plunged into the slop. Limber as a gymnast, Walt landed on the platform in perfect form and ready to shoot. As he fired, the wood dislodged, aiming the bullet skywards. The recoil sent him flying off the side.

In war, a soldier has two daunting choices: attack and die or retreat and be labeled a coward. There is no middle ground on the killing fields. My Army training overrode my instinct to flee. Mired in the gummy dreck, I paddled forward, scrabbling for his slick boot. Although the firearm was no place to be seen, Werner retained control of the sword and kept me at bay.

"Nice match," my opponent groaned, struggling to remain erect, "but it's over now." Vertical, he lunged forth.

I leapt high and used the brace to catapult my feet into his ribcage. The sword flew from his grip, the flashing edge pinwheeling through the air. Overburdened, the decaying board snapped, and I fell again into the gulley. Spasms raged up my spine as my face submerged in feculence. Using his bulk, Walt thrust me to the bottom. Blind in the murk and short of breath, I sensed the sharp outline of his handgun pressing into my shoulders, unable to gain leverage to snag the handle.

In a desperate attempt, I compressed, jamming fingers underneath my back to grab the revolver. Ramming the muzzle into my ex-patrol partner's stomach, I prayed that the cartridges weren't wet. I squeezed the trigger. The water muffled the blast. He convulsed, heaving himself away. At the surface, I gasped and scrubbed the mud from my eyes. My rival collapsed against the wall of the culvert.

Chest shuddering, Werner moaned, "You gut shot me." Coated in waste, he groped in the slime for the terminal wound. "Hank, please do me a courtesy?"

"Sure, Walt." I crawled up the slimy bank and retrieved my sword. I spun the cap of his flask and let him drink. The man grimaced as the rotgut seared his ruptured innards. By touch, I aligned the tip alongside his neck between his collarbone and scapula. "What is it?"

He choked out, "Tell Sallie that I'm sorry. Let her know—"

I moved close to Werner's ear and assisted with the final words, "That you love her." With both hands, I sank the blade through the bones and into his traitorous heart.

Needless to say, I never relayed Walt's message.

Kitch muttered as he wrung out his shirt, "Hank, I'm beginnin' to wonder about you." Ugly marks from multiple lashings crisscrossed his shivering shoulders. He squished against the same decomposing log we sat on after towing Ray Diamond into the shallows of south San Diego Bay. The pimp now had company haunting the shores of Chula Vista. On this damp, overcast day, our clothes refused to dry.

"I wonder about myself, too," I agreed. "Thanks for helping." Glum, I fell into muteness. Walt could be an irritating drunk. Still, I had favored him as an ally, maybe even a friend. This betrayal hit hard. I also mourned for his wife, Sallie. What might Heinrich Braun's reaction be when his personal accountant didn't show up to do his bidding?

"Here," Cane coaxed, tossing me a bag. I hadn't seen him go to the wagon. "Eat this. You'll feel better."

I opened the sac, finding a cheese sandwich and an apple. "Who put those scars on your back?"

Slack jawed, he gaped into the marsh.

"Do you tell her what we do?" I inquired.

"Who, Minnie?"

"Our middle of the night trips must make your wife curious." Unexpectedly hungry, I bit into the crisp bread.

"Nope." Kitch squashed an ant on his elbow. "Not concernin' this stuff. She says a man is allowed keep a few secrets as long as they're not dealin' with money or other women. Why? Are you plannin' to confess your sinful deeds to Miss Mills? I doubt it."

"Laura already claims she doesn't understand me. I 'bewilder' her." An array of bubbles popped above the spot where we scuttled Walt.

Nodding, he asked, "Is the relationship serious? Any thoughts for the future?"

"Remember when we rode out here last time?"

Cane replied, "How can I forget? Every night, lobsters eat me alive in my nightmares."

"I told you I returned from the war and found my wife and kids gone. Laura wants me to move on and get divorced. God knows, I'm willing to make a fresh start, but I have a couple of things to sew up first."

"Such as?" he questioned, buffing an apple on the driest part of his sleeve.

The sun poked a hole in the haze. "I believe I've identified the culprits."

Kitch wheeled in anger. "This Werner fellow abducted your family?"

"Maybe he took part. Walt was an accountant for Heinrich Braun, who led covert raids to cut the Confederacy off at the knees. His band of marauders prowled the South, eradicating everything useful to the military effort." I described how Werner solicited for me to join the Spear of Achilles, the bident tattoo on the president's forearm, discovering the eerie photographs, Till Burnes seeing a similar inking on Levi Naughton, and his interrogation in the cold room. The summary ended with me being nabbed outside the fabric depository. "I can't prove that Braun came to Buzzard Roost or went anywhere near Cedar Hall."

"The guy we jus' buried had that mark on his arm," Cane mused. "That's a boatload of coincidences."

"I'm with you." I stood and pledged, "I won't rest until I expose the truth."

"Let me know what you need, boss." Kitch picked up a stone and skipped the disk across the rising water.

"Sarah would flay me," Alonzo Horton chuckled as he carved the steak and dipped a hunk in Worcestershire sauce. "My wife requests that I drop twenty pounds by summer. She's in cahoots with the doctor—regarding my diet."

"Are you sleeping well?" I inquired. "Is Sarah still hosting séances?"

"The nocturnal concerts are dwindling. With the economic downturn, Jesse Shepard is considering selling the Villa Montezuma and moving to Los Angeles." With a raised goblet, he motioned for more wine.

"Shepard just got here! Who'd buy that property? I bet the upkeep on that mansion is astronomical." Of higher importance, the Villa was possessed—no way I'd live there.

Horton grunted acknowledgement. "I've noticed Laura is unusually moody. She's generally quite chipper. Did you two disagree?"

I never intended to cause her melancholy. "Nothing unsurmountable. We're working it out."

"Make sure you do," he implored. "Henry, I cannot cope with a houseful of mopey women."

"I'll do my best. Alonzo, have you been married before?"

Despair lined Horton's face. "Yes. My first wife perished from consumption. We were both very young." He changed the topic. "How are the apartments coming? I went inside the other day to kick the walls. The building is well-thought-out and constructed."

"Thanks," I beamed. "My foreman designed the layout."

Alonzo buttered a crescent roll. "The colored man?"

"There are several African Americans on the site. Kitch Cane has oversight of the project."

"Tell Mr. Cane that Father Horton thinks he's doing a fine job."

"I will. Kitch is the reason I asked you to lunch. Are you familiar with Chollas Creek?"

He nodded. "That stream feeds into the San Diego Bay. I have explored the vicinity of National City and Logan Heights. There's a black settlement in that area."

"Government attorneys approached Mr. Cane's community, alleging they hold no right to the land. My laborers have families. It doesn't seem fair."

Alonzo's wooly brows wrinkled. "Frank Kimball and the Santa Fe Railroad own most of that stretch. Those evictions would be public knowledge. If you'd like, I will delve into who is responsible. Frank and his brothers are amicable. The train executives—not so much."

"I'd appreciate any help. Please tell Laura that I'll stop by."

"Bring her fresh flowers and a sincere apology."

"But I didn't do anything wrong."

Horton shaved gristle from the edges of the meat and made a wry expression. "Henry, as men, we're always at fault."

Chapter Twenty

"HENRY, I LOVE WHAT YOU'VE ACCOMPLISHED WITH THE YARD," Laura praised, admiring the budding roses. A few weeks back, I awoke to the earthy sounds of Mourning planting rows of flowers. When thanking him, he advised me to, "Keep 'em watered and beware the prickles." As we circuited the house, Hector nipped at our heels.

The tour ended on the porch. Laura and I sunk into chairs facing the coast. The enclosing structure retained the last heat of the afternoon. We rocked in harmony as Hector whimpered in his sleep.

My eyes inched shut as Laura questioned, "What's that over there?" She peered at the adjoining lot. A cawing black bird perched atop a slanting wooden cross. Clapping her hands at the blatant show of irreverence, the raven flew six feet and alighted on the torn tent roof. "Who died?"

"My neighbor's wife. I helped with the burial. He slipped away the next day leaving most of his things."

"That's sad. Was it consumption?"

I scratched the snoring pup between the ears. "That's not clear. The husband implied poor constitution as the cause."

Laura inquired, "Shall you buy the property?"

"Well, I've considered it. I could get the parcel for pennies on the pound, and the foundation is laid."

"Cover up that mound! Nobody can rest easy with a bone orchard in their backyard."

I reflected upon the featherweight bundle we had laid in the dust. Before returning the dirt to the hole, the grieving man recited esoteric Bible passages from Exodus—verses referring to the short life expectancies of sorceresses. "The husband said he needed his wife close-by. Before the grave settled, he was gone. I guess the remains can be transferred to Mount Hope Cemetery."

"Henry, I beg forgiveness for putting pressure on you to file for a divorce. It's not my place to goad you into choosing to be with me. After you left, I felt terrible."

I took her hand. "Laura, I *want* to be with you. I have never known a woman so adorable and so smart. There's nothing I'd like more than to spend—"

"Mr. Gates?" a deep voice hailed from the lane. Our meaningful discussion disrupted, we pivoted to view a rugged man striding up the walkway. "Henry, I'm so happy I caught you at home!"

Unprepared, I sprung from my seat as Heinrich Braun bounded up the steps, palm outstretched and grinning from ear to ear. Hector, awake and growling, strained forward as I anchored his collar. *Too late to send Laura indoors!* I expected this encounter, but not here and not now. This was no time for an altercation.

"What brings you here, Mr. Braun?" I questioned. As I met his handshake, the dog snarled in the back of its throat.

"Hate to bother you folks on such a splendid day." Heinrich removed his bowler and bowed to Laura. With a spurious German accent, he inquired, "I'm here on urgent business. Henry, you were Walter Werner's patrol partner. May I ask if you've seen him recently?"

Here we go! "No," I lied, staring him in the eye. "Not after we tracked down the people on Wilhelm's list. Why?"

Braun looked puzzled. "I'm sure Walter conveyed that he's my accountant? He hasn't come to work since Friday. That's exceedingly peculiar."

"Walt mentioned that you were his boss. You talked to his wife?"

"Of course. Mrs. Werner filed a missing person report with Constable Hurley. Carl's department is understaffed, and so far, they've had no success."

I preferred to hover near reality. "We went out for dinner after finishing our rounds. Walt told me he was leaving for San Francisco. Said Sallie longed to be closer to her relatives."

Heinrich sighed. "Ah yes. Never tying the knot, I can only imagine how long-term absences from dear ones could unravel a marriage." He addressed Laura in a formal tone. "We haven't been properly introduced. Henry, is this your lovely wife?"

Inasmuch as we lacked matching rings to signify a union, I assumed he was fishing. "Miss Cooper is an acquaintance. Martha, this is Heinrich Braun."

Amused, Laura offered her hand. "Hello," she greeted. "Are you one of Henry's real estate colleagues?"

"We're enrolled in the same community-service organization," he answered. "Henry and the gentleman I aforementioned were teamed to support the public. Our fraternity is completely voluntary."

"Very noble." She glanced at me. "Henry is always helping the needy. I wish you a favorable outcome in locating your employee."

"Mr. Werner will turn up sometime and in fine spirits," Heinrich said on his way to the steps. He halted and spun. "I became alarmed when you skipped our last meeting. Is everything alright, Henry?"

"Something cropped up, but I'll be there next month," I promised.

"Bravo! Good day!" Braun tilted his cap and strutted away.

Hector shadowed me as I tread across the veranda. I gripped the railing to regulate my breathing as Laura advanced.

"I see that Mr. Braun isn't a friend. Who is he really?" she questioned. The air cooled as we watched our unexpected visitor recede into the distance.

"Heinrich Braun is the president of the association he cited. His brother, Wilhelm, is the vice-president."

"And how exactly do you provide assistance? Notwithstanding that I just met that man a moment ago, I'm confident he's not who he pretends to be."

I released the bar, swiveling to meet her level stare. Laura lifted the puppy into her arms. I had to choose the best course of action: divulge the nasty truth or shield her from harm.

"Let's go inside," I suggested. In the kitchen, I crumpled newspaper and lit a fire. As the room dimmed, a chill snuck through crevices around the windows and under doors.

Laura leaned on the far end of the table. "Are you linked to your partner's disappearance?"

I marked time as the mantel clock chimed—five o'clock. "Heinrich is an extremely dangerous man."

"That's why you called me by another name?"

"Yes. You mustn't get tangled up in this."

She waved a dismissal. "So you *were* involved?"

There was no way to sugarcoat the hideous facts. "I killed him in self-defense. Walt Werner is dead."

Except for her pale cheeks and flaring nostrils, Laura remained composed. "And he knows?"

"Braun suspects me without any solid evidence."

"Shall I prepare a kettle of tea?" Not hearing my response, Laura licked a finger and tested the range. "Ouch," she murmured. "Start at the beginning and don't you dare leave out one bit."

With Clive and Cherika harnessed as a team, Basil, Mero, and I rode to the wharf to purchase a load of lumber. Their mother expired during the night, and I decided the boys could use a distraction while Mourning managed the funeral arrangements.

I attempted to break up the sorrowful quietude by remarking, "The horses work well together. I think they enjoy each other's company."

"That's a shame, since your mule can't breed," Mero muttered. His eyes were red though dry.

"Where did you learn that?" I inquired, steering past a group of passengers disembarking from an out of commission omnibus.

"In a medical book. Someday, I plan to be an animal doctor," he said boldly. "Mom left us money for school."

Madame Kim's lottery funds would go to a worthy purpose. "That's a commendable aspiration, Mero," I said, speculating if there were any certified African American veterinarians. "How about you Basil, what are your plans?"

He responded sardonically, "All my life, I always dreamed of becoming an orphan." Mero's arm encircled his younger brother's shoulders. "Now that I've reached this goal, what remains?"

Once again, borrowing mankind's well-thumbed lexicon of grief, I said benevolently, "Your mother is at peace. She's in a better place."

"Is there a Heaven, Uncle Henry?" Basil questioned. His wistful demeanor begged for an affirmative answer.

"You're being ridiculous," Mero mocked. "There's no such thing as God." Following a pause, he said, "I do believe in the Devil, though."

I recollected the cloying stench of the ballooning bodies strewn across endless theaters of war and had to agree.

"Shut up!" Basil shouted. "Mom's with Dad!" Tears falling, he jumped off the wagon and raced to the harbor.

"Wait here," I ordered, handing Mero the reins. After a quick search, I spotted the boy sitting by the dock. His jittery fingers held a cigarette.

"How did you get ahold of that?" I asked, plucking the smoke from his fist. I took several puffs before flicking the butt into the water.

Basil sniffled, "Found it." Nearby, flapping its wings, a tall, aquatic fowl landed on a piling.

"I'm the last person you should talk to of the hereafter."

He faced me. "We just die. That's it? Then what am I doing here?"

"From the dawn of time, humankind has tried to answer those difficult questions." I pointed. "See that pelican. Why's he here?"

"To eat?"

"True, the bird is starved. But besides foraging for fish, Mr. Pelican also loves flying around with his pals and taking long naps. Maybe he has a sweetheart at home."

Basil smiled and inched up to the creature. "What's that on its neck?"

"The bird uses that pouch to scoop up food. And those webbed feet help him swim in rough seas."

The fowl allowed the adolescent to come close. "Ha! Mr. Pelican is looking down his nose at me. Does it bite?"

"Every living thing bites," I replied.

From a docking trawler, a fisherman lobbed bait over the water. Beak snapping, the pelican gulped the fish into its gullet.

As we approached the buckboard, I stopped. "Basil, I can't prove the existence of a Heaven or Hell. Despite that, whenever I turn left or right, I behold glorious and amazing wonders.

Somebody smarter than us created all of this, and I'm sure they're taking excellent care of your mother."

Thinking about what I just said, I really wasn't sure of anything.

A messenger delivered a note from Alonzo Horton summoning me to his mansion. We sat across from each other in his extensive library. The custom mahogany cabinets showcased more books than I could read in a lifetime. A sizable crystal ball dominated his desk. Sarah, Gracie, and Laura had gone into town to shop, so barring the patter of servants bustling here and there, we had the big house to ourselves.

"You and Laura must have had a productive conversation. I've never seen her with such energy," Horton commented.

"We've arrived at a mutual understanding, respecting our future. I, myself, am relieved. Your dispatch stated you wanted to discuss Chollas Creek. Were you able to work out who is behind the evictions?"

Alonzo's face clouded. "I contacted Frank Kimball. He disclosed that the United States Navy has surveyed the southern shores of the harbor to attest that San Diego is a viable station for the Pacific Fleet. It shall be necessary to dredge the bottom to accommodate the draft of the newer steel-hulled warships. The grapevine hints that Washington is interested in manufacturing torpedo gunboats here."

"That's tremendous! A military presence is specifically what is required to revive our economy. Think of the quantities of businesses and jobs to be generated." Self-centered as usual, I hoped for an increase in the demand for housing.

"Don't get too steamed up, my friend. The Navy is a ponderous whale—only now admitting that modernization is essential to guard our seaboards. Comparable to the railroad, it will be ages before the boatyard is a done deal."

Coming to my senses, I realized he was right. "And Chollas Creek?"

Horton laid a hand-tinted map on the desk and marked the area with a pencil. "The watershed is smack-dab where the Navy plans to construct the dockyard. Your carpenters need to move."

Dejected, I sat on the chair. "Great," I grumbled. "They have no place to go."

"Didn't you hear me say it'll be years until the Navy breaks ground?"

"So why is Washington instigating the dispossessions?"

"The men intimidating the residents of Chollas Creek are not official representatives of the U.S. government."

Sudden comprehension accelerated my pulse. *Heinrich and Wilhelm!* "Then who are they?"

Alonzo scowled. "That's still to be determined."

On the front stairs, I ran into the women returning from their expedition. After carrying in the bags, Laura and I strolled through the herb garden. I passed on all that I learned regarding Chollas Creek and who I reckoned was stirring up trouble.

She flexed to tug out a bloom of clover. "What's the next step?"

"I'll talk to Kitch and see if his descriptions of the lawyers match the Braun brothers. With no bona fide or immediate threat from the government to vacate, there isn't a rush to pack their bags. That should eliminate some of the tension."

"Is there anything I can do? Will Heinrich send more scoundrels to find you?"

"He's preoccupied antagonizing landowners. Don't worry, I'll be careful." Not desiring to scare Laura, but concerned about her safety, I warned, "Braun saw you at my place. Although he doesn't know who you are, please be mindful of your surroundings."

"Henry, I've already taken precautions," she whispered. Tucked in her purse, a gem-studded dagger snuggled between a comb and mirror.

"Who gave you that?" I seethed, fit to be tied that she perceived the necessity to tote a knife on my account.

"Calm down! Molly lent me this pretty little item."

"That's not a toy," I said.

Laura countered, "And your relationship with Heinrich Braun is not a game."

Chapter Twenty-One

"I SHOULD HAVE KNOWN THE LAWYERS WERE SWINDLERS," Kitch glowered.

We watched the crew nail down the roof above the first set of apartments.

"You had no reason to be suspicious," I said.

He gripped his hammer. "We're goin' after them, right?"

I raised my hands. "Yup, but not now."

Cane paced, ready to explode. "What! Why wait?"

This was the part I hadn't worked out yet. "I need to settle what became of my family."

"We can make Heinrich talk!"

"It may come to that, or—"

Kitch interrupted, "What if those crooks return to Chollas Creek?"

A sheaf of shingles skidded from the roof and broke open.

"Tell them to bring a credible attorney. They won't."

I lay still on the bedspread mulling over how to dig up further dirt on the Brauns. As night softened the room's angles, the ceiling remained a blank slate. Downstairs, the windows and doors had been jury-rigged with strings of pebble-filled cans, my experiment at an early-warning system. Hector was more effective—howling at whatever dared to walk within earshot.

I surmised that Heinrich's morbid photographs held the answers. *Were there others I hadn't brought to light? Where are they?*

Laura stopped by to notify me that the Brauns moved to the Florence Hotel. Fancier than the Cliff House, the establishment was a few blocks north on Fir Street. When asked about the approach she used to acquire this intriguing news, she replied, "A helpful man at the Post Office supplied the address." I could not fault him for his enchantment. Thanking Laura for the research, I firmly prohibited her from entering the premises.

Wary, I varied my usual routine, meeting Daniel Judge at the Oyster Bar in place of the Acme. During dinner, he updated me on the status of the Peabody Mine.

Claude Horrigan kept the workers in line, relaying positive feedback on our rehabilitated thieves. The ever-cautious Foghorn proved his merit by demolishing stone walls using precise amounts of black powder. A human machine, the Mole's muscular shoulders steadily mucked loads of ore from the lengthening shaft.

Judge trickled a jigger of bourbon down his throat and grinned. "Hank, I've got a nugget of sensational news." I pushed away my plate and moved closer. "As you are aware, every two or three weeks we reap an ounce of gold besides our main commodity—copper."

"Did we hit the mother lode?" I joked. Copper paid the bills, but gold—gold made you filthy rich.

Dark eyes glittered as he answered, "Yesterday, Javier forgot his lunch pail in the West Drift. Later on, he went back to have it for the next morning. The hook on the cap light came loose. Javier was in a hurry, and—"

"What the heck happened?" I inquired sharply.

"Keep your britches on! Let me tell the dang story!" Daniel exclaimed. "I'm coming to the exciting part!" Cramming his trap with corn beef and cabbage, the bulbous Adam's apple bobbed as he swallowed. "So like I was saying, Rivera uses an old, rusty, biscuit tin for his meals. For lunch, he takes bread, a scrap of dried meat, and a slice of the Robinsons' pie. Cherry, if the season is right, or fresh blueberry—"

"Okay already!" The man always babbled, forever building up to a climax.

Judge laughed deliriously and thumped the table. "Listen here, Hank. Javier squats to pick up the box, and the lamp crashes to the ground. The spout busts off—you've seen how cheap they are—and the oil spills all over tarnation. Then the wick catches the whole kit and caboodle on fire, and—" My partner lowered his voice, "As the Mexican is on his knees smothering the flames with that blanket he always has on hand for naps, he—"

I stammered, "Rivera struck gold?"

"Hold your horses! The pail is burnt—just ruined. Lucifer can use it to pack *his* lunch. In a cloud of smoke, he can't see his beak, and the blaze is nearly out. With the last flicker of light, Javier notices a glimmer on the wall, and then everything goes black. All agog, yet doubting this wondrous vision, he feels his way topside and gets Horrigan."

"Tell me it was gold!"

"They chipped at the surface to obtain samples." Daniel transferred a cloth pouch under the tabletop. The bright yellow metal warmed my palm and boiled my blood. "Hank, I've been in there myself. The vein is as fat as your waist!"

"Lower your voice! How come we didn't see the gold deposit before?"

"They did some recent blasting. It's a new rock face," he replied.

"Do the other fellas know? Foghorn and Mole?"

"No. Javier and Claude confided in me. Naturally, I wanted to talk to you. What should we do?"

"Do you trust them?"

"Much as I trust you when gold is concerned!" Judge retorted.

"Good. First off, we'll establish how far the lode runs. The fissure might taper, or fade. The Peabody Mine is registered for copper, so no one harasses us. That's an ideal situation. This mustn't become public knowledge or Orinoco Creek could turn into a stinking mining camp overnight!"

"And the men? What shall we tell them?"

Eyelids shut; I imagined a bank filled with glowing ingots. "Nothing for now. I'll go to Julian and take a look for myself."

Brown oxide stains bled from the white quartz. Horrigan swung the massive hammer close enough to ruffle Rivera's hair. Squinting to shield his eyes, Javier methodically worked the chisel along the gold vein, his leather gloves thinning with each impact. To lessen the pounding, tufts of wool plugged his ears. The teapot-shaped "Sunshine Lamps" strapped to our foreheads twinkled in the swirling eddies of the West Drift. The feeble rays paled at an arm's length.

"Stop!" I shouted, stepping forward to check progress. The vein was about three feet wide. After touching the crystals, I dropped to scrape up the fragments. "By golly, we've got the real thing here. We need to lay our hands on quicksilver." It would take a lot of mercury to separate the gold from the quartz.

Daniel identified a complication. "Procuring huge quantities of amalgamate may signal we're up to something,"

Horrigan proposed, "A Scotsman developed an improved procedure to suspend the gold using cyanide. I have no idea how it's done, or if the extraction process works."

"Interesting! Find out more," I requested. "In the meantime, smear this lode with charcoal ashes, and don't let anyone near the West Drift."

Wilhelm Braun sat alone at the bar in the Florence Hotel's ostentatious saloon. I marked his descent into a drunken stupor from a bench in the lobby. A half-hour ago, the bartender had uncorked a virginal quart of Old Overholt. The employee appeared exasperated at his customer's slurred attempts at conversation. When the rye was half-gone, I walked inside and took a seat.

"Mr. Braun, such a nice surprise to run into you. Can I buy you another?" I asked.

Wilhelm turned. "Already got a whole bottle of my favorite. Well, almost anyway. Who're you?"

I said softly, "I'm a member of the Spear of Achilles."

He pretended to recognize me. "You're the avocado farmer. Why are you in here?"

"I came by for a nip and saw you. Figured I should say hi. Are you here by yourself?"

"Jus' me and old Mr. Overholt." Braun motioned the barkeeper for a glass. "Bes' friend I ever had, and the only one I ever kept." Tittering, he flooded our beakers.

"Here's to you," I saluted, and wet my lips. "I lost many close comrades in the War of Northern Aggression. Such a goddamn waste."

Wilhelm's bloodshot eyes widened. "Oh really? You a grayback?"

"As a juvenile, I fought for the cause. These days, I tend the soil, and try not to resurrect the past—too many disagreeable thoughts. What of you? Were you or Heinrich in the war?"

The dumpy man slid into an affected German accent. "*Nein.* Not the Civil War. Back then, we lived in Germany. My brother fought the French. Me? Too young to serve. Following the Treaty of Frankfurt in 1871, my family moved to New York City."

"Your parents didn't reap the rewards of war?"

Braun drank and shrugged. "Guess not."

"Do you recall any of the German language?" I questioned.

He fumbled for a cigar in his coat. "Forgotten most of it, except, *'gute nacht meine liebe.'* Means, 'Good night my love.'" Wilhelm's face veiled as if reliving a humiliation. "Heinrich always says that."

Uneasy, I wondered what other abhorrent actions the brothers' elaborately concocted stories concealed. "I have relatives in New York. They often write and want me to visit. Do your mother and father still live on the East Coast?"

He stared into the amber elixir and mumbled, "They passed away on my twelfth birthday."

I patted his vest and replenished his cup. "How sad! Was it an accident?"

"We lived in a Brooklyn boarding house. My parents' bedding caught on fire when an unattended candle fell over. Herm . . . Heinrich—smelled the fumes and woke up. We used knotted sheets to lower to the street. The entire building was destroyed. Sixteen tenants perished."

"You're lucky to have survived, Wilhelm." I lit his Sensenbrenner. "What year did that take place?"

"March 7th of 1860. I'll never forget that date," he answered. "My brother has taken care of me ever since. Excuse me, gotta shake hands with the vicar."

I waited for his return from the privy, nervous that Heinrich might stop by. Wilhelm stated that he resided in Germany during the War Between the States. Now, he said his parents burned alive in Brooklyn a year before the fighting commenced at Fort Sumter. I drained my booze into his tumbler.

Ready to refill, Braun climbed up on the wobbly stool and slurped my addition. I streamed in more rye and inquired, "Is it true that your brother is an expert photographer? That's a fascinating hobby in which I'd like to gain proficiency."

Temperament frosting, he sat up straight. "How do you know he has a camera? Who you been speaking to?"

Palms held aloft, I asked, "Am I wrong? Is it a secret?"

Wilhelm's lids drooped as he drifted into torpor. "Naw, no secret. Jus' somthin' we don't talk 'bout with outsiders. Your cup is dry. Time for a new bottle." Rummaging in his pants, he pulled free a spotty handkerchief and half a dozen Indian Heads.

"Got it," I volunteered, calling the barman. I filled his glass to the brim. "Does Heinrich prefer nature pictures or portraits? What subject matter engages him?"

"Landscapes, people . . . just the usual." Wilhelm wiped his face with the rag. "Gettin' tuckered out. Think I'll turn in for the evening."

I leaned in and whispered, "Once, a friend gave me postcards of a traveling freak show. At first, the images of deformed or mutilated performers were disturbing, yet on closer scrutiny—profoundly provocative! If I owned camera equipment, I would devote my attention to cataloging the curious, weird, and grotesque. I believe the strange and bizarre should be recorded for posterity!"

Wilhelm unfolded a print from his jacket. "This is the only keepsake I have of my parents." Garbed in a dated style of nightclothes, a middle-aged man and women lay supine in a narrow bed. The linen was drawn below their ankles. "Heinrich took this picture before they died. What's your name again?" Not staying awake for a response, he laid his chubby cheek on the bar.

I perused the long human shadow falling across the sleeping couple. Tucking the sinister photo in his pocket, I replied to the snoring man, "Henry Gates. My wife's name was Elizabeth Gates."

With Walt Werner unavailable—until the day of reckoning—I found myself paired with Doctor Alfred Blume. The June Spear of Achilles meeting was thankfully brief. Without so much as a glance my way, Heinrich voiced that his accountant had departed for San Francisco and bid him a grateful farewell. No new members were drafted. Wilhelm smiled as if remembering me from the saloon. I nodded politely and escaped.

In the heart of Chinatown, my reassigned patrol partner led me directly to the cribs. "Hank, you'll definitely appreciate what you're about to see." The well-primped doctor had unbalanced facial features—his sniffer didn't line up with his mouth—and a sinewy frame. In spite of the unusually short calves, his legs blurred with the voracity of a mongoose. "Over here." We stood at the rear wall of a prostitution shack. At a knothole in the siding, a yellow dot projected through the doctor's monocle and onto his pupil. He moved from the aperture, and breathed, "Take a look."

Inside, a gallery of seated men watched a drama that transpired out of sight, a common act in this part of town. Positioned behind a dinged stereo camera, a hunched figure snapped a sequence of photographs, his identity concealed by black fabric. At a bigger eyelet, I gasped with recognition and shock as Reverend Glazkov's husky forearm wrapped around a naked Asian woman's slender neck. Plainly drugged, her dazed eyes glazed as he cut off her airway.

I backed away from the gruesome spectacle and moaned, "We must stop this!"

Blume butted me aside for a better angle. "What's your problem? I presumed you took pleasure in these 'bizarre' forms of entertainment?" He giggled. "I pronounce the strumpet dead."

Unhinged by the violence, I wandered the Stingaree, heading in the general direction of downtown. Had Wilhelm communicated to his older brother our discussion at the Florence Hotel? When I left the tavern, he seemed incapacitated. Maybe Wilhelm wasn't the village idiot I always judged him to be. Did Heinrich orchestrate tonight's perversion just for my benefit? I vomited onto the sidewalk.

At the Acme, I demanded whiskey.

Steadfast, Tillman Jr. said, "Won't do it, Lieutenant Gates. My dad will tan my hide. How does a teacup of Earl Grey sound?"

"Sounds lousy! Now bring me that drink!" I bellowed at the tormented reflection in the bar's mirror.

Tillman Sr. heard the hubbub and dashed from the rear waving his leather-wrapped baton. He noted my anguished expression and commanded, "Son, give the man what he wants."

As the boy handed me the shot of alcohol, his father slammed the club upon the tumbler. Kessler blended whiskey, advertised as "Smooth as Silk," and glass shards pelted the startled customers. "In the back!" he barked.

As Till turned up the kitchen's gas lamps, vermin scurried into the nooks and crannies. "I had a bad day," I groaned, slumping into a chair. "Saw something I can't erase from my mind."

"That's obvious," the owner commiserated, offering a bottle of water. Rust sediment layered the bottom. "Can't understand how you stomach this hogwash. It's repulsive." Judgmental as ever, he poured himself red wine.

I recapitulated what I had seen in Chinatown and how I assumed Heinrich Braun was the camera operator.

"Told you to quit, didn't I?" Burnes reminded. Distracted, he hurled a potato at a rat sniffing the counter. The missile curved and bowled over a column of jarred tomatoes. "Shoot! Nobody takes heed. It's futile trying to dodge Satan; the Antichrist always returns in one guise or another." He pinched the tip of a paring knife and flung the tool at the scrounger. Piercing the rat, both objects clattered past the edge.

"If I wait to grab Braun, someone else might get hurt," I stressed. The tepid water tasted of sulfur. Cotton-mouthed, I swigged the remainder of the rotten-egg-smelling liquid.

"Can't say what I'd do," Till professed. "Don't binge and go off the deep end. Somebody around this hellhole's got to keep some self-control."

"Perhaps that's why I came to the world-famous Acme Saloon and Billiard Academy, knowing full well I wouldn't be served. I'm sick of self-control. It's driving me berserk!"

The barkeep stooped and picked up the impaled rodent by the tail. "I had a kitty cat, but she run off." He tossed the furry mess in the trash. Burnes rinsed the blade in dishwater, and advised, "Until this is sorted out, you should send Miss Mills as far from here as possible."

I nodded, afraid my friend was right.

Chapter Twenty-Two

ON A BRILLIANT SUNDAY AFTERNOON, I took Laura to Pacific Beach. I pressed her to consider returning to Philadelphia for the time being. The one-sided discussion spun into a debate.

"What you experienced was frightful! That poor helpless girl!" The wind undid Laura's braids as she whirled to beseech, "Henry, you must contact the authorities. Heinrich Braun is a monster!"

I cautioned her that Constable Hurley worked for the Brauns. "The entire department is crooked."

"There ought to be a few honorable men still adhering to the law."

"Can't take that chance. For your protection, I need you safe and sound."

Adamant, Laura asserted, "I'm not leaving. Forget about that. At Smith, I learned to handle myself. Earning a college degree transformed my life."

Peeved that she would not accept my guidance, I punted a knot of seaweed. "How so?"

"In Pennsylvania, my interactions with people of diverse economic and social backgrounds were greatly limited. My family isolated me from seeing the real world—sordid and corrupt as it often is. Going away to Northampton was liberating! In the course of those four years, I lived with fifty other girls in a dormitory. That's where I met Gracie. The Hubbard House is where I dined, studied, prayed, slept, and made lifelong friends. In that intellectual environment, we encountered pressures and opportunities previously unknown." Her eyes charted dolphins herding a shoal of fish. "As an educated woman, I refuse to be a lonesome housewife squeezing out one baby after another and ordered around by a husband who governs the finances. I'm capable of earning a living for myself."

Both fazed and stimulated by Laura's bluntness, her self-reliance brought to mind my zeal to quit school and run off to volunteer with the Confederate forces. How contrasting my days may have been if the North and South had solved their differences with diplomacy instead of lead. "Those are exemplary goals. Which types of jobs do you prefer, and what does your mom and dad think of your independence?"

"My mother loves the notion of moving out here. She despises the interminable winter season. Father has asked me to research the marketability of European-style hats in Southern California. I keep telling him the brims should be wider to shade the fashionable ladies who pursue outdoor activities. As far as a career path, since my vocation is mathematics, Alonzo has hired me to audit his accounting ledgers. With the depressed regional economy, I want to contribute. The Hortons are very hospitable, allowing me to abide so long in their home."

I inquired, "You're drawing a salary?"

"Yes, Mr. Gates," Miss Mills beamed. "Soon, I'll be able to afford my own room and board."

"If you are so determined to put yourself at risk by staying in San Diego, I beg that you remain sheltered under the Horton's roof." I respected that Alonzo had worked as a lawman and could defend himself if boxed into a corner. During a trip to Panama on the *Cortez* in the 1850s, a mob of rioting natives savagely assaulted a group of American passengers. Horton used two handguns to slay eight of the machete-swinging assailants as he heroically led his party back aboard the steamer.

"Henry, I'll live with you," Laura teased, cupping my cheek with a silky palm. "We shall play house!"

"Are you telling me that as a modern woman, you don't anticipate 'squeezing out' any kids?"

"You must talk me into it!"

Seagulls flocked overhead as I chased the girl across the golden sand.

Daniel Judge disregarded the bell and banged on my door. "Hank!" he thundered, rattling the glass. "Hank, it's the mine!"

As I turned the knob, he pushed inside. "Is it bad?" I asked, knowing from his haggard appearance, the reply would be dreadful.

"There was an explosion!" Daniel answered, sinking to a chair. His chest rose and fell. "I don't understand what went wrong. Foghorn is so damn meticulous, almost to a fault."

I imagined being trapped in a lightless cave without air. "How did you find out? Horrigan?"

Distressed, he nodded. "Received an urgent cable and ran straight here."

"Anyone injured?"

Judge frowned. "The telegram didn't say. Just that there was an accident and to 'Bring help!'"

Neither of us spoke on the long train ride to Julian. Daniel stared gloomily out the right window and I out the left, preparing for the worst.

In town, we rented horses and raced to the camp, riding by a thread of prospectors hiking up to aid in the rescue. In the organized chaos, we came upon Claude, shirtless and layered in soot.

"What the hell happened?" I inquired. Mole rolled a wheelbarrow of rubble from the mine's entrance and dumped it down the hillside.

The manager mopped away perspiration with a torn glove. "I wish I knew. Foghorn claims somebody monkeyed with the charges. No one on my team has the knowhow to do that."

We followed Horrigan into the tunnel, jostling past a lengthy bucket brigade of men passing rock fragments to the front. The vapors clinging to the ceiling smelled of almonds—not the usual acrid tang of gunpowder.

"Got something!" an unfamiliar voice shouted. "Get the doc! Hurry!"

Rushing onwards, we stopped at a jumble of boulders. A cluster of frenzied diggers scrambled to uncover a foot, a leg, an arm, and lastly, Javier Rivera's shattered skull.

"Start from the beginning," I stipulated. Rivera's washed and shrouded remains had been transported to Julian. Tomorrow, he'd join the ranks of other unlucky miners carried up the "casket walk" to be buried in the hilltop cemetery overlooking the town.

Foghorn smudged his furrowed brow. "Yesterday, Howka and Archie drilled an array of shot-holes. Javier and I set the charges earlier today."

I asked, "Gunpowder?"

The shot-firer clarified, "Yep. Peabody is a small-scale operation, and using blasting gelatin or nitroglycerine is overkill." Judge scowled at his word usage.

"I've seen receipts for jelly. Do you stock it in the store?" Used to keep the explosives dry and safely separated from the encampment, the store was a secure brick building positioned a hundred yards from the mine.

Foghorn confirmed, "There's five pounds of gelignite. Fifty sticks. We retain gelatin but haven't needed to use it."

Daniel cross-examined, "How were the devices placed?"

As Foghorn talked, his lithe fingers moved, visually recreating each step. "After inserting the compound electric detonators and linking them in parallel to the connecting wires, we inserted four of the gunpowder cartridges. We filled the blast-holes with drill borings and then tamped the stemmings in with a wooden rammer. Rivera and I acted in accordance with all mining regulations."

Judge questioned, "Were there any issues with the cartridges jamming in the tubes and creating friction? Could dampness be a cause?"

"No, sir. Dry as a toasted bone sandwich. We religiously sharpen the drill bits to maintain the proper diameter of two inches. The casings slid in like crap through a goose. Mr. Judge, I've worked at this for a while. I know what I'm doing."

I stuck up a hand. "Foghorn, we'll deliberate that later. Then you ran the firing cable outside?"

"Javier did that. I inspected every inch of insulation for shorts and detected none. As the last man out, I coupled the wires to the blasting machine, inserted the key, gave the handle a half-twist, and *nothing*. No detonation."

"There was a miss-fire?" Daniel inquired.

Foghorn made it clear. "A hang-fire. I severed the cable from the blasting machine, and, as required, we waited an hour. Rivera volunteered to check."

"Why not you, Foghorn?" I asked. "Why didn't you go see?"

"Horrigan has me training Javier as a backup in case an untimely event befalls me." He turned to Claude for corroboration.

The big man nodded. "Javier said he'd take care of it."

I stated the undeniable, "So Rivera goes in, and the ignition is delayed. *Boom!* The whole ceiling collapses on him."

"The burst was too powerful for the explosives we normally use. Rocks and smoke flew from the tunnel entrance—comparable to a bomb." Foghorn flexed his fists. "That *never* occurs with normal levels of gunpowder!"

Daniel's face reddened. "What do *you* suppose took place?"

"Someone tampered with the cartridges before Rivera and I loaded them this morning."

"How can that be?" I questioned.

Defeated, he raised and contracted his shoulders.

Equally mystified, I inquired, "Did you verify the gelignite is in the store?"

The shot-firer responded, "No, not yet. I was busy unblocking the shaft."

Daniel, Claude, and I trailed the miner to the outbuilding. He unlocked the entryway and let us into the cool interior.

Foghorn scoured the chamber from top to bottom. "The gelignite's gone. The gunpowder may have been removed from the cartridges and switched with jelly. It's pliable and hand-moldable." He lifted a cylinder from a carton and peeled off the waterproofed casing. Gray putty replaced the black powder.

"That still wouldn't explain the hour-long delay in ignition," I said.

Foghorn held up one of the shiny compound electric detonators. The tube's crimped end was mangled. "Who is responsible for this treachery?"

Horrigan called from out front, "Come look!" As the manager skimmed fingertips over faint gouge marks in the doorframe, I focused on a sparkle in the scrub. From bits in the pigweed, I pieced together a smashed bottle. I joined the label halves and read "Old Overholt." *Wilhelm Braun's whiskey of choice.*

Chapter Twenty-Three

ALONE WITH PIPE AND COFFEE, I sat in the parlor daydreaming. Hector lay on the rug, gnawing a bone and watching me with large, chocolate eyes. Windswept curtains diffused the light gleaming from Walt Werner's pistol. The Smith & Wesson No. 3 Schofield had polished up like new. No more stockyard crud to gum up the mechanism.

To teach me a lesson, the Brauns killed one of my employees. We were fortunate—a miracle—that more people were not harmed in the explosion. I wondered why Heinrich didn't just come for me.

The West Drift, the shaft where Javier discovered the gold vein, remained blocked by heaps of rock. Daniel and the other miners were understandably apprehensive to enter the mine under the existing menacing conditions.

I released the catch and hinged the barrel downward to expose the face of the cylinder. Pensive, I slid a finger over the six shiny .45 caliber rounds. Locked and cocked, I squinted along the sight. Heinrich and his brother had to die—*soon.*

Ears perked, Hector dropped his toy and padded across the floor. Not hearing the bell, I used the gun to push aside the draperies to see Kitch galloping up on Cherika. I was not reassured by the concerned expression he wore hurdling up the front steps. Of late, my callers presented ill-fated tidings, never welcome gifts. I laid the revolver on an end table and met him on the porch.

"The boys are gone!" Cane huffed.

"Who, Mero and Basil?" I asked, already expecting horrible news.

"Minnie walked them to their house after school. When Mourning arrived, the door stood open, nobody home. When he went lookin', a neighbor said she saw the doctor take them."

"What doctor? Mourning said the physician turned their mother away."

My foreman said with contempt, "He's the louse. Doctor Blume won't treat coloreds."

"That one's a bad penny. Did he give an explanation?"

Kitch flapped his arms. "Said the brothers needed to be quarantined for tuberculosis."

"That's absurd!" I argued. "It's July. Mrs. Ivy died in May. They couldn't be ill."

We collected Clive at Ernie Smoke's stables and rode to Chollas Creek. Minnie huddled with a few women in the lane.

Cane questioned his wife, "Where's Mourning?"

Minnie pointed southeast. "Mr. Dew went to National City to find the doctor. I'm worried. He's crazy."

As the horse and mule plodded along the rails of the Atchison, Topeka, and Santa Fe Railroad, I disclosed my last brush with Blume. With each word, Kitch appeared increasingly appalled.

He glared at me. "Are you sayin' one of Braun's men strangled that woman, and he had Blume kidnap our kids because of you?"

"Possibly." Everything was unraveling, and I had to accept the blame. "Probably," I acknowledged.

"Christ, Hank! What's the matter with you? Always tellin' your stories and givin' *other* people advice. Now, look what *you've* done!"

I felt too ashamed to say anything.

On a spacious, level, plot, Doctor Alfred Blume's residence held a spectacular vista of the glistening San Diego Bay. Blooming shrubs and budding fruit trees edged the grand, recently built, two-story building. We hitched the animals to the windmill tower and stepped onto the stoop. An unmarked manila envelope was stuck to the screen. When no one answered the ringer, I peeped in the windows. The parlor contained formally arranged furniture and a birdcage.

I shook a photograph from the package. In the bottom, something else jangled. Six knucklebones and a red sphere tumbled into my hand.

Cane gulped, "Those are Basil's jacks." He took the print. "What is that?"

"Looks like a mill," I responded, scrutinizing the low warehouse-sized structure on a wharf.

On the avenue, I flagged an elderly gentleman driving a wagonette. Upon reviewing the picture, the octogenarian directed west. "That's the creosote plant," he said. "Vile thing reeks. Just follow your nose!"

In the distance, five pipes belched syrupy smoke. The sharp odor of coal tar intensified as the wind shifted. A railway siding looped back to the Creosote Timber Preserving Works. All around us, neat pyramids of seasoned railroad ties, ship masts, and rough-sawn lumber baked in the late afternoon sun. "Tie buckers," a singular breed of grunts, dipped, stacked, and loaded eight-foot rectangular beams into freight cars for delivery.

At the factory, sturdy gondolas deposited bridge and dock pilings into a humongous processing tank. Once the workers sealed the portals, creosote filled the vessel, immersing the batch in a greenish-brown solution. The aroma was nauseating and headache inducing.

Aghast at the breadth of the premises, Kitch asked, "What do we do now? They may well be anyplace." He studied the photo, turning it over. "And where the hell is Mourning?"

"There's a mark," I noted, indicating the ink spot on the blank side of the paper.

Cane flipped the translucent print and raised the sheet to the sky. An enormous vat overlaid the black dot. Purposely surveying the area, he bellowed, "There!" and sprinted toward a row of fizzing containers.

By the harbor, a dozen topless laborers sheathed in grubby dungarees, cowhide gloves, and inch-and-a-half thick wooden clogs, sprawled across a bank of coke. Steam radiated from their tarnished bodies.

"Did you see any kids?" Kitch questioned, setting his palm to Mero's height.

"We're searching for two colored boys," I defined. "Might be with a white man dressed in spiffy duds—the local doctor?" Break ending, a few shrugged and clambered off the coal stockpile.

Cane cursed under his breath and ran to the tank in the picture. He had climbed halfway up a ladder mounted to the front, when a returning drudge called, "Hey boy, what'chu doin' up dere on my still? We gotta scrape dat out next." Epidermis flaked from his raw face and hands.

I extended my arms in supplication. "Sir, we aren't here for trouble. We're check—" Ignoring me, the throng chucked lumps of compressed coal. "Get down," I recommended. With Kitch's toes rooted firmly on the oily terrain, I removed Walt's firearm from my jacket and shoved the weapon into his grasp.

Arm rock-steady and eyes blazing, Kitch aimed at the leader. "Come any closer and I'll shoot the smarts from the first six numskulls. Then, while I'm reloadin', my Reb compadre will stab whoever remains standin'."

I didn't carry my bayonet, but it wasn't a problem, the crowd retreated out of range. "We want to take a look inside, and then we'll leave," I promised, scaling the rusted rungs bolted to the skirt of the piping-hot still. At the top, I blew on my fingers, and peered into the maw of the mammoth cauldron. I couldn't discern much, except my own reflection at the base.

Cane kept order, as I swung my leg past the iron lip, and lowered myself into the viscous innards. A muffled noise made me hesitate and concentrate. The interior was stifling, confining, and noxious. The steps ended a yard from the nethermost point. I let go, plunging into a scum of near-boiling solvent. After the daily firing of the stills, water tempered the blistering surfaces, enough to allow this menial job to be fulfilled—chipping the leftover coke tar from the floor. I tripped on an object and fell into the sludge. This time I plainly heard rapid respiration. Lugging somebody into the column of sunlight, I pulled off a feedbag—*Mero!*

"Got him!" I yelled, unbinding his wrists and ankles. "Are you hurt?"

"No," the adolescent replied, rubbing his eyes. "Just dizzy and thirsty." Soaked and frazzled, Mero hoisted himself up the rundles into daylight.

Kitch registered that the grimy boy was solo. Anxious, he questioned, "Where's Basil?"

Now enthusiastic to assist, a man bore a pail of water. Mero rinsed his eyes and drank before answering, "Two white men brought us here. They put me in this foul tank and run off with my brother."

"Who took you?" I inquired. "What did they say?"

"After school, a doctor came by the house. Said we were sick and had to go to the hospital. Claimed we'd spread the same disease our mom caught. We stopped on the roadway, and a different man—this one gigantic and mean—jumped into the cart. When the taller guy picked up a rope, Basil and I tried to get away. He moved too fast—put burlap sacks on our heads, so we didn't see anything. Made me crawl into this cooking pot—thought I'd die. Then they. . . . I don't know where Basil is!" The youth broke down.

"That cussed doctor left clues to lead us here," Cane muttered. "There has to be something to help find Basil!" He relinquished the Schofield and traipsed aimlessly around the site. The stills rang with the clatter of the re-energized workforce. Kitch doubled back with haste and instructed, "Turn out your pockets, son!"

Mero dug into his jeans, at first scooping handfuls of dirt. Then the boy's roving fingers retrieved a coal-stained piece of white.

Kitch snatched the paper and smoothed yet another photograph. This print was less distinctive than the image of the creosote plant. Pools of water engulfed a level landscape as seagulls soared above sand dunes reflecting a light brighter than snow. The stark scene could be a section of the voluminous San Diego Bay—*or anywhere.* The back revealed nothing unique.

"Let's go to Blume's," I proposed. "Maybe he's there." Cane agreed and lifted Mero behind the saddle. We were considering various bleak options when Mourning Dew stumbled upon the path. Disheveled and wild-eyed, inky blots streaked the man's shirt and trousers. A machete hung from his fist.

Dismounted from Clive, I asked, "Are you okay?"

Mourning shed the broad knife and hurried to hug Mero. "You're here!" he sobbed, scanning for the younger brother. "And Basil? Where's he at?"

"We're not sure," Cane replied, patting his neighbor for damage. "Are you cut?"

With a shaking hand, Mourning scrubbed gore from his neck. "No, I'm fine. The doc told me Mero was at the factory that waterproofs wood. Is that where you come from?"

"Yup." Giving Mourning the picture, I described how we arrived at this place and time. "What is this? Did he tell you about Basil?"

"The salt flats south of here," Dew gasped. "Go!"

Both animals overloaded and at a canter, we departed National City to enter the undeveloped town of Chula Vista. As we proceeded by the trailhead that Kitch and I used as a funeral route for Ray the Panderer and the Judas, Walt Werner, I quizzed Mourning to learn if the repugnant doctor continued to walk with the living.

"Oh yes sir!" he growled into my ear. "When the doc wakes up, nobody will hear, since I locked him in his pantry. In case we need more answers, I let the sawbones keep his lollipop-licker." He shot me a mischievous smile and opened a jeweled box. The small casket held five amputated fingers, one in a gold band. The words "Cooper Medical College" circled the oval ruby. "That vulgar so-and-so's a southpaw now."

Past the pitted tracks of the National City and Otay Railroad, we neared the lowest part of the lagoon. The white substance in the photograph was actually salt, not sand or snow. Tons of shimmering alkali dried in the onshore winds. Beside a sign hand-lettered with the name "South Bay Salt Works," I aligned the print to the horizon, endeavoring to duplicate the same angle of perspective. The steam-driven conveyor belt that mounded the peaks of crystals towering over us did not show in the frame. *Where should we go? There are no employees here! This property must be a thousand acres!*

Emotional, Dew paced wearing a visage of heartache. "It's too late. The tides coming in!"

"Why does that matter!" Kitch exclaimed. "Talk to me, Mourning!"

"The boy's underground! *They buried him alive!*" Roaring Basil's name, the carpenter waded into intertidal wetlands toward several man-made ponds.

"Hold up!" I hollered. "Why didn't you tell us that?" Mourning splashed ahead, his reply inaudible.

Gravel levees separated the seawater from the bordering marsh. Metal guillotines regulated the flow of saltwater channeled between the pools.

Dew shouted, "Before passin' out, the doc confessed to buryin' Basil by a head gate! He's breathin' through a stalk of bamboo!"

The ascending Buck Moon steadily towed the tide higher. Twenty floodgates transferred brine from one pond to the next. When enough water evaporated, the pure table salt was harvested. Lost and at wits' end, I again raised the picture.

Mero tapped the print. "That's the stick there!" He skated down an embankment of eelgrass to a green stem with ringed joints protruding from the submerged mudflats. Numerous footprints stamped the shoreline.

"We're here Basil," I cried into the bamboo.

The four of us burrowed into the clingy gunk. As we dredged deeper, water streamed into the depression. Mourning exhaled as he hit wood. The old shipping crate resembled a medium-sized coffin.

"Careful!" Dew spat through clenched teeth. Chafed hands scratched silt from the Winchester trademark branded into the lid. His shoulders hunched as breaking fingernails clawed the edge.

In the course of a lifetime, I have identified the sodden carcasses of drowned mariners fished from the sea, and thankfully only once the ravaged corpse of a young girl smothered by an abusive uncle. With no kicks or screams originating from within the box, I lowered my expectations, ready in body and mind to find Basil breathless, his pallor the color of granite and puckered from submersion, or eyes bloodshot and bulging from asphyxiation.

With one plank splintered loose, the nails gave up, and the other fasteners pried off with ease. My jaw dropped, not prepared for the look of abject terror contorting Basil's face as he flailed in six inches of cloudy water.

As if giving birth, Mourning wrenched the child free as the sea surged into the empty tomb.

We weren't getting anywhere. Alfred Blume had nothing else to surrender. Mero, Basil, and Kitch waited outside the pump house as Mourning and I interrogated our captive. On the roof, the windmill's screeching blades turned to meet the feverish Santa Ana gusts. Now stoic, but stippled with fresh blood, Dew had attacked the doctor with a vengeance I had never witnessed, even on the barbaric battlegrounds of Chancellorsville.

When challenged on the faded Spear of Achilles tattoo adorning his forearm, although Blume admitted to serving in Heinrich Braun's unit during the Civil War, he didn't recall ever being near Buzzard Roost. He added to our frustration by not providing a reason for the burial site photographs, or letting slip where the brothers took refuge. After seeing the physician's teeth sown across the ground like ivory seeds, I believed his memory loss.

"He's all yours," I said, dropping the bent pipe in revulsion.

Mourning rose from the pump housing and stood before the trussed man. On the earthen floor, he gently slapped Blume. "Wake up—you need to be here for this," Dew whispered, using thumbs to raise the sagging upper eyelids. "You shouldn't have took my kids." He requisitioned my help to uncoil a rubber siphon hose coupled to the water storage tank. "Mr. Gates, please hold open the doc's pie hole. We're gonna let him drink deep from the Well of Sorrows."

Chapter Twenty-Four

AS FAR AS I COULD DETECT from the daily newspapers and my informal inquiries around town, Alfred Blume's body remained concealed. I envisioned the doctor swimming in the murky solitude of his own water tank and got a chill. At some stage, the physician's patients might file a report with the law, or maybe the degenerate bachelor will never be missed and eventually dissolve into paste.

After disposing of Blume in the cistern, Mourning took the kids home to rest. Kitch and I traveled to the Florence Hotel. We learned that the Brauns had checked out at sunrise without leaving a forwarding address. The despicable pair drifted in the wind.

This news may be taken as good or bad, depending upon one's viewpoint. Laura was ecstatic upon hearing the brothers had fled; still, I found it hard to swallow that the psychopaths had given up so easily. Cane now had his own bone to pick with Heinrich and Wilhelm, swearing no letup until inflicting his own brand of justice.

Days passed, and then a month. The Spear of Achilles disbanded with the members not knowing what became of their leaders. I cautioned Laura to stay on guard. The unified community of Chollas Creek kept close watch on Mero and Basil. The boys were resilient, and Mourning was a caring father. Whenever I dropped by, the brothers acted unscathed by their traumatic ordeals. From my own harrowing war experiences, I knew this carefree indifference to be a defensive shield doomed to crack.

Daniel Judge and I spent our waking hours at the renamed Rivera Mine. We trucked out debris and installed sturdier bracing to shore up the roof. A new stout door and robust lock fortified the explosives store. Foghorn controlled the only key and kept on the lookout for "dirty anarchists."

To keep our crew from defecting to another claim, we organized a company meeting. At a reserved private table in the Acme, Daniel astonished the men by announcing Javier's gold deposit. Reassured that each would receive substantial stipends to work the vein, the revitalized miners kept their mouths shut. Judge sought a stable income to quit his secondary jobs. I brooded that analogous to a sudden case of the shingles, the Brauns patiently lay dormant, ready to outbreak at the most inopportune moment.

Neither eating nor sleeping well, I continued rambling the bawdry thoroughfares and sunless alleyways of the Stingaree. Disturbing and befuddling nightmares filled my catnaps. Ghouls of yesteryear mingled with breathing—or recently breathing—foes, specifically the Braun brothers, Ray Diamond, Walt Werner, and Doctor Blume. Many mornings, I flopped into bed as the sun scraped over the horizon.

Of late, I seldom intervened in a scuffle, much less a brutal crime. Visualizing Basil in that salt-encrusted shipping carton focused my energy. I couldn't be bothered by the inconsequential.

With little luck, I ventured to ferret out other Spear of Achilles members. The few I located shed no light on the locale of the president and vice-president. One of them, a cattle breeder agonized that pirates had abducted "God's messengers." Carl Hurley, the bribable constable, was one of the men I wanted to find. Higher on my list, the homicidal Reverend Glazkov. Heinrich's flunkies had to know their commander's whereabouts.

When in town, I took lunch at the plentiful restaurants packed along Market Street. In the past, Constable Hurley had also dined in the same area. I assumed that his regular beat must be here or nearby. Not interested in arousing suspicion, I didn't dare ask for his schedule at the marshal's station.

Ensuing fruitless weeks of monitoring the ebb and flow of humanity, animals, and mechanical transports washing through the city streets, I almost gave up. Traffic was sluggish the day I spotted the pudgy lawman.

On the opposite planked sidewalk, a band of spirited children caught my eye. They ringed a dog playing dead. Lolling on its back, the Saint Bernard wagged a stumpy tail and welcomed tummy rubs. The glint of brass buttons on a blue jacket distracted me from Bum's outstanding performance. A matching helmet restrained Carl Hurley's unruly mop as he strolled by an outdoor grocery. I paid the bill, traversed the boulevard, and followed from a distance.

Hurley deftly twirled a baton as he patrolled the neighborhood. Courteous to passersby, Carl tipped his cap to ladies and once retrieved a lost ball for a blubbering toddler. The man entered a French bakery. I spied his reflection in a shop window as he accepted a bag from the baker. *Graft payoff?* On the curb, powdered sugar flecked the officer's lips as the doughy cruller disappeared.

The patrolman savored the next snack at a public park. Dutifully sharing crumbs with a bevy of squawking pigeons, he hardly noticed me sit beside him on the rusting bench.

"Constable Hurley," I began, "do you remember me from the Spear of Achilles meetings?"

With a sleeve, the bluecoat wiped frost from his mustache as recognition hiked his patchy eyebrows. "You and Walter Werner were partners. Henry Bates, right?"

I did not correct my surname. "Yes until Walt moved away." The Smith & Wesson pressed against my abdomen—this weapon much more convenient to stow than a three-foot long sword. "It's disheartening that the group dispersed when Heinrich and Wilhelm hit the road. I believed we accomplished something special."

"Hrmph," Hurley snorted. The birds scattered as the empty sack hit the ground.

"What's the matter?" I questioned. "Weren't you grateful for our support in lowering the crime rate?"

Carl stood to whisk off his uniform. "Nothing personal, sir. I am sure you started with admirable intentions, but I'm glad that is over now. Good afternoon."

My gut told me the man lived a virtuous life, or tried to. "Then why did you help the Brauns?" I called as he exited under a vine-covered archway. "They're evil people."

The constable paused and assessed me. Fear aged the round face as he answered, "They never gave me a choice. I have a family to consider—just had a second baby. Thank God, those hard cases are gone."

"How about Reverend Glazkov? Where might I find him?"

Hurley acted surprised. "In church of course! Where else?"

Scaffolding encased the First Baptist Church. Planted on the corner of Tenth and E Streets, the structure swarmed with carpenters. Hammers were the only sounds ringing from the seventy-five-foot-tall bell tower. I presumed the modest home on the boundary of the property acted as the rectory. When I approached, a man in his early thirties came to the door attired in a starched clerical shirt and collar.

"If you're here for the roofer's job, the foreman is in the office." The spectacled minister pointed at a shack surrounded by quantities of lumber. "However, if you're seeking salvation or hunger for a receptive ear, I'm Pastor Harper," he greeted, extending an unflinching grip.

"Appreciate the offer," I said. "But, I'm here for someone—Reverend Glazkov?"

"Come inside," the pastor requested, swinging the screen wide. "Mrs. Harper is at a Woman's Missionary Society luncheon. I apologize for the clutter. We relocated here from Wichita."

Harper sat on a matching side chair. The cozy domicile smelled of oil paint.

"Is Reverend Glazkov a member of your congregation?" I inquired, contemplating an illustration of the Messiah in the Garden of Gethsemane. Beneath a gnarled tree, the Savior's clasped hands pleaded across an unmoving boulder. Lighter pigments accentuated a golden halo.

A perturbed expression etched the pronounced cheekbones. "I never got your name," he responded. "Why are you looking for this man?"

"It's a delicate matter. Do you know of whom I speak?"

"Yes," the minister replied. "Viktor Glazkov is *no* reverend though he *is* working to raise this church. Again I must ask, what is your name and purpose?"

"Henry Gates. I need to talk to him."

"Mr. Gates, I preach the Word to parishioners from all walks of life. As I deliver the sermon, I behold both disciples and atheists overflowing the pews. In the first row, the fervent stare with rapture, accepting each utterance as Gospel. After the service, I shoo these zealots outside. Agnostics are dragged in every Sabbath, coerced by a spouse. The cynics try their best to stay awake—chins bobbing—despite my admonishments of the eternal damnation of Hell. Since these wage earners toil so hard, and loyally fill the alms collection plates, I cannot condemn their inattention or lack of faith. Then there's the sheep that have wandered astray. These are the wretched souls I am destined to redeem! Rich or poor, healthy or infirm, God in his almighty wisdom has guided these fallen angels to the sanctuary of my parish—*or* my front door."

"Pastor Harper, no offence, today I'm not here for redemption. I'll go see the foreman about Glazkov." Rising from my seat, his stern bearing stopped me.

"Henry, I sense you're a righteous man. Regardless of that impression, I perceive you intend to violate God's will by doing Viktor harm. In my line of work, I have become an excellent judge of character and an ardent student of human nature. Tragic events from the past haunt your waking hours. You are one of Jesus' lost and wandering sheep. Am I right?"

"Perhaps, yet even King David executed common murders."

Harper nodded. "True, the Old Testament is full of fascinating contradictions. The scriptures document much bloodshed before Christ died for our sins."

On the stoop, I said, "Once consecrated, this place of worship shall be a beacon of hope."

"Someday it will. Now it's merely a shell—four walls and a leaky roof." Pastor Harper laid a palm on my shoulder and murmured this benediction, *"May the Lord bless you and keep you. May the Lord make his face to shine upon you and be gracious to you. May the Lord lift up his countenance upon you, and give you peace."* Straightening, the minister stroked his clean-shaven chin and made a decision. "Tell August, I sent you. If you ever wish to confess your mortal transgressions, my door is always open."

The roofline of the unfinished nave cast ridged moon-shadows on the construction site. I ascended the front stairs and accessed the narthex from below the silent bell tower.

August, the foreman for the First Baptist Church project, informed me that he allowed his employees to stay overnight on the premises as long as they didn't bring in women or booze. He said on most nights, Viktor Glazkov bedded down in the vestry. When queried for his opinion, the surly boss muttered, "He's a decent journeyman, but I wouldn't invite him over to play cards."

As I stood in the passageway between the main entrance and the nave, I weighed my alternatives: wait for the occasion to tail Glazkov to the Brauns, haul the hypocrite from the church and wallop the answers from him elsewhere, or throttle the lying snake in his sleep. I let the ballgame play out naturally.

On edge, I drew my sword and tiptoed into the sanctuary. Through glassless windows, the Earth's only satellite highlighted rows of skewed pews. Sporadic snoring buzzed from a bundle in the south transept. Blindly stepping around the contractor's supplies, I toppled onto a different sleeper curled by an unfilled baptismal font. Pores oozing grain alcohol, the man didn't wake. I moved toward the chancel separating the congregation from the altar.

Beyond the choir stalls, a hallway led to chambers at the rear of the edifice. A row of crated religious relics clogged the corridor as I crept by an unoccupied office and a functional kitchen.

With one more place to reconnoiter, I tensed. Door ajar, I leaned against the frame and peeked in the gap. In the future, the vestry may secure Pastor Harper's sacred robes and liturgical items, but tonight, the alcove contained the few necessities a migrant laborer might shoulder from field to field, or a veteran soldier to each campaign. These shabby articles consisted of a mangy bedroll spread on the floor, a flannel overcoat hanging from a peg, a crinkled wad of clothing, opened ration cans, assorted toiletries, and a haversack to tote the gear. To my touch, these trappings felt tainted.

Scrubbing my palms on my denims, I pondered where Glazkov could be. Alert for an unexpected return, I again searched his belongings for leads. A key was wedged into a chink in the wall. Near the makeshift bed, my shoes crunched grit. I crouched, sniffing a sweet, fruity fragrance. As I swept away the top layer of sand, pungency evocative of iron and peat moss agitated my gorge. At the brightest side of the room, with tacky fingers I held the key to the light—*blood!*

I inspected a trash bin behind the church. Squeezed into a poke, I unraveled a worn Bible wrapped in the vestments that Glazkov wore to the Spear of Achilles conclaves. The pages tore—glued together with red body fluid—as I attempted to read the holy book.

With the West Drift cleared of wreckage, Horrigan and his men mined the pocket of gold. Unable to concoct a method to use cyanide as a leaching agent, we settled on the proven treatment for amalgamation—quicksilver. Daniel confidentially contacted sources in the western region of California's Central Valley to requisition seventy-five-pound flasks of mercury. The heavy, silvery-white liquid mixed with the granulated ore and formed an amalgam paste. Distillation left a residue of precious metal. We kept the copper output at a consistent rate of production, restricting ourselves by withdrawing the gold in small batches. So far, no one had distinguished why our miners constantly smiled.

I purchased the vacant plot on my block. Kitch and I exhumed my neighbor's wife and carted her over hill and dale to Mount Hope Cemetery. For eternity (or sometime sooner), she rests in peace on a grassy slope between the Dunn and Ford families. Cane thought up the simple, yet poignant epitaph for the tombstone: *Somebody's Darling Lies Buried Here.*

The forty-eight apartments on B Street were nearly complete. Young families rented the finished units, and a waiting list held additional names. No buyers for houses, but the leasing market did well. With this project drawing to a close, Kitch designed the layout of the property next door to my cottage. My supervisor seemed happy with the continuous work and the daily obligations of managing the men.

An attorney advised me that since seven years had lapsed from the time I had last seen my wife, he could petition the courts for a judicial declaration of presumptive death. Once authorized by a judge, the divorce paperwork would be filed. I had mixed feelings listening to the lawyer outline the procedures. It was satisfying to take action; nonetheless, my heart ached as I wrote Beth and the kid's names on the legal applications.

Chapter Twenty-Five

In my dream, wolves wormed from a fathomless sinkhole in a hollow world. The feral creatures raced in figure eights, iridescent scales scintillating in the flickering of a million torchlights. Called to order, the flock hunched on muscular haunches, yellow eyes trained on their leader, a hulking biped who—

I roused, gradually cognizant of Hector's barking. The bedroom smelled of smoke and the curtains to the north and east blazed orange—but not from ordinary daylight.

I tore away the coverlet and moved to the window, elevating the sash. Along the foundation, a sea of flames belched black fumes redolent of kerosene.

The dog's yelps turned shrill. I pulled on pants and shoved the revolver in my belt. Mirroring an inverted stream of water, grey fog seeped below the doorframe and upwards, extending tendrils across the ceiling.

Coughing, I entered the hallway. No longer hearing Hector, I yelled—*nothing!* The crackling grew louder as the exterior shingles kindled. At the head of the stairwell, I wrapped my mouth with a towel, and mounted the top step. Under bare toes, the planking ran a high fever. From a loud progression of crashes in the attic, I knew the roof was gone.

At the foot of the stairs, I rushed to the porch, my hand jerking as the doorknob raised blisters. Through the pane, I spied the white-hot outlines of the two rocking chairs, the nearest crumbling into a pile of embers, and flying off. As I retreated, the upper panel imploded, cutting my cheek, and coating the rug with sizzling fragments. Sucked inwards by the spiraling draft, sparks devoured the floral wallpaper.

The lower level broiled bright as if an angry star pressed against the glass. I cried Hector's name and bolted to the kitchen. Lungs stinging from the fuliginous air, I dipped the mask in the basin, and yanked on the rear door. I fell as a burning cord of wood tumbled inward and ignited the linoleum.

Shouts from outside lured me backwards. My elbow pushed a full bucket as I slithered to the stairway. I doused water on the steaming treads and climbed into unconsciousness. Awakened again by Hector's cries, I lifted my chin to sense him nudging his snout against mine. The cocker spaniel bayed insistently, prodding me higher.

At the bedroom window, with Hector in my arms, I prepared to leap.

"Throw down a blanket!" an urgent voice hollered.

Eyeballs smarting and vision fuzzy, I made out five firemen near a hand-drawn hose cart watching the bonfire. Heat roasting my backside, I flung a quilt.

"Jump!" a different man directed. "You stupid, not the animal!"

I strained past the sill to release Hector, who landed on four paws in the safety net and howled. Then I dropped my sword, which nose-dived into the ground. As the ceiling collapsed spilling attic rummage onto the bed, I swung outward and let go. Caught by the volunteers, and lowered to the turf, I scooped up the puppy and held him close.

"Somebody must really be out to get you," the chief remarked as his department lit cigarettes. "We have no water. There aren't any hydrants over here." Using his boot, the fireman stomped Mourning's smoldering rosebushes. "Looks like you owned a fine house!"

I had to agree with everything he said.

I spent a solitary night in an empty apartment and then moved to Turner Hall. It took no time, considering I only possessed the dirty clothes I wore, my sword, Walt's shooting iron, and a growing puppy. The Turnverein kept cots in the changing room available for members too fatigued or drunk to go home. Captain Wiedemann convinced the director to give me permission to stick around until I got back on my feet. Hector entertained himself by investigating the vinegary odors emanating from the gymnasium's sweat-infused floors. As for myself, I wasn't having as much fun.

Sleepless, with pistol and sword by my side, I listened to the old building settle. I brainstormed on where the Brauns had holed up. Since the inferno, the brothers always felt too close for comfort, and I yearned for an additional set of eyes in the back of my scalp.

Constable Hurley stopped by my property one morning as I sifted the ruins for anything of worth. The officer of the law expressed happiness that I was not mixed with the ashes. He told me to be careful and withdrew.

In the soot, I excavated the key that Viktor Glazkov hid in the vestry. Listlessly rotating the shiny instrument in my hands, I had no inkling how to find the matching lock.

Multiple gold and money caches had been secreted in my yard, the main stash buried under the eucalyptus tree. I carried enough cash to live on and left the rest. Not trusting the banks, I couldn't think of a better place to squirrel away the nuts.

I avoided everyone, not willing to put my friends in harm's way. Concerned for my wellbeing, Kitch advocated sheltering at Chollas Creek. I declined, knowing that for me, asylum remained nonexistent. Mourning raged when he saw the dwelling we built in shambles. In spite of my pacifying efforts, I was not sure what he might do. Frightened of another bombing, Daniel added more security to the mine. Till advised me to leave town, confident that if Heinrich or Wilhelm ever showed their faces, he would personally exterminate the pair.

Laura? A whole other matter. Without argument, she accompanied the Hortons on a business trip to San Francisco. The scorched gash in the earth left little hope for a long-term relationship. I missed her desperately.

Hector and I arrived at the Concordia Turnverein after a relaxing early morning walk throughout our new neighborhood. Except for the whooshing wings of barn owls soaring skyward, G Street slept. The dog darted between my boots as I opened the door. Inside, I turned the latchkey, hearing an inhale and sharp growl before glimpsing a dumbbell curving overhead.

My wrists and ankles smarted from the unyielding restraints. The dripping side of my skull throbbed. Levi Naughton arranged lanterns to dramatize the mechanism of my bondage—the same Sargent Combination Pulley Weight machine Captain Wiedemann had demonstrated on our initial tour of the facilities. Straps cinched my waist to a seat on the bottom rail.

Ten feet away, Hector wriggled against his collar, the attached rope fastened to a rowing device. Crimson ringed the cocker spaniel's muzzle. Blood trickled from a nasty puncture in the man's thigh. In defiance of this calamitous situation, I swelled with pride—the scrappy hunting dog had spunk. Maybe he'd rescue me a second time.

Not making sense of how our roles had reversed, I inquired, "Did you jump ship, Levi?"

He laughed. "Very perceptive! Was it in the papers?"

"Just guessing," I responded. "I let you go. You ought to have stayed in Mexico."

Pegging his hat on a stand, Naughton slid over a chair. He crossed his legs. "Thanks for getting me shanghaied into slavery. I was down at Snug Harbor lifting a few with the boys when someone offered to buy me a drink. Seemed like an honest chap, so I said sure. Next thing I know, the skipper of the *Peking* has got me chained to a bunk. We sailed three hundred and fifty miles to the guano islands. At Elida Island—a barren, hellish rock—we shoveled enough bird poop to fill the schooner with a thousand sacks. That's a mess of crap and a mountain of riches if you are a ship owner. The farmers use guano for fertilizer, and the U.S. government needs the saltpeter for gunpowder. When the seas swelled, we scudded to Vizcaino Bay to ride out the storm. Smoke appeared on the horizon—Mexican custom officials looking for poachers." The man aimed my Schofield. "Pull up those weights."

"Why should I?" Feeling bite marks in my tongue, I ingested a blood clot.

"Do it," he warned, "or I'll shoot the dog."

Already affixed to the hooped handles, I drew back the cables. The wheels squeaked as ten slabs of iron—*all of them*—ascended the metal frame of the apparatus. My biceps bulged from the exertion and a vein somewhere upstairs pulsated.

Levi ambled across the gym and unleashed Hector, who resisted by dragging his paws. "Let's find out how much you love this mutt." He grinned and tied the animal below the hoisted counterweights. "That's two hundred pounds. Not as heavy as that tower those Frenchies are erecting in Paris, but still a good test of a man's stamina. We'll see how *you* enjoy being tortured." Seated again, Naughton continued the story. "So the steamer gets closer, and Captain Moodlin screams, *'That there's the Pacheco!'*"

Hector panted as I exercised. Even if I lowered the burden gently, he'd be crushed.

Observing my struggle, Naughton chuckled, "Nice and toasty in here. You nearly froze my stones off in the Acme's cold room."

"Set him loose," I begged. "Shoot me, I don't care. Let the dog go."

He shrugged and yawned. "Moodlin concluded that safety comes in numbers and altered our course to the gang's headquarters—a hidden bay at San Martin Island. That's where the *Hongkong* and *Alta* are moored."

Molly Doyle glided from obscurity gripping my sword. Grim as the Reaper and cloaked in as dark a shade of black, the barmaid mouthed, *"Keep him talking."*

In an awkward attempt at light conversation, I asked, "What's with your lip? That must hurt." A jagged pink line replaced the walrus mustache.

Levi skidded a callused thumb over the scar's stitch marks. "Yes, that was unfortunate and also your fault. On the third week out, I felt woozy—no sea legs—and split my kisser on the fiddley."

"Fiddley?" I moaned as the rectangular blocks unceasingly lowered. Hector rose and uttered an uneasy yowl.

"Hank, it's the brass framework around a hatchway. Skipper called me lucky to not to lose my tusks." Flashing his canines, he rubbed the fur underneath his snoot. "This ain't filling in right."

In stocking feet, Molly slinked into the circle of illumination. I repeated Hector's name to hold the animal's attention.

Naughton reenacted the naval battle by floating his hand alongside the other. "When the steamer overtook our ship—I thought we were goners! The custom officers threw grappling hooks, missing our bulwarks because of the large waves. Moodlin fired off a couple rounds and told those imbeciles he'd rather die here and now than rot in a Mexican prison. That captain's got some *cojones!* The *Pacheco* pursued us under full power to Santa Rosalia Bay. Blocked and on the reefs, we ditched the *Peking* and boarded the longboats."

Weapon raised, Molly balked as if losing courage, or incredibly, just curious to hear the end of the story. Although my arms dislocated from their sockets, I too became intrigued.

"In drenching rain we pulled ourselves up the steep cliffs and hid in the brush to watch the patrol boat anchor. I whispered, 'Farewell fellas!' and took off into the hills. Weeks later, the authorities arrested the skipper and two sailors for horse wrangling. Those toads are serving eighteen months in an Ensenada jail. Like you, they won't make it out alive."

With slick palms, I almost let go. "How did you survive without food or water? There are so few settlements on that section of the coast. Did you expect your poacher friends to save you?" After this last question, I nodded imperceptibly.

Instead of stabbing—which I would have done, or gone for the neck—Molly carved Levi's back, from shoulder blade to kidney. And for extra measure, she cut a horizontal slash across his hips. Ribbons of red sprayed the hardwood floor.

The man bawled, "Gowd!" and twisted to shoot. A grunt parted the girl's lips as she charged forward, ramming the sword into his chest, the tip decelerating as the hilt's cross-guard smacked ribs. The gun discharged into the ceiling and flew from splayed fingers. Naughton lumbered toward the exit, abruptly veering with unknown intent to the middle of the gymnasium. Halfway to the boxing ring he mumbled, "Billy, is that you?" and fell sideways, head bouncing on one of Dudley Allen Sargent's health machines.

"Untie Hector," I implored. Three bent digits on each hand were all that kept the dog from becoming a pancake.

Molly kicked the firearm aside and sped to free the pup, which enthusiastically clawed his way into my arms. The iron fell with an echoing clash.

As she extricated me, I exhaled, "Why did you come here?"

The barmaid smiled shyly, "With Laura out of town, I wondered if you were lonely."

"I needed a friend tonight," I admitted, massaging my aching forearms. "What should we do with Mr. Naughton?"

"Dump him in the Stingaree with the other garbage," Molly answered. Using her foot for leverage, she plucked the blade from the dead man's breast. "Your chum isn't the first to wind up as hog food."

Chapter Twenty-Six

AFTER MOLLY MOPPED THE CARNAGE FROM THE GYMNASIUM'S FLOOR, we disposed of Levi Naughton's bisected body into two of the multitudinous pigpens populating Chinatown. I applauded the girl's timing and saluted her bravery. We both swore to forget this troubling event. On the threshold of her flat on Seventh Street, she asked me to come in. Successfully curbing my need for human companionship, I thanked Molly again and went home to feed Hector.

Laura's curt note described San Francisco as a progressive city and said she and the Hortons were returning to San Diego in a few days. I couldn't wait to see her again and prayed we'd be capable of rebuilding our relationship.

Over the "Catch of the Day," I told the tale of Levi's unpredicted escape from the *Peking*. "Till, I counted on never laying eyes on Naughton again. We gave him a break."

"That was a mistake." Burnes tapped mugs of sudsy beer, shaving off the excess with a knife. "We should have gutted that son of a bitch when we had the chance. Done here?" he inquired, indicating my half-eaten meal.

Arms and shoulders still sore, I pushed the plate of rubbery fish across the bar. I pointed at something sweet. "What's that?"

"What the sign says—cider cake," the barman responded and cut a wedge. "The kid baked them this morning."

"Then they're fit to be eaten." The dessert proved to be delicious and cleansed my palate. I presented Viktor Glazkov's key. "Any idea what this is?"

The Irishman fingered the key and tossed it back. "You tried the lockers at the Santa Fe Depot?"

"Yes. I also went to the Post Office."

"What exactly are you searching for?"

I licked the fork. "Not sure. I'm hoping to recover the missing grave photographs, though I don't get why Heinrich Braun would entrust Glazkov with his prized possessions."

"Your defrocked preacher may have stolen the key for insurance—blackmail." Burnes slid a pencil from his ear and traced the opener on a scrap of paper. "I'll check around. Meanwhile, try to stay alive."

Of the same mind, I knocked on wood and ordered a thicker slice of cake.

Laura looked ravishing in the brand-new clothes she had purchased in San Francisco. The woman expressed happiness to meet me; however, I sensed a gap widening between us. Compelled to reveal the incident at the Concordia Turnverein, I refrained, not knowing how she might behave learning of Molly's entanglement.

"What's vexing you?" I asked. We sat on an iron bench in the plaza fronting the Horton House. A crew of stooping gardeners pruned roses along the fence.

"Whatever do you mean?" Laura replied, straightening the hem of her skirt.

"You're acting different—distant."

She met my gaze. "Henry, I'm considering moving back to Philadelphia."

In light of my ongoing circumstances, this news arrived as no huge bombshell. Even so, I felt queasy. "When?"

Laura registered my demeanor and touched my hand. "Simmer down. Not for a while. I am obligated to wrap up the validation of Alonzo's financial records. Anyway, ever since we met, you've been dying for me to leave."

"For your own protection. There are thunderheads of woe shadowing me."

Her laugh was fleeting and without humor. "'Woe' is a mild way of defining the jeopardy you—and those surrounding you—are steeped in."

"I'm aware of that fact."

"Come with me to Philly," Laura proposed. "Together, we'll start a new life there."

Ants inched up my ankles and the brothers' faces came to mind. "That sounds great, but. . . ."

In preference to chiding me for manifesting the indecisiveness of a foolish child, she requested, "Let me see that key again."

I placed the shiny object in her curved palm and updated, "Till says it's commonly used for safety deposit boxes."

"And you think this key belongs to the Brauns?"

"I doubt Viktor Glazkov had anything of value."

Laura dropped the key into her bag. "Which bank?"

"Dunno. I assume the office is nearby where Heinrich and Wilhelm lived. What are you going to do with that?"

She closed the top and sighed. "Henry, I need this to get what you want."

To keep myself occupied and to prepare for reconstruction, I hauled the remains of my cottage to the junkyard: charred studs, blackened pottery, and the tattered remnants of my wardrobe. Sweating and foul-mouthed, I humped the Grand

Quaker range onto the front lawn. With the nickel-plating polished clean of residue, I resolved the stove might be salvageable. With my paraphernalia reduced to ash, it didn't take long to lose interest. Dejected, I sat under the flowering gum tree. Watching clouds shroud the sun, I took a siesta.

My eyes opened to find Kitch and Cherika gawking at me. "Sorry to wake you from your sweet dreams boss, but you've got to decide if I should begin here or over there." The crook of his arm cradled the rolled plans.

Groggy, I pulled myself upright and against the peeling bark. "What would you do? And does it matter anymore?"

My foreman clenched the mare's reins and hunkered in the crabgrass. "Work on the other house—something new. This place is still too—raw." He tethered the horse to the tree. "Any news on the Brauns?"

I shook my head no and questioned, "How's Minnie?"

"Scared to death. My wife has been through trials and tribulations—that woman's tough. Minnie doesn't understand what is happenin' to you, and to us. She demands an end to it."

"Amen to that," I murmured. "There's no way I'll stumble upon them myself. We must formulate a method to draw those rats out of the woodwork—a trap." I stood and grasped the diagrams. "Show me the drawings, Mr. Cane."

As a team, we finished the day building on top of my neighbor's solid foundation.

No longer in custody of the safe deposit box key, this afternoon, I aspired to determine which institutions provided this service and calculate the distances relative to the Brauns' most recent residences. There weren't any banks in Ocean Beach near the Cliff House, and when I queried the desk manager of their last address at the Florence, he said the hotel did not offer lockable containers.

After peering in the large windows of the Consolidated Bank of San Diego, the place of George Pomroy's employment, I crossed F Street making my way to the next office.

In a square diagonal to the First National Bank, a lady dabbed a handkerchief to her cheek. Her chestnut-colored hair reminded me of Laura's, so I took a second glance. The weeping woman *was* Laura. The other gloved hand clutched a single photograph, the rest cascading from her lap to the bench.

"You found them!" I exclaimed.

"Henry!" she blurted, shoving the prints into her accounting satchel. "How did you know I came here? Were you following me?"

Seated beneath a king palm tree, I responded, "Laura, I was walking by trying to work out which bank the Brauns might have used to open an account. May I see Heinrich's pictures?"

She held the pouch tighter. "No you mustn't. They're—ghastly."

"I believe you," I said. "Without official documentation, how did you talk the bankers into opening the case?"

Laura's lip curled. "That part was easy. I went to every financial institution and showed the manager the safe deposit key. Most informed me I was in the wrong place. An executive at the First National Bank recognized the key, so I told him my name was Ingrid Braun and my husband Heinrich had asked me to retrieve important papers from our box. I signed the signature card, and a clerk escorted me into the safe." She blew her nose. "Holding them now, I wish I had left these disgusting things where they were."

I smiled reassuringly and extended my arm. Laura repelled my advances until I snatched the bag's strap from her grip.

The envelope enclosed a stack of stereographs. I fanned the edges of the stiff cards and counted at least eighty. Each albumen print measured three and a half by seven inches and incorporated two pictures mounted for parallel viewing. Self-developed, no stamps marked the margins to identify or advertise the photographer's studio. Faded with age, the copies were speckled sepia, corners bent from frequent handling. These images differed significantly from the empty grave negatives I discovered in the Brauns' hotel room at the Cliff House.

The first monstrosity featured an older man trussed to a wagon wheel. Judging from his tattered overalls and the surrounding cornfields, this victim was a farmer. With hands lashed to the steel tire, barbed wire fixed his neck to the spokes. Clearly experiencing a slow demise, his gaping mouth and wide eyes reacted to the guts ejecting over his belt. The photographer had written a number, the locale, and date on the negative. These details displayed as white handwritten text on the bottom of the stereograph: 803 Georgia 1882.

"I didn't look at them all," Laura said. Her quaking voice and the bustle of traffic sounded far away. "Only a fiend could be so ruthless!"

In the subsequent photograph, a boy of fifteen or sixteen leaned against a wall. Outfitted in a Confederate uniform, his arms had been constrained behind his back. The adolescent glowered into the lens, the smirk a frozen study of defiance. Lead slugs pockmarked the spattered stucco. The succeeding print recorded the devastating results of a firing party: once insolent, now merely dead, the lad stared into eternity. A close-up of the infantryman's rictus of agony culminated this three-picture set. The place and year: South Carolina 1863.

I scanned the vicinity to be sure bystanders did not observe our detestable activity. Screened by a hedge, the park remained vacant. My breath hitching, I analyzed the next series of photographs. The malignant images promenaded the still-cooling bodies of those poor mortals whom had gasped their last: waxen-faced patients in hospital beds, bloated blue and gray soldiers littering smoking battlefields, carved-up hussies in forgotten alleyways, outlaws and coloreds hanging like rotten fruit from trees or gallows, and the worst—young children, these cruel debaucheries, unspeakable and unforgettable.

"This is Mr. and Mrs. Braun," I informed. The label stated: Ella and Grover Brown 1860. "In Wilhelm's photograph, his mother and father were asleep. Here they—" Nothing I said could communicate the senseless viciousness leading to this act of parenticide.

I stopped at the 1864 print that Heinrich arrogantly flaunted to Levi Naughton, claiming the little girl's injuries resulted from a rampant horse. Someone's daughter *did* lie in the damp of an open grave. She *did* wear a pretty dress spotted with blood, and her hands *did* clasp a bouquet of wilted daisies. Yet, the dark bruises encircling the tiny throat told of a more human cause of death.

Laura wrapped the morbid keepsake in a handkerchief and put it into a pocket. "Somebody should memorialize this hapless child. Henry, I must go." She stood.

With a hug, I consoled, "I'm sorry you had to see these, but I appreciate your hard work finding them. Will you be okay?"

"No, and neither will you." Laura dried her eyes and offered a Holmes stereoscope. "Here, use this. It, too, was in the box." Then without further words, she abandoned me with my handful of abominations. A red mist of anger fried my brain as I examined the concluding set of photographs.

Head down and blinders on, I arrived on Fifth Street. Any establishment not owned by Till Burnes would suffice. Adjacent to the Paris Chop House, the lighthouse on the top of Pete's Cassidy's infamous saloon radiated a magnetic beacon for lost souls. I shouldered past the battered swinging gates, leaving daylight and descending into smoky gloom. The place stunk of stale vomit and the unwashed masses. Chairs, tables, and a rough-hewn bar were the disorganized room's sole appointments. Seated between two inanimate longshoremen, I threw coins and asked for whiskey. The tumbler held my undivided attention as the tavern's owner poured Tanglefoot from an unmarked bottle.

"Haven't seen you in here before," Pete remarked. When I didn't answer, the brute known for rolling sailors, scowled and walked away.

I swirled the jigger of dirty-brown spirits. Even with my eyelids scrunched, the ungodly pictures of Beth's crucifixion persisted—all the more visible.

The stevedore to my left lobbied for me to buy a round. I ignored the incessant needling. This was my party, and I craved every solitary drop.

Pressed to my nose, the rotgut smelled of sweetened turpentine. I returned the venom to the counter. Beloved wife . . . cherished Robert and Alice . . . my devoted sister Grace . . . doting mother . . . the whole family . . . *violated, ravaged, and defiled by a demon using the mortal name of Heinrich Braun.* As I drew the liquor to my lips, I locked eyes with the gold-framed seductress reclining on the bricks behind the bar. The oil and canvas jezebel whispered for me to surrender. I raised the beaker and toasted, "Long life." This was my first drink—and certainly not the last—in thirteen years.

The tinkle of shattering glass awoke me to a new day and the corresponding blaring hangover. Although the sun had risen hours ago, the blind cubicles attached to the twenty cribs were stuck in permanent eclipse. A man on the next straw mat hacked up a lung and rolled onto his back. The vagrant stuttered the Lord's Prayer and hawked into snoring peace. I navigated a honeycomb of conjoined rooms, lurching past men, women, and carnal combinations of both. God's fallen festooned the dens with good-luck talismans: horseshoes, tinsel, strips of colorful paper, and statues of the Virgin Mary.

Lifting my wrist to shield the glare, I entered the "bullpen." Fruitlessly masked with cheap perfume, the fetid compound abutted Cassidy's saloon. In recent years, this ugly stain on the map became a miserable home for whores, pimps, and fugitives. The Stingaree was an abyss for nameless wretches—such as I—who never wanted to be found. I waited in line with "Lacy," "Jade," "Cinnamon," and "Tamale Fanny" to wash under the single faucet. The grey water refreshed my brow, yet I forbid the odoriferous sewage from wetting my parched mouth. I didn't know how many days had elapsed in this earthly purgatory as nobody kept a calendar.

"Move on!" a bouncer slapping a white-ash club yelled from a flimsy runway bridging the roofs. Another giant oaf blocked my path. Armed and full of himself, he collected two dollars for an additional night in Shangri-La. I threaded my way into "Wildcat Alley." This congested passageway connected the rows of board-and-batten shanties crowded into the blocks spanning Fifth and Third Streets.

Within the relative seclusion of McInerney's public house, I bought a bottle and limped to the dreariest corner. The inferior bourbon upset my insides. Later—maybe—I'd find something greasy to coat my stomach.

I obsessed over innumerable hateful thoughts, all related to the gruesome pictures and the intensity of my malice for the Brauns. Not having the opportunity for revenge, I felt like exploding. Tucked against my chest, the grungy shirt concealed the packet containing the stereographs. The revolting lump pierced my core. I comprehended that the prints must be destroyed, but for some abnormal reason, I hadn't gotten around to lighting the match. No one—not even a judge, jury, or priest—should ever be forced to gaze upon these atrocities.

Laura's distraught expression as she walked from the park tore at my conscience. My disappointing actions generated her mental anguish. I pondered if Kitch, Till, or Daniel looked for me. What about the welfare of Mourning, Mero, and Basil? Adrift at sea without a rudder, I deliberated whether I had the discipline to pull myself together and return to Turner Hall. I hoped someone took better care of Hector than I did. This particular failure earned me a healthy swig, chased by a deeper swallow. Then reliving the deaths of the people I had annihilated during the war and afterwards, I imbibed again. Praying for amnesia—*I still remembered everything.*

I had Werner's gun. Perhaps today was my time to pay the piper. I rubbed my fingers on the handle.

"Can a gal get any service in here?" a female voice squalled. Annoyed at the intrusion into my exclusive depression, I pressed my face into my hands. In the midnight darkness, I captained a phantom ship rigged with moth-eaten sails and a beetle-infested hull toward the starless seas of oblivion. The ultimate destination—Davy Jones' Locker—was in sight.

Molly Doyle reversed a chair and sat with her elbows resting on the back. "I was in your debt, now *you* owe me. If I had a father, I imagine he'd resemble your drunken ass. Before she boarded an eastbound train to run away with Mr. Embry, Ma said Pa was a lazy drunk who got himself stabbed in a bar fight over a whore. To be truthful, I have little faith my mother knew whose tallywag poisoned her belly. The person I see in the mirror is a stranger."

I closed my eyes and stared at nothing. The world spun topsy-turvy. I begrudgingly acknowledged her existence.

Molly grabbed an unwashed cup, filled it to the rim, and consumed my booze without delay. Holding her nostrils, she duplicated this motion four or five times. "What a day I've had," she griped. "Till worked himself into a tizzy. My boss thinks everybody is out for his blood—and maybe it's true. He is allowing you a couple of days to pull yourself from this funk. Till said every man has the God-given right to fall down the rabbit hole once in a while, but he trusts you'll crawl from the bottomless pit on your own."

Temporarily distracted by a topic besides alcohol, I asked, "Burnes read *Alice in Wonderland?* I wasn't aware he learned the alphabet."

"Oh Hank," she said condescendingly, "Till is more educated than the simple barkeep he portrays to the muttonheads guzzling swill at his taphouse. He is fascinated by many subjects—always reading. That menagerie of wild animals is amazing."

"You watched me?"

"From a distance." Molly drank like a fish, implying she had a hollow leg. She grinned. "Guess I'm *your* angel now."

"How long have I been here?" I was afraid to hear the answer. It seemed like forever.

"Nearly two weeks. Laura busted into the Acme and explained what happened. The girl's worried sick."

"She told you about the pictures of my family?"

"Laura wasn't able to look at them all. She reckoned those are the ones that sent you spinning over the edge."

My fingers stretched for the bottle. Stopping short, I lay my palms on the pine. "Those bastards killed everyone I care for."

"Everyone?" Molly challenged. *"Are you sure?"*

This time I did not hesitate. Akin to a sympathetic friend wielding a sledgehammer—invited and welcomed—the liquid fire helped me achieve tonight's goal. I blacked out.

Chapter Twenty-Seven

"USE THIS," MOLLY GOADED. "It's not the Taj Mahal; still, I try to keep my palace from reminding me of the Acme."

I retched into the pail and lay on the bed. "Water," I rasped. Lips clamped, she carried the spew into the hallway and returned with a full glass.

The small flat was homey. The Son of God hung over the headboard, and a hooked rug covered the worn flooring. A Philadelphia Deringer rested next to a vase filled with nightshade. John Wilkes Booth used the same pocket-cannon to assassinate Lincoln. Through the raised window, I saw rows of apartment houses across the street. Carriage noise and the cries of rambunctious children percolated into the room.

Molly sat facing me; her rapt countenance signaled that she wanted to talk.

"Thank you for taking me in," I said. "How are *you* feeling?"

She pushed a runaway lock from her brow. "Fit as a fiddle."

I peeked under the sheets, and then to the folded garments on the chair. "Did we—?"

"Don't be silly. I sponged off your stench before dragging you into bed. Remember our hot bath?"

"*Hmmm.* Where's the—?"

At a bureau, Molly opened a drawer and produced the envelope. "I'm throwing these damnable pictures in the fire bin."

I nodded, relieved that she had the mettle to do what I could not. When the barmaid reappeared pale-faced and empty-handed, I questioned, "Did you look at them?"

"Curiosity killed the cat," Molly answered. "I've never seen such despair. It's no wonder you lost yourself in the bullpen."

"What now? What should I do?"

She passed me the laundered slacks. "Are you ready for what's next?"

"What do you mean?"

"Are you done fucking around?" Her hand rose as if to slap a naughty child.

Seated on the mattress, the breeze felt agreeable to my scrubbed skin. I stood.

"Good, me too," Molly Doyle muttered and came closer. "Laura has a plan—an outlandish plan, but it might just work."

Reinvigorated, I ran to the gymnasium. My clothes were gone and so was Hector. I combed the town for him—sidestepping the gin mills—without luck. Miraculously, I no longer lusted after alcohol's self-inflicted decay of memory. I prayed for Hector's safe return.

High on a scaffold in the lot cater-corner to my demolished home, Kitch and Mourning built a house. The framing was done and most of the siding. The two men bantered with somebody on the other side.

I called, "I thought you'd be putting on the finishing touches by now."

The laughter ceased as the carpenters turned. Roundhouse Mike squinted past the wall and shouted, "Mr. Gates, everybody figured you croaked. Does this mean we're gonna be paid?"

"Tomorrow morning. As long as you're pulling your weight."

"Roundhouse is bustin' his rump," Cane endorsed. My supervisor slid down the ladder and joined me by a carton of tiles.

I asked, "Is he getting along with the crew?"

Kitch snorted. "Mike's comin' around. Once in a while, he buys the gang lunch. The man's tolerable for a cracker."

"The place looks impressive. You guys are fast. With me away, why did you keep at it?"

"Mike was kiddin' about the pay. Miss Mills has been stopin' by each week with our wages, and sandwiches."

"Sandwiches?" I questioned.

"Ham and cheese, sometimes turkey. She makes tasty sandwiches."

This dumbfounded me. "You spoke to her?"

"Sure. Said you saw those pictures and then vanished—*poof!* The woman's awful sorry she left you alone."

I leaned forward and inquired, "Laura told you that?"

"Uh-huh. One afternoon, she showed up at our house with Miss Doyle. First white women I've ever seen in Chollas Creek—'cept for the Baptist church ladies tryin' to deliver us poor colored folks from evil. My wife had no clue what to do, so she invited them to stay for dinner. Minnie even gave Laura a pie to bring home to Father Horton."

"What did they discuss?"

Cane chortled. "Not you—girl stuff. I went outdoors with Aaron and played ball with Hector."

I jumped to my feet. "You have my dog? He's okay?"

"Hector put on a few pounds. Didn't Laura tell you she retrieved him from Turner Hall?"

"Kitch, I need to go see her."

"Then what the heck are you still doin' here?"

I stood across from the Express Building. Top hat in hand, the real estate tycoon exited his office. Horton seemed perplexed.

"How are you doing old boy?" Alonzo asked. "Haven't seen you in a while. Why are you here on the curb?"

"I'm waiting for Laura," I replied. "Will she be long?"

"She'll be out shortly. I don't recollect how I balanced the books without her. That girl's a godsend."

"True enough!" I professed as he went on his way.

The door opened, and, wrapped in an ankle-length, box-pleated skirt and navy-blue, puffy-sleeved bodice, Laura sailed down the steps. As usual, she was gorgeous. Her eyes bored into me. "Fully recuperated, Mr. Gates?"

"Yes, Miss Mills. Except for my bum leg, it's all working normally." In the mud, I danced an ungainly jig to prove my agility.

Withholding her amusement, she questioned, "Why are you here?"

Back on the sidewalk, I answered, "That's precisely what your boss asked. May I talk to you?"

"Does that infer you're taking me to the Acme?"

I grimaced. "No, no. You hate that place. We'll go somewhere nice. Anywhere you want."

Indifferent, Laura stated. "For a saloon, the Acme is not so deplorable. The rude and brawling atmosphere grows on you. Plus the food fits my budget."

"Too bad Till is such a lousy cook. And what makes you such a connoisseur of bars?"

"Molly's the expert. When we searched for you, she brought me to every watering hole in town. There are ten dens of iniquity to each house of worship. The Acme is high-class compared to the joints you patronized. I witnessed things, strange—"

I stopped and interrupted, "Laura, will you marry me?"

Her mouth dropped. "What did you just say? We're standing in the middle of Sixth Street."

"In a heap of horse dung. I asked if you would marry me."

Laura regained her poise. "Buy me dinner and we'll exchange views on that subject."

Till Sr. and Molly were not on duty. Tillman Jr. provided unusually good service by guiding us to a table next to the front window. He also handled our food orders. The sights and sounds of fellow dipsomaniacs merged with the tantalizing malty tang of beer.

"Are you okay?" Laura questioned. "Is it too soon? Should we leave?"

"No. I'm alright," I misinformed. My fingers quavered pulling out the tobacco pouch. "I'll be better once we eat." Stoking the pipe, I puffed the peppery burley. "Laura, I meant what I expressed earlier."

"Henry, your proposal is impulsive. My suitors have been very proper: a formal dinner with the parents, weeks of beautiful flowers, and an engagement ring. A few minutes ago, while dodging a cab, life-changing words spilled from your lips. Most women presume their men will climb over Mount Everest and swim through a hurricane to love them forever. Admittedly, you've experienced a shock. Nevertheless, I dismiss being a transitory diversion."

The declaration, "I love you, Laura," stuck in my throat like a broken sugar lozenge. I did not understand why these elementary words were so reluctant to release. "You're not. My lawyer notified me that the divorce paperwork is signed. I'm free of the past."

"Henry, you barely found out the horrendous truth regarding your wife and children. Frankly, you need to recover from that trauma. And you still have business with the Brauns."

"Molly told me of your ploy. I must go along with her—it's crazy. Why would the brothers fall for your ruse?"

Laura answered with confidence, "From what you've exposed—and the depravity I've seen firsthand—Heinrich is obviously enthralled by death and the supernatural. That beast won't be able to help himself."

I shivered as black widows scurried up my spine and laid eggs in my neck. "Are you really up to this?"

Till's son served two hot plates of pot roast with an edging of carrots and potatoes. The meal looked and smelled edible. Flabbergasted, I inquired, "Who cooked this?"

Timid, he responded, "Please taste it. What's your opinion?"

"First-rate. I'd get this again," Laura replied. "Did you make this?"

Tilly grinned. "I prepared this dish for you to try. The recipe for braised beef was in *Mrs. Beeton's All-About Cookery* book. It's easy—I followed the instructions. A cup of cooking wine does the trick. You can't tell my dad."

"Why not?" I questioned. "This is much tastier than your father's slop. He doesn't use fresh ingredients or add seasonings."

"Pop never listens. He believes he knows everything."

"That's a universal parental trait," I said. "I'll try to talk sense into him."

The cook shrugged and returned to his domain.

Readdressing my previous momentous proposal, I tried again, "So your answer is yes?"

Pensive, Laura responded, "Are you referring to luring in the tiger for slaughter or planning a wedding?"

"Wedded bliss. And the tiger hunt, too."

"Affirmative on trapping big game. The other? I must think on it. This can't be a hasty decision."

A mite snippy, I asked, "How long will it be?"

She didn't say.

In the brilliance of mid-afternoon, the facade of the Villa Montezuma appeared less ominous. From the pavement, one could still spot the gargoyles roosting on the roof, yet these chiseled goblins looked more wooden than alive. A gardener with a handsaw amputated thorny branches from the blood-red bougainvillea reaching over the walkway.

As Lawrence Tonner answered the bell, the same reddish Ethiopian cat slipped out the door, bounded off the stairs, and dashed into a ventilation hole in the foundation. Inside the entrance hall, walnut wainscoting and intricately coffered ceilings absorbed any light not trapped by the thick draperies. Cooler than expected, he led our party along a hallway to the drawing room. Laura took an armchair, and I alighted on a divan below a portrait of the mansion's owner. Devised for lounging rather than sitting, the elongated, low sofa had no back or arms. The secretary itemized our drink preferences and assured us that Jesse would be down at once.

Artisans had inlaid the ebony wall panels with bas-relief sculptures of mother-of-pearl and ivory. Cabinets, bookcases, and shelves exhibited the souvenirs and rare oddities collected on Shepard's travels. Art glass likenesses representing Shakespeare, Corneille, Goethe, and other celebrated playwrights, painters, and statesmen adorned the oversized bay windows. Their noble silhouettes cast a spectrum of colors on cases housing awards from the Czar of Russia and the Prince of Wales.

The world-renowned musician materialized through sheer curtains wearing a mink shawl. A red and white-banded skullcap topped his head, while an enormous diamond ring glittered on a pinkie. Although peculiar for summer, his ostentatious ensemble was fabulous.

"Miss Mills and Mr. Gates, I've been on pins and needles awaiting this visitation. Your letter sent my mind racing in so many directions." Always hyper-observant, he must have seen my shifting contortions. "I apologize for any backaches caused by my furniture. We chose these antiques for their history and elegance in lieu of comfort or functionality. Marie Antoinette sat on that very divan while confined in the Tuileries Palace. Those spots are her tears. Lawrence says I should get it reupholstered."

"The couch is fine," I said moving away from the dark stains. "Last time we were here, it was evening, and I wasn't able to take account of what you've accomplished. I am positive that the Villa Montezuma is the grandest house on the West Coast."

Jesse beamed. "Your flattery is well taken, though I credit the spirits who inspired the design and furnishing of my home. It shall be my pleasure to give you a tour of the premises."

Tonner entered the room carrying an engraved sterling tray laden with bread, little cakes, butter, jam, cups, and a teapot. He completed the English teatime custom of preparing and conveying the refreshments before asking if we wanted anything else.

"Lawrence, please stay and hear this," Shepard invited. With everyone settled, he continued, "From your cryptic message, I gathered you desire my specialized services?"

"Yes sir, I direly need your help." The brief letter had summarized my quest to apprehend the two brothers responsible for committing a streak of heinous murders. I illustrated how the killers fixated on learning the blackest secrets of the occult and should come out of hiding if the acclaimed Spiritualist offered a public demonstration. "Your only involvement is to perform the ritual. If the Brauns attend, the proper authorities will bring them to justice."

Underneath the bull's-eye cap, Jesse's unblinking hazel eyes hypnotized as he probed the depths of my being. Not entirely unpleasant, the effect was nonetheless unnerving.

Tonner watched closely, breaking the glamour by surmising, "Mr. Gates, I suspect you intend to execute these men. Am I right?"

I rose and paced the silk Persian rug. "I can't wait," I snarled. Laura told me to sit. I sat.

"There is more that you haven't divulged," the secretary speculated.

From my breast pocket, I removed a fragment of one of the albumen stereographs rescued from the incineration bin behind Molly's apartment. Composed with the clinical eye of a deranged medical photographer, the grotesque picture captured the final moment of Beth's life. The staged image epitomized all the pain and suffering that mankind had instigated since leaving the Garden of Eden. With shaking fingers, I laid the singed print on the table.

The men inhaled. Laura gasped and bit her knuckles.

Lawrence calmed himself and inquired, "Is your objective to let this act of retribution take place here at the Villa?"

I directed my response to Shepard. "Yes, I'd like to use the same room where you gave the last séance."

Self-effacing in company, forceful in private, Tonner stipulated, "You must find another site. This house already has enough poltergeists keeping us up at night."

Jesse nodded in agreement and asked, "Do you want me to contact your wife?"

"Is it possible?" I questioned.

He cleared his throat. "Mr. Gates, much of what I do is for entertainment. There has been a smattering of times—"

Lawrence interjected, "I've seen it for myself. When the conditions are ideal, Jesse has phenomenal powers—"

"Of suggestion," the Spiritualist concluded with a wry smile. "Wisdom necessitates me to advise you to treasure your dearest at their finest. Individual wraiths may be disinclined to cross on to the afterlife, but it's the living who struggle most with the loss. Miss Mills, please tell us what you have in mind. If feasible, we will implement your concepts to the best of our abilities."

Laura spoke for fifteen minutes describing her scheme to draw in and ambush Heinrich and Wilhelm. Shepard listened intently, requesting clarification on a few minor points. When she came to an end, he walked to the window. Stroking his mustache, the musician gazed into the pale blue sky.

As my mouth opened to seek the maestro's assessment, Tonner cut me off with a raised hand.

Jesse swirled dramatically and exclaimed, "Your wish shall be granted! What you ask for *will* be dangerous. These are the items we'll need."

Chapter Twenty-Eight

LAURA AND I STOOD IN FRONT OF HORTON HALL at the junction of Sixth and F Streets. Closed for business, the two-story brick building formerly housed a roller skating rink and, until recent years, various shops. Above the spindled balcony shading the double entrances, white stenciled letters advertised "General Merchandise." The auditorium filled the second floor.

She unlocked the door using Alonzo's key and entered the vestibule. Startled by intruders, a sparrow flew in circles and out a broken window. I felt we had unearthed a time capsule. Behind a wall of glass, the market that once traded in groceries and dry goods still stocked—albeit expired—canned and boxed staples on long shelves. Thankfully, for the benefit of our noses, someone had purged the meat display cases, vegetable bins, and fruit baskets of perishables. The clock-like dial of the antiquated Ritty Model 1 cash register recorded the last sale of one dollar and ninety-five cents. Starched aprons hung from pegs, ready to be tied on by tardy clerks.

Laura vanquished the hush with an echo. "Alonzo said the Gales up and left town during the onset of the recession. He expected another firm to lease the space. So far, nobody is interested." She crossed to the granite ticket booth and traced a finger in the grime. "This place will require a thorough overhaul before the opening."

I spied dots of bird poop and black mold stains as a consequence of the cracked pane. With less than a week until the performance, many tasks needed undertaking. "I'll ask Kitch to have his crew get everything shipshape. They can also post the flyers around town." Earlier in the day, we had stopped by a print store to order handbills, programs, and tickets.

A pair of staircases book-ended the vaulted lobby. The right set of steps squeaked as we ascended past yellowed posters of cancelled plays and concerts. Heretofore the main venue in San Diego for artists to showcase their talents, the twenty-year-old theater—outdated by today's standards—retained much of its appeal and class. Decorative cornices bordered the flaking ceiling mural portraying noble Kumeyaay Indians presenting bushels of gifts to the Spanish explorer Juan Rodríguez Cabrillo. A gilded proscenium arch framed the sixteen by thirty-two-foot stage at the end of the chamber.

We mounted the platform and faced the sooty footlights. The hall held four hundred spectators. An additional two hundred folding chairs could be squeezed in the back and along the sides. I imagined the Brauns seated in the front row, the brother's faces upturned—necks ready for slitting. If they didn't make an appearance, this sketchy enterprise might develop into a huge waste of time and resources.

Created by a well-known San Franciscan artist, a vibrant grand drape separated the apron from the acting area. Laura parted the overlapping halves of velour. Backstage, set pieces swayed from the overhead fly system constructed to move backdrops between acts: a pastoral landscape, war ships battling on the ocean, and a picturesque village from the Middle Ages. Close up, the painted scenes looked phony.

I stared up at the array of ropes, pulleys, and counterweights. "Will this work with no injuries?"

Laura lifted wooden replicas of a shield and sword. "If everyone is careful, and nothing goes horribly wrong—maybe, just maybe we'll succeed."

The next few hot August days became a frenzy of preparations for the production on Saturday. Laura and I met several times with Jesse and Lawrence to iron out the fine details. Buttoned up and as mysterious as a magician, Shepard kept the technicalities of his processes under wraps. Forced to trust the musician's experience and expertise, I prayed that on opening night the complicated contraptions would not fail.

A reporter for the San Diego Union published a series of favorable articles on the upcoming event. Theatrical advertisements were posted outside businesses, and enticing flyers had been handed out all over town. In the depressing days of the financial crash, the remaining populace anticipated any pretext for a thrill.

Years of human neglect allowed Mother Nature to gain a strong foothold inside Horton Hall. Rat and bird nests needed to be swept away. Creaky boards and shaky railings had to be nailed tight. Cedar shingles must be purchased to fix the leaky roof. Kitch and Mourning toiled until the small hours renovating the theater. A technician from the gas company refurbished the lighting fixtures. Roundhouse Mike chopped up the accumulated clutter and lugged the scraps to the curb. Earnest to play a part in snaring their kidnappers, Mero and Basil scrubbed floors, brushed seating, beat dust from draperies, polished brass fittings, oiled woodwork, and cleaned mirrors. Curious pedestrians tried to review our restorations through the soaped windows. After countless hours of hard labor, Horton Hall appeared presentable.

There was a dress rehearsal on Friday evening, and finally—*we were ready.*

"Hank, without the beard you look ten years younger," Kitch remarked.

Touching smooth skin, my fingers lingered on the scar carved across my jaw. "I don't feel ten years younger," I carped. My backbone protested as I smushed an eyeball to the peephole. To complete the transformation, the barber had sheared off six inches of hair. I had faith in my basic disguise.

We sat on stools inside the vacated grocery at Horton Hall. A lone flickering candle brightened the room. The blackened windows facing the lobby served two purposes: the painted glass screened the dreary state of the vacant market, and the observation ports scraped in the pigment afforded covert positions to survey the queue of patrons entering the auditorium. A number of avid customers bought tickets. At nine-thirty, they were early. The curtains would rise in an hour and a half.

Cane whispered, "Hank, how did you earn that slash? Did it happen in the war?"

"Yep, I received this beauty during that period. This insult to my pride was not a direct result of combat." A stressed laugh burst from my lips. "You know of *my* addiction to alcohol. I have never seen *you* take a sip of whiskey or heard you express any enthusiasm in indulging. Envious of your willpower, I'm always drawn to the intoxicating solace of fermented beverages and quite often reaped the repercussions."

"Minnie puts up with lots of grief, but not booze." He turned to inquire, "You fell off a horse and landed on that sword?"

"Nothing so heroic," I responded. "One morning I awoke to discover that I had the new ability to poke my tongue into a hole in my cheek."

Cane leaned elbows on the windowsill and peeped into the aperture. "What was that?"

"After a three-night bender on the outskirts of Mechanicsville, I came-to in the basement of an uninhabited farmhouse. I fell straight through the rotting floor and crashed onto a hill of moldering potatoes. A sliver of wood stabbed me on the way down. *Surprise!* Two Union cadets were camped in the root cellar."

"Did they make you their prisoner?"

"Nope. Those kids were deserters in hiding, more scared than I was. I told the Yanks to return to their posts before the sergeant realized his men ran off and lined up the traitors before a firing squad."

Confounded, Cane asked, "You let the enemy go?"

"Those boys supplied food and sewed up my face. Letting those Yankees live is the least I could do."

"No wonder your mug is so dang crooked," he chuckled. "If those blue-bellies survived the war, I'm sure their offspring hear about Henry Gates—the drunken Johnny Reb who mashed the taters."

"And you?" I questioned.

"My back?"

"Yes."

"Not as funny a story, and I'm not as keen to tell it."

"That I can see. What did you do?"

Kane clenched his teeth and hissed, "Why do you assume I deserved a scourgin'?"

"Then how come they punished you?"

"The first whippin' occurred after I sassed Mass'r Bragg—don't recall what I said. Got a birching—eight times—once for each birthday. Then a few years later, Mister Triche found me asleep in the barn when I was supposed to be milkin' the cows. He used a cord to tie my thumbs to the rack in the courtyard."

I frowned and remembered the method I used to bind Levi Naughton's thumbs to the rafters in Till Burnes' cold room. *Had I learned this torture technique from my father at Cedar Hall?*

Cane resumed, "That was a real lashin', so the overseer had everybody watch and take note. Let me tell you, that man knew how to lay on that rawhide horsewhip. Whupped me to the bone and forced my brother to rub salt in the cuts for good measure. Our women purified the wounds, stitched 'em up, and made healin' salves with herbs from the secret gardens. The next day, I still had to till the fields. Thereafter, that devil flogged me for no reason—didn't matter if the sun shined or it rained cats and dogs. On the other hand, Ol' Miss was an angel. On Sundays, she brought the colored children up to the house and taught us to read bible passages. Ol' Miss baked biscuits and—"

"Don't lose that thought," I breathed. A man with a felt eye patch peered into the front entrance. I recognized him as one of Heinrich's thugs from the night Walt Werner accosted me at the Spear of Achilles meeting hall. In the lobby, he bought a ticket, and went to smoke on the sidewalk. "That guy works for Braun!"

"You're confident?"

"That's him! There were two others, but I never got close."

Without a word, Kitch hurried out the side door. Sounds of a disturbance drew me to the exterior window. Through rippled glass, I saw him pressed against the hooligan, his knuckles grinding below the stringy hair. As they pirouetted, Cane lifted his kicking partner by the neck using a cord with handles attached to the ends. The one-eyed man's last vision featured wide-eyed me.

I exhaled and rushed into the alley. Together we hauled the body into the market.

As Kitch tucked away the garrote, he gulped, "Shall anyone miss him?"

Except for a fistful of silver, the corpse's pockets were empty. "Hard to tell," I answered. "His mother might. You had to kill him?"

"This is definitely an occasion where swift results are needed."

"Well, you did the right thing. This substantiates that our quarry will be here tonight."

Posthaste, we deposited Braun's henchman under the cash register and continued to monitor the foyer. At ten-thirty, the floodgates opened. People filled the waiting room with excited chatter. The ladies turned out in festive colors; however, the gentlemen wore undistinguishable black suits and hats. I concentrated on the single men, not sighting either of the perpetrators.

The upper doors were unlocked, and the theatergoers filed up the dual staircases.

Anxious, Cane inquired, "Are they inside?" Never having seen the brothers in person, he used my descriptions as points of reference. "The men all look like penguins."

I scrutinized my pocket timepiece. "They may have gotten by. The show is about to start. I'm going upstairs. Check on Mourning and be ready." Dew guarded the rear of the building and the external steps leading up to the second floor.

Giving Kitch a nod, I exited to the street and joined the line out front.

Chapter Twenty-Nine

IN THE REAR OF THE HORTON HALL'S GALLERY—the cheap seats—men's hair and women's hats blocked a clear view of the stage. This inconspicuous position allowed me a vantage point to skim the hall for Heinrich and Wilhelm, plus any additional suspicious characters.

Halfway through Jesse Shepard's piano recital, and in the depths of a transcendental operatic adaptation under the harmonic influence of the late Giacomo Meyerbeer, I still could not find a trace of our prey. Celebrities filling the front row included Governor Waterman, Wyatt Earp, and the musician's famous cousin, General Benjamin Grierson—a Civil War hero who now commanded the integrated Buffalo Soldiers.

Replicating his preceding encores, the talented artist ended the musical portion with the stunning "Grand Egyptian March." As the booms of cannons faded, so did the footlights and sconces lining the walls. Lawrence had turned off the main gas valve. The standing ovation shifted to jittery giggles and nervous whispers. In spite of knowing that the deepening tension lasted a mere three minutes, the disquiet seemed endless. A woman behind me panicked. Complaints resulting from crushed toes tracked their steps as the husband escorted her from the room. Blind and palpitating, I myself fought claustrophobia.

A dim glow illuminated a figure on the dais. Jesse hovered, apparently weightless, although I knew a velvet-covered box supported his feet. It was midnight.

"Welcome ladies and gentlemen. I hope you enjoyed the first act of our presentation." Shepard expounded on how friendly metaphysical energies adopted his corporeal manifestation to convey their ever-maturing melodies. "Critics have labeled me as a Spiritualist or a heretic. I confess to mentoring under a few of the famous European mediums of our time, but furthermore, I sought the truth right here in San Diego at Searchlight Bower with the open-minded Ebenezer Hulburd and Justin Robinson. The dead long to communicate with the living. You just witnessed the esteemed masters using me as a conduit for your entertainment. I'm blessed with an intuitive musical talent, yet lacking formal training; I'm not capable of delivering these stirring compositions without the cooperation of my accomplished shadow guides." Jesse chuckled. "Perhaps *I am* the reincarnated English version of Wolfgang Amadeus!"

As the crowd hooted, a cord pulled the crate sideways. Shepard landed nimbly and marched the platform. Grandiose gestures accentuated his exhilaration. "Naysayers classify modern Spiritualism as witchcraft or trickery—even the cause of the War Between the States! I thank Professor Sidgwick and the Society for Psychical Research, along with Henry Seybert's Commission, for debunking the many imposters swindling our grieving military widows. I'm sure you've heard of the Fox sisters and the Davenport brothers?" He held out both hands. "I must challenge the rationalists. What is organized religion other than the belief in a supreme intelligence, God's natural creations, and the promise of a rewarding afterlife for our eternally evolving souls? These are the tenets—the principles—of Spiritualism."

Center stage, alone and with lid closed, the piano played an eerie refrain. The pianist's fingers twitched imperceptibly, as if directing the instrument. A frigid cyclone whirled around the gathering as clappers struck a carillon—the sources of the wind and chimes hidden from sight.

"Please come forth and give the names of the beloved family members or friends you wish to speak with once again. While I cannot guarantee their spirits will be available or accommodating, I shall attempt contact." Jesse assessed the room. "You ma'am," he selected. "In the straw bonnet with emu feathers!"

I turned left. A stout female in her early thirties lowered a hand and shouted, "Mr. Shepard, I'm desperate!"

"Your name?"

"Helen Foster." In a quivering voice, Helen disclosed how her husband, Jacob, had perished in a terrible boating accident. Washed overboard in the midst of a typhoon, his body was never retrieved. Mr. Foster had buried their savings in the backyard without divulging the exact locations. The wife had tried digging everywhere, finding a handful of puzzling objects, but nothing of significance. "Can you ask Jake where to look? I need the money to pay the rent and feed my kids."

Sensitive to her predicament, the medium beckoned for the widow to sit on a chair screwed to a marked spot. Jesse stood behind the same "mother" he had coached this afternoon. Shepard laid palms on her shoulders and chanted incantations in a throaty Middle-Eastern dialect. Helen's face slackened as her eyelids fluttered.

An indistinct blob of bluish fluorescence appeared on the ceiling, entwining with swooping auroras. Tonner produced these phantasmagoric sprites by operating multiple banks of Luke bi-unial and tri-unial magic lanterns. The limelight-powered machines rear-projected hand-painted or photographic images onto gauze screens or smoke. A few mechanical slides even simulated movement.

Accompanied by the plucked strings of a harp, the angelic flashing lights merged and sank into the woman's head.

Helen's eyes widened in recognition, then understanding, and shut as she toppled to the floor.

"Stay back!" the Spiritualist implored. *"Do not touch her! Mrs. Foster remains in a fugue state!"*

When the subject became responsive, the wailing commenced. Inconsolable, Shepard led the actor offstage to be reimbursed and reunited with Jake.

A young couple whose baby relinquished life at childbirth petitioned next.

"Was the boy christened?" Jesse questioned.

"No time for that," the father sighed. "The midwife spanked Sidney, he took a breath, cried once, and—"

"Please!" the mother shrilled, holding high a mourning portrait "I want my son!"

Shepard apologized, "Folks, I've never contacted anyone who is not spiritually cleansed. Unbaptized children abide in the Limbo of the Infants, the boundary between Heaven and the edge of Hell. I pray that Sidney lives in a world of pure happiness and not in a region of everlasting punishment."

Burbles of an innocent cooed from an array of invisible horns. Exalted, the gallery gasped as a winged cherub flitted across the wall toward the awaiting parents.

"Praise God!" the husband lauded as he caught his swooning spouse. The wondrous illusion was very realistic.

"Death is the ultimate mystery!" Shepard announced, "Your son is free from original sin!"

"Cure me!" an aged man begged. An adolescent served as a crutch. "My bones ache something fierce! How they burn within! Lay your hands upon this penitent sinner."

"Sir, I am not a faith healer," Jesse insisted. "God has not endowed me with divine powers, and I have no capacity to ease your misery. Grandfather, you must consult a physician."

"Pretender!" the geezer accused, buckling into his seat.

Disruption averted, a man yearned to apologize to his dead wife, followed by a woman who aspired to interview Abraham Lincoln's ghost. Committed to writing a biography on the Civil War president, the author had queries regarding the "Great Emancipator's" state of mind during the production of *Our American Cousin* at Ford's Theatre. The medium instigated dialog with both parties: tempestuous allegations of infidelity for the former and humorous homilies from the latter.

As a youth, Shepard attended the prairie lawyer's debates against Stephen Douglas. Impressed by the sixteenth president of the United States, he briefed the audience that after losing her sons, Mary Todd Lincoln conducted séances in the White House.

It had been a long, worrisome day of expectancy, and by one o'clock, my head nodded. There would be a final summoning before the exhibition ended: a woman concerned about the celestial wellness of Mr. Jingles, her furry lap cat.

The Brauns had not taken our bait. The situation discouraged and depressed me. Despite this defeat, feeling so exhausted, I didn't care. Maybe the two had left town—*good riddance to bad rubbish!* At least the musician/Spiritualist had made a profit, and the public received stimulating entertainment. Even knowing that the divinations were scripted, I admitted that Shepard possessed an uncanny ability to enlighten.

Also displaying signs of weariness, Jesse confirmed that this was to be the last inquiry. He identified a fidgety lady in a pink sweater sitting by the aisle. I grinned, picturing Lawrence backstage coaxing the herd of hungry strays with fresh tuna.

"I have a request!" a booming voice interrupted. My intestines knotted and lungs seized. Jolted awake, I craned to pinpoint the source. "Mr. Shepard, I'm not convinced that what we observed here tonight is legitimate. Much of your routine is contrived." A man in the third row stood, revealing his profile: beaked nose, pitted cheekbones, spiked mustache, and the same icy reptilian eyes. *How did I not see him?* Heinrich Braun addressed the spectators, "This trickster is making you into dupes." Grunts and nods of agreement filled the room.

Jesse smiled and said, "Sir, I never professed to be a prophet, yet with the Creator's guidance, I've converted hard-nosed cynics and despondent misanthropes into accepting that human beings retain dormant capabilities. Exercised with practice and proper judgment, employing the sixth sense can persuade most lonesome phantoms to walk into the photosphere—nirvana."

My prayers were answered when the eldest Braun looked to his brother and said, "Prove it. Show us our parents."

"What are your mother and father's names? When did they pass to the astral plane? You must miss their encouragement and loving embraces." I assumed Shepard realized these were the men we stalked, but I was not sure.

"Loving embraces?" Heinrich spat. "That's a laugh! I refuse to tell you their names or when they kicked the bucket. Figure that out yourself!"

"Helping you will be my privilege," the medium proclaimed. "I shall send a message to the umbrae." He fell to his knees. "Let it begin."

A low rumble originated at the rear section of the stage. These reverberations increased in volume and rotated to my right. Proceeding behind me in a clockwise motion, the thuds became booms and to my left, the clamor grew into an ear-shattering barrage. This cacophony circuited the theater immeasurable times, each revolution blending in the keening of more earthly voices. As suddenly as the noise started, the disconcerting babel ceased.

Aware—from the rapid motion in my field of view—that people were exiting the auditorium, I focused on the apparitions floating twenty feet above the stage. Jesse used a salvaged photograph to clad Till and Molly in similar styles of bedclothes to what the senior Brauns wore as their children bid them a permanent *gute nacht*. Pulsing magic lanterns superimposed the dead parent's faces upon the living mannequins.

Hooked onto unseen wires, Burnes drifted in and out of a swirling miasma. He called in a frail voice, "Herman!"

Authentic tears streaked Molly's cheeks as she sobbed, "William how could you!"

As Heinrich and Wilhelm goggled at the stupefying spectacle, gigantic flames bellowed from the whistling ports of gas pipes. The mounting blaze formed an orange background for the hanging man and woman. Molly, closer to the heat, shrieked in feigned or genuine distress.

"Mama!" the younger brother exclaimed. "Herman did it! He lit the match!"

"Quiet!" Heinrich blustered. "You itched to know what would happen, same as me!"

The Irishman propelled forward, endeavoring to distance himself from the furnace. "Turn it off!" he pleaded. "Get Molly out of the way or let us down!"

Shepard ran backstage instructing his assistant to cut the gas. As the musician heaved on a rope, Molly's harness advanced with rattles and screeches on a metal rail bolted to a cantilever. No longer under the luminous guise of Mrs. Brown, her relief was evident. Progress halted when an unlubricated roller bearing stuck.

Distracted by the stream of frenzied cats scampering up the aisles, Jesse yanked harder on the cord. “Lawrence, shut off the gas now!” Overtaxed, the rusted axle of a pulley wheel snapped loose.

Molly sliced the air, the pendulous arc curving into the proscenium arch. The barmaid hit the corner’s edge, the sickening ricochet sending her careening over the Brauns. At the apex of her flight, the fire extinguished.

Pupils adjusting to the murk, and heeding Heinrich’s curses demanding vengeance, I grabbed my sword from below the seat and pushed past patrons fleeing in the opposite direction. The brothers leapt on the stage and rushed to Molly. Crumpled, her arm bent at an unnatural angle. Dangling aloft, Till cocked, aimed, and pulled the Bull Dog pocket revolver’s trigger. The .44 caliber rimfire blew a crater in the wall above Heinrich’s head, sprinkling his hair with plaster. The gun’s recoil sent Burnes spinning, and he struggled to line up another shot.

I heard a small pop, and Heinrich stumbled backwards. Still smoking, the walnut stock of the Philadelphia Deringer slipped from Molly’s grip.

The Brauns staggered upstage as I cradled Molly and pledged to find a doctor.

“Go after them!” she insisted. “Laura’s back there!”

Confused, I asked her to repeat herself. To my knowledge, Laura remained at home, tended by the Hortons.

“I’m sorry. She wanted to help.”

“It’s okay, Molly.”

“Hank, I put a slug in the meanest one.”

I applied pressure to a gash on her forehead and praised, “You did good.”

Schofield in my left hand, sword in my right, Jesse, Lawrence, and I searched the stage area. No Brauns. No Laura.

Kitch joined us as we explored the empty dressing rooms. "Mourning's outside," he alerted, waving the Enfield. "He won't let anyone get by."

"Get me down from here!" Till reminded us. "Without dropping me!" Tonner turned a crank to lower my friend from the rafters.

"Take care of Molly," I yelled to Shepard as Cane, and I barreled through the gaping door.

In the alley, beneath the waning Sturgeon Moon, there was no sign of Mourning. A blood trail led to the street, trampled in the sand by a passing dairy wagon. We crouched in the dirt and listened.

Chapter Thirty

"WHERE DO YOU THINK THEY WENT?" Kitch questioned. "To the harbor? He won't get too far with that bullet hole. And Laura will bog them down."

If she is still alive! I buried that paralyzing fear and fixated on the options. The brothers might go north. With Los Angeles over a hundred miles distant, and the rail lines not running for another four hours, this route seemed improbable. I assumed Heinrich retained the strength to clamber onto a horse. Thirty miles south, the unrestricted Mexican border welcomed—a common haven for wanted expatriates. The mountainous towns to the east—Ramona, Julian, Cuyamaca City, and Descanso—were remote, but a rough ride for someone with a serious injury. The deserts lying yonder eastward? During the summer months, the Montezuma and Borrego valleys remained places of intolerably high temperatures and low humidity. The San Diego Bay, gateway to the Pacific Ocean, was only one mile west. Or, they found refuge downtown, and obtained medical aid.

I answered, "You're right, from the waterfront they could sail north or south."

Kitch sprang to his feet, and I pursued. As we passed a tuna cannery, a volley of gunshots stopped us in our footprints.

"Where was that?" I asked, attempting to home in on the fading echoes.

Under the dreamlike radiance of the arc lamps, he yelled, "West! Two came from a shotgun."

An individual slouched in the gutter on the corner of J Street. Lanterns flared in the neighboring windows.

"He took my Browning," Mourning wheezed through blood-flecked lips. Between stores, a door burst open, and a male robed in a soiled nightshirt inquired about the commotion. I waved the newsmonger away.

Conscious of the gaping chest wound, Cane questioned gently, "Are you in pain?" He scanned the clusters of townsfolk clogging the sidewalks. "Who did this to you?"

Comprehending that he was taking his last breaths, Dew raised his head and pointed across the intersection. "Him." Slumped against a pillar, and clutching the stolen lever-action shotgun, the man's chin stuck to his sternum. I threw the John Browning to Kitch. With a boot, I pushed the corpse on his back. A red hole centered Wilhelm's forehead. As if to explain the current grave state of affairs, the younger Braun's mouth yawned, and, as if realizing he had nothing worthwhile to say—reflexes clacked the teeth shut.

"I winged the older brother," Mourning gurgled. "Then this bald dunce got me. That bastard basted me twice with my own gun before somebody nailed him. I heard a rifle shot. The girl—" Gasping, his watering eyes dilated, and then squeezed out tears.

Frantic, I jerked his arm. "Mourning, where's Laura?"

"They're goin' to the Fifth Street wharfs. Hurry, the Devil took her," were the carpenter's final words.

Shipyards, lumberyards, trading posts, and squatters' lean-tos clung to the shoreline. An array of piers, the longest being the five hundred-foot Pacific Mail Wharf, spanned over the mudflats into deeper waters.

Tramp schooners and steamers anchored in the bay or berthed at the landings projecting into the inlet. A few saloons remained open for those coherent enough to buy one more round.

"Let's split up," Kitch proposed. "I'll scout out the side-wheelers." He followed the row of railway cars brimming with coal.

I reminded him to call if he found anything and inspected the wind-powered ships near the embankment. The rigging of the three-masted *Eurydice* creaked as the swells lapped against her hull. Except for the sailors snoring in hammocks on deck, the embarcadero was quiet.

A night watchman snoozed in a shelter. Poking his torso, I asked if anyone had recently passed.

"Who wants to know?" he slurred, wiping the drool from his lip onto the tight-fitting uniform.

I pulverized the flagon of rum and hissed, "I'm the guy who's gonna tell your boss you ain't doing your job!"

Insulted, the lookout sat upright and tucked the wrinkled shirt into his pants. "Buddy, I need the dough. The Mrs. loves whatever sparkles. You cannot fathom what it's like sittin' here all alone listenin' to your mates whoop it up in the bars. I also work as a stevedore durin' the day!"

Irritated by his excuses, I used a shard from the broken bottle to emphasize my question. *"Did you see a man and woman?"*

The guard snickered, "A bloke came by with a whore, and I must declare, that gal wasn't overjoyed. They boarded the *Ancon*."

In the distance, the "All Aboard" signal, a prolonged toot of the ship's horn, notified of eminent departure.

Exhaust wafted from the single stack of the *Ancon.* Fitted with brigantine rigging and black hulled with white superstructure, the two hundred and fifty-foot-long vessel floated at the terminus of the Pacific Mail Wharf. I saw Kitch halfway out. Driving my gimpy leg to its limit, I hollered and pointed to the ship. He turned and dashed forward.

Dockhands untied the moorings from bollards and hurled the cables to deckhands. The gangplank was pulled onto the cambered platform. White clouds belched from the slanted funnel as steam filled the vertical beam engines' behemoth cylinders.

"They're leaving!" I panted. Installed on both sides, the louvers of the thirty-foot paddle-wheels rotated faster as the boat moved away from the wharf.

Cane sprinted, gaining velocity as his lengthy strides gained traction. I thought the man would never make it in time, but he did. Kitch dropped the shotgun and vaulted beyond the churning water, grabbing the starboard railing. His boots scrabbled the hull as an arm curled over the edge. The Enfield plunged into the foam as he climbed aboard.

Gone for an instant, Kitch returned with a life preserver. He slung the Kisby ring underhand and urged, "Jump Hank!"

Carrying what momentum I could muster, I took one last glance at the skimming buoy and dove into the ink. Sometimes Fortuna—Lady Luck—deals you a good hand. Most often, the Greek immortal is oblivious to the plight of humankind. Tonight, the flighty goddess heeded my plea. My face bore the brunt of the impact, yet my thrashing arms hooked into the white circle of cork. Seawater flushed my sinuses and stung my eyes as the connecting line skipped me through the waves.

"Hold on!" Cane screamed as he reeled me to the *Ancon's* stern. Yanked up the transom, I plopped to the poop deck.

Hoisted on the flagstaff, an American flag flapped against the phosphorescent band of the Milky Way.

"My pistol is lost," I sputtered. I blamed Fortuna as I groped the chestnut planking.

"Mine, too," he admitted. "You still got the sword."

I silently apologized to the deity and scrambled up a ladder to the hurricane deck. Clanking loudly, the rocking motion of the diamond-shaped walking beam transferred the engines' ten-foot strokes to the side-wheels. Under striped canvas, I wedged between the radial davits used to lower lifeboats in emergencies. Even though it was a three-day voyage to San Francisco, it would take us forever to search the whole ship.

Kitch, registering my consternation, inquired, "What the hell are you doin'? We can't quit lookin'."

"I'm trying to guess where Heinrich is. Hurt and dealing with a kidnap victim, he's staying away from public areas."

"No kiddin'. Why did he go to all the trouble of bringin' Laura this far? He doesn't know we trailed him here."

"You mean, why not just kill her after his brother died?"

Cane met my glare with determination. "We'll find her. Let's check below."

Amidships, we entered a bulkhead hatch and descended a companionway to the boiler. In the stokehold, muscled stokers shoveled coal into insatiable fireboxes. Accessing an aft passageway, we hugged hot pipes leading to the thumping propulsion plant. The humid, low-ceilinged chamber housed the mechanisms used to power the *Ancon*. Crew members lubricated grease cups while monitoring water levels, steam pressures, and temperature gauges.

A bell rang once, and a marine engineer approached the engine order telegraph in the control room. When the indicator on the pole-mounted brass dial clicked to the top "Stop" position, the officer acknowledged the command by setting the responding pointer to a duplicate notch on the instrument. He directed a worker to shut the main valves. As the man pulled on banks of levers, the massive vertical shafts of the port and starboard reciprocating engines chugged to standstills.

The heavy ship pitched sideways and then steadied.

Again, the telegraph clanged. Thrice this time—the cavitate bell.

Now the metal needle slid to "Full Ahead." The officer scowled upward as if disputing the order. He barked to open the regulators to the maximum positions. The steamship groaned as the mighty engines gulped superheated air.

The *Ancon* trembled and canted starboard. I heard something scrape along the hull. The baffled engineer snatched the speaking tube and squawked questions into the horn. Not receiving an answer, the man yelped louder.

"To the bridge!" I exhorted. I grasped the worn rails and hauled myself up the narrow stairway. On the upper deck, the thundering paddle wheels drove us into the dank fog. On a platform before the smokestack, and behind the front mast, the vacant windows of the wheelhouse reflected an enlarging image of the Point Loma peninsula. *Where is the captain?*

I scaled a short ladder affixed to a paddlebox and eased into the pilothouse.

Kitch chased my heels as I crept into the shadowy room. By the helm, the skipper sprawled senseless or, on closer examination, bled-out—dead. Heinrich Braun operated the ship's wheel—fiercely twisting the spokes landward with his right palm. Already past the sandy shores of La Playa, he steered the *Ancon* directly into the projecting rock jetty of Ballast Point.

Yet, this suicidal trajectory was trivial compared to what he clasped in his left hand. The shark fin sight on the extended barrel of a Colt Peacemaker jabbed into Laura's neck. Ignorant of our presence, both appeared mesmerized by the blurry lights of the few buildings inhabiting Point Loma.

Trained to strike first, I prepared to lunge with the Foot Officer's Sword. As I flexed, a portal slammed open on the far side of the pilothouse. The marine engineer barged in, red-faced and ready to defy his master.

Restraining Laura by the arm, Braun spun and fired twice. The officer tottered back outside and teetered over the safety chain. Except for a small splash, it was as if the chief of the engine room never existed.

Noticing us, Heinrich laughed. "Mr. Gates!" He indicated with the weapon for me to drop the blade—which I did.

"Let her go," I warned.

The man we had hunted for so long peered into the haze, gauging distance. Maintaining his grip on Laura, in a monotone he informed, "It doesn't matter anymore. We'll all go down together."

The engine order telegraph—still set to "Full Ahead"—looked a mile away. If I could get to the device, would anyone below hear the bell or be able to slow the boat before the hull splintered into a million pieces?

I stared at the blue bident tattooed on Braun's forearm, wanting to ask about his obsession with death. Then again, we were quickly running out of bay.

The wound's dark stain from shoulder to elbow became evident as the murderer shifted the Colt from me to Kitch's chest. "You there! Are you friends with the old colored fool who pegged me? Which of you sons of bitches killed my brother?"

I had no idea who shot little Wilhelm.

As Cane composed his belligerent reply, Laura drove Molly's gaudy dagger into Heinrich's thick throat. A freshet of blood showered the girl's hair and face. The huge man pivoted and bashed the Colt on her skull. Eyes rolling, she crumpled under the chart table.

The three-inch slash bubbled as Braun turned to finish us; however, the lovely Fortuna had one crowning favor to bestow. The angled prow of an anchored sloop emerged from the mist. With the deafening roar of a derailing freight train, the vessel's bowsprit grinded along our main deck, flinging folding chairs and umbrellas into the sky. The thirty-foot white spar crashed into the front of the bridge, smashing every window before splintering in half and spiraling off the side.

Heinrich Braun flew at us in the tempest of glass and wood fragments. I took up the sword and swung at what I hated most. This I must swear to you, the photographer's crocodilian eyes tracked me as his head sailed across the helm, through an open porthole and into the briny deep.

"Engine Room!" I shouted. Kitch twirled and raced downstairs.

I revolved the eight spokes of the ship's teak wheel hard left until the rudder jammed in its furthest position. The vibrations underneath my feet paused as the reverse gear engaged. Losing thrust, the *Ancon* continued to move forward as the starboard side drifted toward the reaching arm of Ballast Point. The paddlebox clipped a fishing dock as the bow beached on a sandbar.

On the bloody floor, I nearly jumped out of my skin as Laura whispered softly in my ear, "Henry, sorry it took so long, but the answer is *yes.*"

Epilogue

AT LEAST FOR NOW, Mr. Mills hasn't opened a millinery shop in San Diego, and Mrs. Mills isn't basking in the warm Californian sun.

For a few weeks, Laura and I endured the unwanted status of hometown celebrities. The San Diego Union announced that I, Lieutenant Henry Gates, single-handedly saved Miss Mills and the steamship *Ancon* from certain death and destruction at the hands of a deranged maniac. The reporters refused to hear that without Kitch and Mourning's assistance, I couldn't have located the brothers or performed these tasks.

We pulled a tattered notebook from Heinrich Braun's pocket. The pages cataloged the scores of innocents he senselessly executed. There were dozens of Southern plantations on the list—my family members inscribed under the entry for Cedar Hall.

I often speculate upon why Heinrich committed those atrocious acts. Over the tiresome months seeking my adversaries, I always imagined a decisive showdown, concluding with a full confession. I thought this revelation would somehow clarify the reasons for killing my loved ones.

To this day, I cannot explain who carved—or the meaning of—the word "Gates" next to the pitchfork symbol on the Buzzard Roost Creek Bridge. If forced to guess, I'd have to say it was my son. I gave Robert a pocketknife the last time I saw him. Had Heinrich remembered his visit to Cedar Hall and realized my connection to the people living there? With the insane tactics he used to toy with me, I believe he did.

Maybe it is best I never know the monster's motives. Heinrich's total madness is a disease I have no intention of catching.

And we did not find out who gave Wilhelm Braun the third eye. I thank the sharpshooter for their good deed.

Our wedding planning was spontaneous and modest. Laura and I applied for a marriage license and traveled in a rented carriage towed by Clive and Cherika to the Point Loma Lighthouse. As the clouds moved out to sea, the future shined bright for us and the metropolis spreading far below. Pastor Harper officiated over the short but sweet ceremony. Father Horton and his wife Sarah; Till Burnes and his family; Molly Doyle; Daniel Judge; and Kitch Cane and Minnie, along with Mero and Basil attended. They applauded and cast rice after we exchanged vows. I am sure Mourning Dew watched approvingly from somewhere above.

With Laura six months pregnant, we got as far away as possible from the horrors that took place. We packed our bags, caged Hector, and rode a cross-country train to her hometown of Philadelphia. Arriving in the dead of winter and having had no previous experience with a "Nor'easter," at first, this Southern boy had difficulty adjusting to the leafless trees, three-dog-night temperatures, and blinding blizzards. During the daylight hours, donning a fleece parka, weatherproof boots, and a coonskin cap keeps me snug. On nippy evenings, Hector and his close pal Marcus the tabby cat sleep at our feet.

Laura and I remodeled a brick row house near her parents in a thriving Philly neighborhood named Center City. We take the cocker spaniel for long walks in the forest and look forward to bringing our child to play along the banks of the Schuylkill River. These four walls do not contain an equal level of pride as the cottage Kitch and I built with our own two hands on Fourth and Beech Streets. Those days of camaraderie I will not forget. Just the same, the peal of my wife's voice resonating throughout these hallways makes me love this home even more.

As spring approaches, the expected date of birth races toward us. Laura works nonstop. At City Hall, she holds a position as a tax-examining clerk and perseveres to establish a regional chapter of the International Council of Women. As her belly grows, I plead for her to relax. My wife smiles, locks fingers with mine, and says she is fine.

I have made headway by taking small steps. Dissimilar to San Diego's stagnant real estate industry, the local market is healthy. I will never be Alonzo Horton's equivalent as a salesman or entrepreneur. Still, my eyes are on several noteworthy properties. To be specific, a chain of hotels and restaurants.

My prevailing passion is to supply electricity to Philadelphia's citizens. Partnered with one of Laura's cousins, our fledgling company is contracted to string power lines in the northern parts of the city using the latest Ganz transformers. As each avenue is spliced to the electrical grid, I am delighted to witness modern incandescent lights erasing the shadows.

The Rivera Mine continues to produce varying amounts of wealth. Daniel sends my share of the proceeds with personal notes. His newest letter held a nugget of unforeseen news. At our wedding dinner, Mr. Judge and a fully healed Miss Doyle discovered themselves seated together. Thanks to cupid—Laura—they are now a couple. Daniel and Molly are both independent and strong-willed. It will be interesting to see how their relationship develops.

Claude Horrigan relinquished his post as Mine Manager to Foghorn. The big man shoved off on a sugar boat to Puerto Rico with cash in pocket and the lure of free land. I sincerely think the gravity of Javier's demise became too much to handle, and he needed a fresh start.

Kitch's unwavering work ethic and attention to detail has paid off. He founded his own construction business and is doing well. The afternoon Cane and I parted ways took a toll on us both. He was glad I learned the fate of my first family and elated that Laura and I began a life as one. My friend's jaw dropped when I handed him the deeds to my holdings. I advised him to rebuild over my burnt foundation. The parcel should make a nice home for Minnie and the three boys. Cane writes regularly, apprising me that many of the folks from Chollas Creek have moved into his apartments. I am relieved they had someplace safe to go. In the summer, Kitch and Minnie plan to travel down to Lafourche Parish and search for her daughters.

I gave my john mule to Mero and Basil. Clive stables with Cherika and gets extra tender loving care. He is a lucky fella.

Till Burnes, his wife, and son spent a few restful weeks in Hawaii. Mary would have been jubilant if the trip had been a family vacation rather than a hurried escape from a grand jury's indictment for gambling. A Superior Court judge later dismissed the charges. After Tilly took over the kitchen responsibilities of the Acme Saloon and Billiard Academy, the dining room is filled to capacity every night.

My sword? The weapon rests at the bottom of the San Diego Bay. Nobody was there when I threw the damn thing into the waves. Let it rust.

One hundred and fifty-two days have passed since I last lifted a drink. Are my nightmares filled with stalking bogeymen? Insomnious, do I wander Philadelphia's dark streets seeking redemption? The gravitation to roam has weakened; however, I cannot claim the specters of the departed have left me in peace. To my surprise, I laugh a lot. With Laura beside me, I am less restless. She wraps her arms around me, whispers words of comfort, and I slip into pleasant dreams. When I awaken to a sunny dawn, any ugly visions fade like the aftertaste of bittersweet wine.

As I stare at the walls in the baby's room—painted with ducks and geese—I question whether our child will be forced to live through the inhumanity of another war. If Laura gives birth to a boy, is he going to be so eager to enlist? If it's a girl, I pray she never has to brave the hardship of burying a casualty of bloodshed. Although I am apprehensive of what might come, I count my blessings for what I have.

Did Jesse Shepard grant me one final supernatural communication with my dear wife's ghost? No, I took his advice and moved on. Elizabeth and the children, Robert and Alice, shall always live in my memories—eternally young and happy.

As I lay still in the dead of night or rock on the front porch in silent moments of reflection, I sense the gentle tug of the vast Pacific Ocean. I long for miles of dazzling coastline, lofty mountains capped with snow, and the natural mystery of the desert. Will we ever return to San Diego? God willing, it is merely a matter of time.

www.ingramcontent.com/pod-product-compliance
Lightning Source LLC
Chambersburg PA
CBHW020558310726
48979CB00008B/1265/J

* 9 7 8 0 9 9 1 4 2 4 8 6 3 *